Society of
STEPMOTHERS
BOOK ONE

You Knew He Had Kids
When You Married Him

LISA ADAMS

Published by

Pixie Ears Press
Menlo Park, CA

For permission requests or more information, please visit:
pixieearspress.com

ISBN-13: 978-1-939157-08-9

Library of Congress Control No: 2014910744

✧✧ for my ninjas ✧✧

Also by Lisa Adams

For young readers

The Evil Sweater and Other Stories

Feshy's Dreamworld

For hungry people

S'mores: Gourmet Treats for Every Occasion

For book nerds

Why We Read What We Read:
A Delightfully Opinionated Journey
Through Contemporary Bestsellers

(co-authored with John Heath)

Contents

Prologue

NO ONE EVER dreams of becoming a stepmother. Yet millions have done it already. Hundreds are at the altar *right now*.

This is, if you think about it, fairly remarkable. How many other never-desired roles do people take on in droves? Only widow, only survivor.

I don't mean to be morbid. But with the birth of almost every new stepmother there is loss. And it all comes back to the simple fact that this life is not, almost ever, a juicy first choice for anyone involved.

We refuse to acknowledge this difference when we fall in love. We pretend that the flummoxed children and lurking exes are scenery, incidental. We pretend they can't batter and dent us. This is a mistake.

For even if the new life proves wonderful, and it may, the loss on which it is built makes it so very different from the life we dreamed about when we were small—and not so small.

Shall we meet the latest pretender?

August

1

TWO DAYS BEFORE my wedding, I had a yeast infection and a crapload of work to finish. Real life isn't a bridal magazine, to be sure, but hunkering in my cubicle like a mangy hoarder wasn't exactly how I'd wanted to bid adieu to the single life.

My office phone warbled. "*Rhiannon Delesio!*" I screeched into it.

"Dude, you sound worse than yesterday," said my best friend Summer.

The sleep-deprived cackling erupted from my throat. "NO! I'm a multitasking hyena!"

"Well, some of us would love to take you out for drinks tonight. Are you going to have time?"

And just like that, the laughter burbled toward tears. I gulped it all down. "Oh Summer, that would be so great. But I'm stuck here until I finish and it's going to be a long night."

"Come on, you can't take a break?"

I hesitated. As it was, I'd be here until at least two a.m. My boss was sizzling with displeasure over my ten-day vacation, lacing our every interaction with sweet little threats about what might happen if I left certain projects undone. I just couldn't let a couple of drinks de-shoe this workhorse. I had to decline.

"Okay, well I thought I'd try," Summer said. "See you Saturday?"

"If I live that long," I sighed, hanging up.

And then, just as I plunged into email, the phone pealed. I swooped up the receiver without checking caller ID.

"Annie! Where have you been? It's your mother."

Oh, God—the One Who Must Be Avoided, the gloom-and-doom nitpicker herself! I tried not to groan audibly. Why had I *ever* told her that my cell phone didn't get reception at the office? "Yeah Mom, I'm at work and I have a *ton* of stuff to do, so—"

"Annie, you're getting *married*. Every other bride is out shopping with her mother at this time in her life. And you just *work*."

"Yeah, Mom, I'm working because I love it so much," I shot back, knowing that only the stickiest sarcasm could contend with this latest narcissistic nugget. "Shopping sounds awful compared to this awesome *work* on my desk. Poor *you*."

Long pause. "Every other mother," my mom wailed on, "gets to spend time with her daughter before her wedding—"

And then deliverance came with a couple of beeps. "Oh, sorry Mom, that's the other line—gotta go."

Begone, foul beast! I hastily clicked over to the incoming call. "This is Rhiannon," I answered gratefully.

"So, don't be mad," came my fiancé's voice.

This was, of course, my cue to be mad.

"London's going to bring Evie to the wedding."

"Oh, Will," I groaned. "Why?" As if I didn't know the answer.

"She's really having a hard time, Annie," Will said. "It would really help her, having her best friend there." I heard the judgment, the reproach, beneath his dopey dad-voice.

I let my head fall into my hands, rubbing my pulsing temples. At ten, London Tyler had already earned a teenage-grade merit badge in the sassing and snubbing arts. She had no desire to be my stepdaughter, now or ever, and had made it clear she would not go gentle into that good night.

Yet we had tried so hard already to respect London's understandably conflicted feelings. Will, of course, had wanted both of his daughters *in* the wedding. I'd reluctantly agreed, only to be surprised by the intensity of my humiliation and relief when London had adamantly refused.

Josie, Will's bushy-tailed six-year-old, had accepted the flower girl post with elation. But Josie's eager participation hadn't softened London's convictions. So Will had dangled other carrots: a pre-wedding manicure, a custom-made gown. With each inducement, London had been temporarily mollified.

But now this. I didn't care much about London's *actual* request— another kid at the wedding? Whatever. The heaping buy-offs just turned my stomach, made me want to dig in my heels and refuse London even one more molecule of generosity. But the kid had us over a barrel. I could only leave the negotiations to Will.

"Fine," I gave in. "But *you'll* have to figure out the seating arrangements. I've got to get back to work."

I hung up the phone shakily, trying to pull myself together. Was every bride's wedding this stressful? *Of course*, I told myself brusquely. *Don't be stupid, Annie. This is real life!*

"It's not going to be perfect. It's not a fairy tale," I whispered aloud, trying to remain, as always, one step ahead of my fantasy problem.

But Facebook wasn't helping. (And of course I was still checking it—no matter how busy I was, my obsessive little fingers couldn't stop flitting back to the screen every few minutes.) Everyone I knew seemed to be experiencing unmatched bliss and an unreasonable level of attractiveness.

I took a deep breath.

Facebook is fake, Facebook is fake, Facebook is fake, I reminded myself. And I should know—I'd been the one posting nothing but wedding updates and cute pictures of the girls with captions like "my future daughters!!"

I shuddered to think how social media would have warped my already-fanatical childhood. At age eight, I'd learned that I shared the name of the Welsh moon goddess, and I was off to the fantasy-land races. Was I a goddess too, imprisoned? Like a Calvinist hunting for proof of predestination, I'd spent dozens of hours looking at my face for signs of impending divinity. I'd filled note pads with drawings of crowns and scepters, weeping inconsolably when my puppy mistook my sketch pad for newspaper and drenched my whole collection of casual-wear tiaras. I'd penned coronation speeches and thought excessively about mermaids. Flat as a flounder, I'd dreamed of binding up an ample bosom, flashing creamy cleavage to snare a beautiful prince.

Imagine all that plus constant comparisons between myself and the other girls in class: their outfits, their parties, their ponies—their parents.

Well, I had boobs now, and I had a prince of sorts. I'd made something of myself. I'd trounced my crummy childhood. Life wasn't going to be like my fantasies, but it was close enough—wasn't it? *Just be content, Annie,* I admonished myself in disgust. How could I be surprised that a man this perfect had been loved before?

Just get through work and the wedding, I ordered myself, wrenching my mind back to the job. *Once we're married, everything will be fine.*

2

THOUGH MUSICAL TASTES surely vary, few would argue that "Who Let the Dogs Out?" makes for a stellar wedding march. Yet some kind soul chose it for me, neglecting to turn off a cell phone that blasted its guttural woofs at top volume just as my rickety father delivered me to the altar of our garden ceremony.

But once the gasps and laughter faded, I was back in the moment. *It's not a big deal,* I reminded myself, settling my hands in Will's as the officiant spouted some fluff about wedlock everlasting. Then it was vow-time, and in Will's words and eyes I forgot entirely that a hundred friends sat behind me, that anyone might begrudge me this long-sought ring.

It was my turn. "You are the person I always dreamed of," I said tearfully, junking my stilted script and finding in that moment the elusive, earnest eloquence I had wanted so much for my personal vows. "You are the man I used to sketch in my heart when I was just a child, and the man I want now more than anything in the world."

And then the giggles started.

At first it was just a twitter, one I barely heard as I continued my impromptu gushing. But as it continued—a whisper, a snigger, a snort—I couldn't keep myself from hearing it, and the more I tried the more I got derailed. I stumbled over my final words as the spigot in my heart cranked closed.

But even this I shook off as I felt Will's cool ring, Will's warm mouth, and with a disbelieving shiver heard myself declared his wife.

It really happened! my heart shrieked as we strode happily back down the aisle. The rude and thoughtless couldn't take that away.

Later, delicious buffet fare consumed, guests still chuckling over the best man's send-off speech, my sister Stacia rose to extend her congratulations. Perhaps Stacia was a bit mousey, lacking the best man's impeccable delivery, but that was not the reason none of our guests heard the punch line of her appropriately humiliating prom-night anecdote.

Sobs—racking, phlegmy sobs—exploded over Stacia's soft voice, sending every head in the direction of the kids' tables, where Josie had begun spraying into the air like Old Faithful. Tears spurting, blond curls bouncing, Josie streamed across the room in her pale blue satin to fling herself on her father.

The crowd erupted in applause and laughter. *Look!* they were all clapping, sighing. *How adorable!*

I had to laugh too. This child, this instant family, was nothing to be hidden; it was what I had inherited when I said *I do.* I tousled Josie affectionately, offering the crowd a shrug and grin. What, really, could have been more appropriate? Life with kids was all about surprises. And the effect on my guests was certainly warmer than the conclusion of Stacia's speech would have been.

But as the guests cooed and sighed, as our flower girl hiccupped off her tears, I looked across the room at the kids' table, and saw London give Evie—her best friend and final bribe—a congratulatory high-five. And I just *knew*.

All of it, every interruption, had been London's doing—the cell phone, the tittering, and the working of little Josie into hysterics. Every time I, or someone representing me, had spoken, London had intervened.

What a little bitch, I thought helplessly, too shocked and furious to care that I was inwardly swearing at a grieving ten-year-old. Pouting, whining, pushing back: these were the expected behaviors of stressed-out children. But trying to wreck a wedding was inexcusable.

With a deliberate effort, I took a deep breath and forced my rising shoulders down, adopting a placid bridelike expression. *London hasn't ruined anything,* I reminded myself. The wedding had gone on; Will and I were married now. We would have to deal with all this later. Hearing the tinkling of forks against glasses, I looked away from my stepdaughter's triumphant smirk and drew whoops from the guests when I jumped into Will's lap and showed him just how happy I was to be his wife.

3

THE DANCING, THE caking, the flinging of flowers all went off hitch-free, and once again I relaxed. Even London had lightened up, sliding around the floor in her stockings with her fully recovered sister and the other kids. Now in this late hour, when the old and boring people had gone home, when London's friend had been fetched and the drinkers were just starting to confess how much they all loved each other, I looked around the room and found it absent one groom.

He must have gone out for some air. Or was he helping his elderly Aunt Mamie to her town car?

"Oh *swee*-tie…?" I murmured to myself, feeling a sudden flash of silliness. "Where *are* you…?"

I skipped out to the garden where the ceremony had been held. It was gorgeous and heady in the moonlight, its animal allure not lost on the unidentified couple screwing rowdily in the bushes.

Okay, no.

I went back inside, but Will wasn't there—not at the tables, not on the dance floor, not lounging against the wall with his best man. I managed to brush off a horde of well-wishers, promising deep and magical conversations when I got back in just a tiny little moment.

Out front then? It was that Aunt Mamie after all. Well, I thought, I should say goodbye to the old lady too. I stepped through the arched double doors of the entrance, and my heart sank.

Despite my romantic leanings and divine name, weddings had never been the focus of my fantasies—I had no bulging matrimonial scrapbook tucked beneath a dust ruffle. It was the *man* I'd dreamed of, always, not the orchids and the white dress. But was it too much to ask that, on this day—on my *one* wedding day—I might be spared the sight of the woman whose vagina had slopped out my husband's only children?

Apparently not. Apparently I'd been a fucking idiot to think my husband could have connected those particular dots.

They stood there chatting, my groom and his ex and the golden-haired products of their union. Fairies danced and angels warbled; sparks flew from immaculate teeth. They all looked so cozy together. They looked so *complete*.

God, how I wanted to escape. Or vomit. But if I flounced off now, they would probably notice; if I puked, they certainly would. Crap crap crap. I set my shoulders and walked over. "Hi, Gianna," I said, forcing a smile at Will's ex-wife. "Thanks for picking them up."

"Of course," Gianna said smoothly, then added: "Congratulations. You look beautiful."

"Oh," I blinked. "Thank you." But even in that compliment there was Gianna's constant cool smugness, the unspoken addendum: *but not as beautiful as I did.*

Gianna turned her attention to the children. "Did you have fun?" Josie nodded eagerly, chattering about the quantities of Shirley Temple she'd downed, while her sister just shrugged with pre-adolescent fatigue. "Well, off we go then."

"Hugs!" Josie shrieked, throwing her arms around her beloved father and then, for a touching instant, flinging herself against my dress. By the time I had kissed the six-year-old, London had already hugged Will and turned away.

"See you tomorrow!" Will called after them, waving. I stared at him for a moment, feeling his brimming happiness, his palpable pride. Guiltily I swallowed my dark feelings. This was my husband now. These were my kids. For better or worse, there was no going back.

I was one of the family.

4

IT HAD SOUNDED so sensible and mature when I'd justified it to my friends. This marriage wasn't just the bonding of a couple, I'd explained airily; it was a forging of a *family*—and so what Will and I needed was not some decadent honeymoon but a family vacation, a fresh tablet of shared memories that would help put some of those difficult moments behind us and launch the new Tyler clan off on the right close-knit foot.

What a fucking joke.

Now, in Hawaii's early morning hours, on the fifth day of my familymoon, I sat on the toilet sobbing inconsolably.

It had been such a little thing, really. I'd dealt well with London's mood swings, Josie's need to hold her father's hand every-fucking-where we went, the girls' frequent bickering over cereal-box prizes and radio stations. And we'd truly had some fun moments, snorkeling and body-surfing, even swimming with dolphins. Touching the squeaky bottlenose, London had softened so marvelously that I'd felt for the first time a maternal stirring toward the child.

So it really was going pretty well. The Rhiannon who, I could now admit, hadn't really believed her own bullshit monologue to her friends was standing back a little freaked that the whole thing was coming together.

Yet there were still these little whispering demons. *Send them to the kids' camp for a day, just one day*, I silently begged, knowing that since Will hadn't voiced the idea himself he'd be aghast if I mentioned it. I would have killed for a quiet hour to read or talk; I would have killed for the explosive celebratory sex we still hadn't had. Yet Will seemed invigorated by the constant activity and chatter, content with the one hushed pair of orgasms we'd shared the first night here. I couldn't bring myself to dampen his ebullience. I didn't say a word.

So I stuck with the family agenda, smearing on sunscreen and playing board games and taking refuge once a day in a forty-minute shower in which I struggled mightily not to touch my pent-up privates. I smiled, laughed, did the dishes, and tried hard not to hate the bedazzled, childless newlyweds strolling through the resort. Yet still came the flickering demons. *Wouldn't it be nice if they weren't here with us?* I'd think guiltily, making way for the even deadlier admission: *Wouldn't it be nice if they weren't here—like in this universe—at all?*

But even the simmering nastiness wasn't what sent me over the brink. I didn't let myself think about the demons: I was too afraid, really, to face what those terrible thoughts might mean.

No, what triggered my pre-dawn meltdown was the simplest little thing.

I'd wakened—sort of—flopping myself over in a somnolent haze to press my body against Will's prone one, to tangle my sleepy fingers in his hair—

Except his hair was long and curly and I couldn't have jolted out of bed any faster if I'd slid my hand over scales or slime.

I stood there trembling, blinking my eyes to clarity in the ashy dark. And yes, there they were, father and daughter, totally conked and side by side, both on their faces like murder victims or—*for God's sake, Annie, what an image*—discarded dolls.

Lip quivering, I went to the bathroom to pee and began to bawl. It was nothing, this little invasion, yet it symbolized everything— the no romance and no sex, the no honeymoon and no time, the crazy-making inanity of nonstop kid-blather. It was the claustrophobia of being surrounded day and night by children I was supposed to love but barely knew. It was the horror I felt at my own hateful, unmotherly thoughts, the rising panic that I had made an unworkable and atrocious commitment. It was the fact that I'd nearly humped my stepdaughter and my husband didn't seem to notice through his invincible euphoria that I had never been more miserable in my life.

Finally, when my tears tapered off and I suspected that another five minutes here would see my butt permanently welded to the toilet seat, I peeled myself up, rinsed my face, and tiptoed back to the bedroom. Josie had rotated diagonally; she seemed to be impersonating a starfish. Too tired to argue, I threw a robe over myself and curled up to sleep in the chair.

5

"DADDY, DADDY, SUGARPLUM Daddy..." I heard distantly from my spine-mangling armchair. There was nothing for a moment. Then, louder: "Sugarplum! Daddy!"

Somewhere across the room, Will groaned. "Hey JoJo," he mumbled. "Whatcha doing in here?"

"I came to sleep with you, Daddy, don't you remember?"

"Oh. Right." But I suspected he had no memory of whatever had brought his youngest daughter to our bed. It might go down as an unsolved mystery. "Where's Annie?" I heard him yawn.

"I dunno!" Josie said brightly. "Get up, Daddy, let's get up!"

"Okay, okay," Will said. I peeked open an eye and saw Josie hauling at her father's arm like a fisherman at a bursting net. One more second and the bed would be mine.

"Oh no!" Will said. "There's our Annie!"

I opened my eyes. Will and Josie were sitting on the bed staring at me with adorably identical concerned foreheads. "Oh, hi," I said, as though I hadn't been awake from the first cry of the Sugarplum.

"Are you okay, Annie?" Josie asked, hopping down and running over.

"Yes, I am," I said. "I just thought there was more room for me out here." I slapped a hand down on the seat and sent Will a you-owe-me-one smile.

Will cringed back at me apologetically. "Do you want to get a little more sleep, hon?"

I nodded gratefully, already on my way. I slid beneath the cool sheets and sighed with pleasure as the door clicked closed.

When I awoke, the house was silent. *Now this is a vacation,* I thought happily, wandering out to the kitchen for a cup of coffee. Stuck to the fridge was a note:

Annie, we've gone down to the beach. Come meet us!
We've rented a sailboat, so be there by 10!
Love you, Will

Hmm, I thought. Hmmm.

It was 9:20. I could certainly make it. But this silence was so luxurious, so thick and dreamy I could almost scoop it with a spoon. I could just go out on the balcony, sip my coffee, flip through a magazine, close my eyes…

I looked at the note again, pondering. Then I went to get my phone.

"*Hi!*" Summer cried. "How *are* you?"

I took my best friend through the last several days, trying to pitch my retelling toward the humorous. Now that I'd slept, it all seemed like a sitcom-script, my crisis in the bathroom more overdramatic than agonizing.

Still, as soon as I'd finished, Summer asked wryly: "Still think it was such a good idea to take a family vacation instead of a honeymoon?"

I caved at once. "No way," I said. "It was completely idiotic. Why didn't you tell me?"

"You were not to be argued with," Summer said. "You made me feel like such a self-centered slut for having a honeymoon and not sharing it with homeless children or something."

I groaned. "Ugh, I'm sorry. I didn't mean it that way." And I hadn't. But I'd felt so pressured to justify my every decision, especially to myself—and to those, like Summer, who proudly displayed their beautifully rounding bellies.

"I'm joking," Summer said. "It was fun listening to you make your case. You're such a cute little weirdo."

"Uh, *thanks?*" I laughed. It had been such an odd case to make. All of our friends were parents, pregnant, or dating the young and childless; none had ever had to ponder the far-reaching implications of skipping town without the step-moppets. Of course *they* would never want to share a honeymoon with someone else's children; who would? And yet they'd never say so, for they all instinctively grasped what grievous personal consequences would result from that kind of disclosure.

I, on the other hand—well, by virtue of my decision to marry Will, I was supposed to want, indeed to *prefer*, that family vacation. If I didn't, my friends would wonder, even frown; they'd doubt my generosity, my character. What else could I have said? And so they'd all gushed about how wonderful I was, how maternal, the only kind of person who should ever leap into stepparenting.

"Sooo..." Summer glinted, "how was the wedding night?"

I groaned again, admitting the terrible truth.

"What?" my friend cried. "I thought you were staying the first night at a hotel?"

"We did," I said. "The suite was all very lovely for the five minutes we were awake. Then we got up at six the next morning and jetted out here."

"Well, you *have* to get some tonight," Summer insisted. "Or that guy does *not* deserve to be your husband." She paused, then said impishly, "He was *very* cute, by the way, at the wedding. And, oh my God, how cute is Josie?"

"She's great," I replied honestly, about to reveal how not-great her older sister's antics had been…but at the last second bit back the words. "They're both great. How are you?"

"Good!" Summer said, summarizing the past several days of an achy-but-glowing pregnancy. I could tell she was caressing her taut skin. "I can't believe I'm almost a mommy," she giggled.

"Me either!" It was hard for me to fathom that my scabby-kneed neighbor had become a married woman, about to make life with the very body she always worried would doom her to perpetual virginity. "You're going to be great." I paused, staring out the window at the tranquil blue. "But God, it's hard, Summer. It's really hard."

"Well, of course it is," Summer said. "But it's different when it's your own."

"Sure, of course," I said at once, and I knew that it was. But I was still miffed at Summer's superior overtones when, five minutes later, I hung up the phone and pulled on my swimsuit, reluctantly forgoing another orgasm-opportunity so I could make it to the sailboat harbor on time.

6

WILL AND THE girls were just clambering into their small boat when I came skittering down the slope and out to the dock.

"Hi, sweetie!" Will called, while Josie jumped up and down, clapping and shouting *Annie! Annie! Annie!* Even London offered an abbreviated wave.

"Hi, guys," I huffed, stepping into the tiny craft. "Thanks for waiting."

"We didn't know if you were going to come," Josie told her.

"Are you kidding? I wouldn't miss it!" I insisted brightly, tousling the girl's hair. And with that simple gesture I felt my feelings turning a half-rotation, clicking into place at *glad to be here after all*.

We launched out into the crystalline water. Though I hadn't sailed since an ill-fated episode at Girl Scout camp twenty years previous, London and even Josie seemed comfortable with the thwapping and creaking of the whole strange apparatus. It was Josie's job, she made clear through frequent and zealous demonstration, to scream out *DUCK! DUCK!* whenever the boom swung, perilously swift, across the hull.

"I don't want you to get bopped in the head like I did," Josie explained, placing a serious hand on my knee. "I don't want that at all."

"So where did you learn so much about sailing?" I asked. "Are you some kind of sea-captain?"

Josie clapped her hands together with the hilarity of my suggestion. "NO! I'm just a kid. But we go sailing with Mommy and Ren alllllll the time."

"We've been like *twice*," London corrected her sister, then explained to the adults: "Ren got a new boat."

"The *Flying Clint!*" Josie shrieked.

I sneaked a glance at Will. Gianna's second husband—the tall, sandy-haired real estate millionaire—was not one of Will's favorite subjects. Nor was Ren's son, the four-year-old athletic prodigy whose name now festooned the side of their family yacht.

But if Will was bothered, he didn't show it. "Well, if I had a boat, I'd name it after my kids too," he said. "I'd call it...hmm...the *Whiny Butthead.*"

"Daddy!" Josie screeched, and London socked her father's arm.

"That should be the name of Ren's boat too," London declared. "Clint is *such* a pain."

"Yes," Josie glowered. "He always acts like a big stinky baby."

I knew how hard it had been for Josie, the beloved youngest, to share her mother and stepfather's affections with her four-year-old stepbrother. Peevish and wrong as it certainly was, I was relieved to think there could be tension at Gianna's house too—that Will and I lavished upon Josie the special treatment that she now lacked from her own mother. *You were the one who was always there for me,* I imagined Josie saying to me one day, a vision of verklempt loveliness. *You were my* real *mother.*

"—Earth to Rhiannon!"

I blinked. Oh, geez. Lost again in the most predictable and unachievable of stepmother fantasies. "Sorry," I shook my head. "I spaced out."

"I was just saying," Will repeated, "that the girls will always be the favorites at our house. Isn't that right?"

There was a line, fissure-thin, between Comforting the Children and Bad-Mouthing the Ex; it was not Will's style to straddle it so unabashedly. "Yes, of course they will," I said anyway, wondering at my husband's insistence. Then London spotted a spray of flying fish and we all turned to gape at the breakneck hurtling. I could only marvel at their easy balance, their effortless sailing between sea and sky.

After lunch, Will had a surprise.

"Snorkeling and sundaes!" he'd shouted, and I had girded myself for another afternoon of hardcore Funning with the Family. But as I'd begun to paw the box of snorkels for something that would fit me, Will had coiled an arm around my waist. "No, my darling," came the low and devilish whisper. "This is just for the kids."

"What?" I'd asked, bracing for disappointment even as my hope flared. But in his face was my own hunger and I felt myself flooded with hormones and glee. *Oh thank God.* My fingers began to play at the knot on my sarong.

Later, endowed with the tender nipples and vocal chords befitting a newlywed, I lay in my husband's arms and dared to slip on my old confidence. *Of course I made the right choice,* I thought dreamily, feeling the wonder and relief lap against me like a calming tide. *We are meant for each other. Nothing can touch that.*

7

"MOMMYMOMMYMOMMYMOMMY!" JOSIE SHRIEKED across the room as the phone rang. "Mommymommymommymommy!"

Why the girl had to be constantly ashriek was a mystery I had yet to solve.

"MOMMY!" At last Josie had flipped open the phone. "HI!"

"Yes!"

"Yes."

"Yes. We went to the pizza store. Yes."

And then came the flood, Josie's great daily vomiting of every single thing any of us had said or consumed or undergone. Standing at our kitchenette sink, I gritted my teeth and scrubbed some dishes, trying madly to tune out the exasperating play-by-play. "…Daddy spilled on his new shirt," Josie recounted, then launched into an agony of incertitude as to whether the soup she'd ordered at the beachfront grill had smelled more like cleaning spray or pee. "Oh! There was a big fat lady in the pool…"

Scrub scrub scrub. Ignore ignore ignore. I am not listening. I am not caring.

"…then Annie farted and we all laughed!"

"*Oh*-kay, JoJo, that's enough," Will said, snapping up the phone and ending the scatological adventure as I quietly died in my dishwater. "London? Do you want to talk to Mom?"

Wordlessly London took the cell into the bedroom while Josie howled at the injustice. "You can say goodbye after London is finished," Will said, the magic words instantly drying the tears on Josie's cheeks. She skipped off singing to play with her dolls.

I scrubbed, hearing Will approach. I felt his lips on my neck, his hands slide down my thighs. "Sorry about that, sweetie."

I kept working the saucepan. Should I be mad, humiliated, over it? "Can we, uh, have a talk with Josie about what we share and what we don't?"

"That's an excellent idea," Will nuzzled. "Although, you know..."

His lips were giving me the chills. I leaned back against him, letting the pan float back into the murk. "What?"

"It *was* a pretty loud fart. I think the public has a right to know about it, don't you?"

I turned around and smacked him with a sudsy hand. "Shut UP!"

"I think *you* are the one who needs to be quieter!" he guffawed, and then I was scooping the chunk-filled water out of the sink and into his face, and he was shaking the rinsed and drippy plates over my head, and London had emerged from the bedroom and handed the phone back to Josie, who resumed her sportscasting duties with gusto.

"Mommy, they're having a water fight, Daddy and Annie! And now he just *kissed* her!"

Well, sometimes full disclosure had its benefits.

8

WE *LOOKED* LIKE newlyweds.

Will wore a blue dress shirt; my shoulders overflowed with forty-dollar lei. Petals peeked from my French twist; earrings glinted and dangled; our fingers entwined across the creamy tablecloth that children never tugged or stained. Twenty-eight and thirty-four, eating grilled polenta and butter-drenched clam linguine, we looked like any couple here: young and fresh and unencumbered, setting out on a path yet to be carved.

Except that we couldn't stop talking about the kids.

"So did you find out about Josie's camp next week?" I asked in spite of myself. It was pathetic: we'd start to talk about something adult, something *else,* and within moments were back to silence or another observation about Josie and London.

"Nah," Will said. "I'll have to ask Gianna when we get back."

I gazed at my husband. Dark hair, blue eyes, caramel skin after these seven days in the sun. He was stunning, everything my fantasies could ever conjure, and he'd made these reservations as another surprise—our last Hawaiian evening preciously alone and romantic while the girls watched movies with a resort-endorsed babysitter.

And yet—and yet—

"Do you know what was wrong with London?" I had been afraid to ask earlier, afraid to taint the date with unsavory conversation as we'd strolled away from our suite and left a sulking London behind a locked bedroom door. But now—hell, it was time for dessert, and despite the potential discomfort I really wanted to know.

"It's just hard for her, Annie," Will sighed, as though he'd hoped too that I would leave it be. "It's hard for her to see us together, hard to be left behind."

I nodded with more sympathy than I felt. Yes, it was hard, but London had now had *two years* to adjust to her father's new life with me, two years as the beneficiary of every possible effort and peace offering I could whip up. To begrudge us one dinner alone on our goddamn honeymoon? The girl had serious nerve.

"I just don't understand her," I confessed. "She's so hot and cold with me. Nice, friendly, then mean and cold. I guess I thought she'd be reserved at first, but then warm up to me. But it changes every day. Every few minutes."

Will smiled sadly. "Well, she is her mother's daughter. Gianna can be quite the ice queen." Thankfully, he didn't elaborate on his ex-wife's hotter side.

"But has she been like this with other people?" I pressed. "Maybe she needs to talk to someone. You know, a therapist. She seems to have…a lot of strong emotions about me."

Will brushed off the suggestion with a shake of his head. "Just give it time, Annie. She *will* get over it. She *will* love you as much as Josie and I do. You just have to be patient. Remember, she's just a child."

I stared at him. Was London "just a child"? Was she a child when she blasted reggae dog-barking over our wedding ceremony? Was she a child when she deliberately mucked up my vows? Something about Will's dopey apologia made all my bridely anger rise from its shallow grave.

"Will, she's not that innocent," I said, my annoyance showing. "She was trying her hardest to ruin our wedding." I'd intended to bring this up another time, when we were safely home and alone on the mainland, but…well…

His expression was both disgusted and incredulous. "That's preposterous," he said. "She was having a great time."

"Open your eyes, Will!" I hissed. "Didn't you hear her giggling during my vows? I *saw* her high-five Evie when Josie started crying at the reception. And the cell phone going off?"

"That could have been anyone," he insisted.

"Yeah, maybe in 2001," I rolled my eyes. "Nobody plays that song anymore. Nobody but London."

Will sat back in his chair. "You're accusing my daughter of, what, not turning off her cell phone? Who cares? Plus a bunch of other things that didn't even *happen* except in your head?" He looked absolutely revolted by me. "It's really low, Annie. So beneath you. What's next, boarding school in Switzerland?"

The tears sprung to my eyes. True, I'd gone about this all the wrong way, practically inviting Will to the defensive, but I'd never imagined he'd reject my proof. Then again—God—*was* it even proof? *Was* I being a wicked stepmother, inventing reasons to condemn a moody but faultless ten-year-old? All I could do was shake my head numbly, trying to restrain my streaking mascara.

"Look." His voice softened. "I thought our wedding was perfect. It was one of the best days of my life. None of those little blips ruined anything. Nothing could have."

Oh, nicely played, Will. I looked up at him for a trembling moment before my mascara just resigned and I blubbered into my napkin, head bobbing with apologies and accord. He was right; he was so right. *Why* was I being so petty? Blips made us human; they'd made the day our own. Nothing mattered but the joy and love that had prevailed.

9

ONLY AFTER A 168-hour family vacation, culminating in an over-ripe flight brimming with whiners, did I truly understand the claw-ing, screeching desperation of the clinically claustrophobic.

"But I'm *hungry,*" Josie was saying, cranking into a session of fake-crying and seat-punching that quickly turned to genuine sobs as Will grabbed her arm roughly and gave her a dressing-down, sotto voce. I put my head in my hands, fighting off the foaming desire to kill. Finally, just as Josie's moans began to ebb, the infant across the aisle started squalling.

It was unreal. When the plane finally shuddered to a halt, it was all I could do not to squash the departing grandmas in a crazed dash for freedom.

Then it was baggage hour, and London's turn to go sour as she vainly begged Will to let Evie spend the night. Josie, meanwhile, had long since recovered and was *vroom*ing around the turnstile spitting happily on all the weary travelers.

I have inherited the two most mercurial children in the world, I thought in bewilderment. Tears to sunbeams and back again in zero-point-five.

The same black bags circled around and around. The same babies bleated. I stared longingly out the window at the mass of taxis, pic-turing a quick sprint and a hasty getaway. I could be back to the child-free sanctuary of my apartment in twenty little minutes…

I sidled over to Will. "Sweetie, I still have a lot of packing to do," I murmured quietly. "I'm wondering if I should spend the night at my apartment."

He looked so surprised, so wounded. "But I can help you pack tomorrow."

This was true. He could. The kids were set to leave at nine A.M. And yet the whole plan would go quite awry if I dismembered them before then.

"I'm just worried I won't have time to get it all done," I said, but Will was having none of it.

"Stay with me, Annie, please?" He grabbed my hands. "You're my wife. It's you and me together, from now on." He flashed me the googly eyes. "Come on, please?"

"All right," I relented, my insides stabbing with guilt and disappointment in equal measure. *I shouldn't be feeling like this,* I thought with a rising pulse. I was a married woman, for God's sake, linked to this man and these kids for life; after tomorrow I wouldn't even *have* an apartment. Yet the lure of alone-time winked and dangled; I felt like a convict salivating over a looming jailbreak.

Finally, finally, our luggage appeared and we staggered over to wait for the shuttle and then, back in the car, the greasy deliverables of a McDonald's drive-through. At home we squeezed wordlessly onto the couch while Will popped in a movie. Within ten minutes, surrounded by balled-up wrappers and squandered fries, our whole family was asleep.

10

"WHERE *IS* SHE?" I asked Will discreetly. It was 9:45 and the kids were still in our living room. I had exceeded my family-time limit by forty-five minutes; it would truly be tragic if I'd managed to hold it together all last night only to disintegrate as the clock struck ten.

Will was clueless. "Is she late? Oh, I'll call."

He called. But there was no answer.

"Will, we're supposed to pick up the truck at ten," I said anxiously. "We have to go."

"Okay, well, you go get the truck and leave your car at the rental place, and we'll pick it up later. I'll meet you at the apartment as soon as Gianna shows."

I nodded, grabbing my purse. But at the door I hesitated, turning back to London and Josie, who were both too ensconced in cartoons to acknowledge my pending departure. Despite how grievously I wanted a break—how much stronger the eye-clawing instinct had grown with each of the passing forty-five minutes—I felt sudden pangs that I wouldn't see the girls for a whole week. There, at the door, footsteps from freedom, I almost wanted to stay.

This was the thing that no amount of thinking or calculating had prepared me for: the emotional spectrum collapsing in on itself, the self-directed and interconnected and childless and child-blessed and wanting and not-wanting all mixing together like so many noodles in a soup too weird to be put on the menu.

I walked back into the room. "JoJo, I'm going to start packing my things, sweetie, so I'll see you when you come back next week, okay?" I smoothed the girl's hair.

"Bye-bye, Annie!" Josie responded, jumping up and throwing her arms around me. "Now kiss me!" she cried, and I laughed and smooched the little rosebud mouth.

Now the hard one. "Bye, London," I said, taking an awkward step closer but not sure whether to force a hug. "Have a fun week with your mom, okay?"

"'Kay," London answered distantly, eyes still fixated on the screen.

That was it. Okay then. I reached out and hastily rubbed the unsociable shoulder, then left without another word.

Hours and boxes and rolls of tape later, Will finally called me. "I'm really sorry, honey, but there's been a change in plans."

11

I SAT IN the moving truck, seething out the window. Will was at the wheel, just a short rubbery slide across the seat yet an icy acre away.

We had barely spoken since Will had finally showed up, already checking his watch, to put the finishing touches on my long, lonely day of packing. And only now, halfway to my new home, could I bear to hear the details.

"So what time exactly?" I asked.

"I don't know," was all he said. "Pretty soon."

We drove in silence, swaying and bumping with the road.

"Annie, I'm sorry," Will finally said. "I really am. But it's not my fault, okay?"

Oh, yes. Poor little helpless Will. "It was your decision to say yes," I reminded him tightly. "You don't have to say yes to everything."

"I have to keep the peace," he said wearily. "If you don't understand that, then..."

"Then what?" I snapped.

But he didn't answer.

When we reached the house, dusk had fallen. In the driveway, Gianna sat waiting in her white BMW. The very sight of her made me nauseated with fury.

Will parked the truck on the street and we walked wordlessly up to the house. Gianna and the girls had emerged from the car. "Daddy!" Josie squealed in ecstasy. But London looked as though she'd been crying.

"All right, then," Will said, his gesture somewhere between a wave and a surrender. "I hope it goes well."

"Thanks," Gianna said. "I really appreciate it." But gratitude, I wagered bitterly, was not the primary emotion flickering behind Gianna's aquamarine eyes.

It was eerie how effortlessly Will and I fell into that time-honored technique of managing a household and children without once speaking to each other.

I thought this was probably not a good sign. But there was not a chance in hell I would make nicey-nice without having thrashed through what had happened today. I would ignore my marriage before I would fake it.

I hate that smug bitch, I thought in bed, letting my fury percolate while Will tooled around in the bathroom. Gianna's self-satisfied face floated before my eyes, the golden hair billowing around in shampoo-commercial flurries.

After Will climbed in beside me, a moment of silence passed. Then he finally spoke.

"What can I say, Annie? What can I do?"

But I didn't answer. "She did this on purpose," I said instead. "She waited until the last minute to spring this on you."

"Come on, Annie—it was a work thing."

I snorted. Since marrying Ren, Gianna donated her time to a smattering of charities. She didn't *work.*

"Look, part of this whole shared parenting thing is that you have to be flexible sometimes," Will said. "Now she owes us one. If something like this ever comes up for us, we can ask Gianna—"

"But we *wouldn't*, Will," I said. "That's the difference. We *wouldn't* ever do that and if we did I guarantee you she would say no. Because she'd have plans. Just like *we* had plans. Do you know how hard it's going to be to get everything moved tomorrow with the girls under-foot?"

"That's life with kids, Annie!" Will said, exasperated. "You have to roll with the punches. It's not going to be your perfect little orderly life anymore. You've got to grow up here, stop being so selfish—"

Oh no he didn't! I had a fleeting, marvelous image of myself whooping Will on daytime TV like some unkempt cavewoman, riot-ous crowds cheering me on.

Without saying a word, I switched off my light.

12

I HAD THOUGHT I'd done a pretty good job with the pre-move weeding, but as I stood before a spindly tower of boxes whose zenith seemed to blot out the sun, I began to have my doubts.

"It's bigger than the tree in *The Nutcracker!*" said Josie in awe.

The kid had a point. There was no way that this stuff was fitting in that house.

"Holy crap!" London chimed in as she emerged from the house. "What do you *have* in there?"

A lifetime—that was all. My former roommate had kept her own things, of course, but—as I had proved the better accumulator—the apartment had looked sufficiently pillaged once I had boxed up my booty.

"This will be fun," Will beamed to the girls. "Annie has lots of nice things. When we have duplicates, we can decide whose is better and keep that one. We'll get a whole bunch of new stuff this way!"

It sounded good. But as they started to comb through the pickings, somehow it always seemed to be my model that got voted off the island. My beat-up coat rack? Okay, good decision. My calcium-crusted vases? Sure, that was fair. Since Will hadn't showed for the packing, I had kept more than I'd intended to, not knowing exactly what the Tyler home already had. But when Josie opted for their ravaged Scrabble board over my pristine collector's edition, I knew there were some serious errors in either the girls' taste or their criteria. As the family continued to critique my cache of worldly belongings, I began hovering around the throwaway box, discreetly salvaging the unfairly condemned.

Soon, of course, both girls had lost interest and wandered off, leaving Will and me to drudge through the rest. At long last we had an approved hoard to distribute, an equally large pile to release to the garage-sale crowd.

"Girls!" Will screamed into the house. "Come help!"

Josie was there instantly, proud to be helpful and swift with the anecdotes. "When we moved into Ren's house," she told us, "there were lots of men who moved *all* our stuff. We just had to say 'put it there, put it there' and they did whatever we wanted!"

Will tried his best. "Wo-ow," he said flatly.

Six-year-olds weren't great at picking up on tone. Josie gushed on, "My room was soooo big that we had to buy more stuff just to fill it up!"

"Well, lucky for us, that's not going to be a problem this time," her father answered, mostly succeeding in keeping the sarcasm out of his voice. "Who'd want to have to go *shopping?*"

The plan was to transport each item from the driveway to its rightful place. But between cabinets that were too crammed and children that were too bewildered, the pile just re-accumulated inside the front door. "Girls," Will said, rapidly losing patience, "this isn't helpful. We need you to put these things *away.*"

But after a chorus of *but but buts* it became obvious that no one under twelve was going to be unpacking a thing.

I was secretly grinning. It was almost apology time!

I set about putting my things away, swapping out items and re-boxing the Tyler discards. For a couple of hours it went pleasantly enough. But the pile was endless, the crevices of the house so grubby and disorganized and *full of crap.* Will's temperament, in steady decline now, was no longer a source of told-you-so glee but only a chafing nuisance.

"Where do you want this?" he barked at me, holding up a serving platter. "What drawer do you want this in?"

"Will, it's your kitchen," I shot back. "I don't know what drawer. My guess would be with the other serving platters."

He went muttering off.

"No! You can't put that there!" Josie suddenly cried out as I tried to find a spot on the mantel to display a beautiful sculpture I'd scored from an acclaimed local artist. "That's where Mommy's statue goes!"

I looked in surprise at the dinky little figurine I had displaced. It was a ceramic piece of dollar-store quality, a slim and shapely woman with lopsided eyes and painted yellow hair. It looked like something a dirty television orphan might be clutching. The stricken look on Josie's face, however, suggested innumerable riches.

"How about here, then?" I offered, restoring Gianna's tacky effigy and scooting aside an even uglier piece of junk.

"Nooo!" Josie screeched, fat tears welling in her eyes. "Not there! That's my Daddy's special Disneyland ashtray!"

"Well, what would be a good place, then?" I asked through my teeth.

Josie considered. "Maybe the bathroom?"

"Okay," I patted Josie, returning the sculpture to its box. We'd have to decide this one later.

And Josie wasn't the only one. As I tried to force my linens into the overflowing hall closet, London's teary voice floated from the kitchen: "I just don't like her touching Mom's things—"

"Mom doesn't have things here," I heard Will answer tersely. "Mom's things are at Mom's house. These are our things."

"But stuff that you had when Mom was here," London pleaded. "All our stuff. Our family *heirlooms*."

Jesus. If that Gianna statue was an heirloom, this family was trashier than Jerry Springer's entire studio audience.

"Aaaagh!" I screamed at the linen closet, flinging a chunk of towels onto the floor. My every neuron shouted *escape.* But I had no apartment, no room of my own—and, God Almighty, there was still so much to *do.*

My clothes! I thought suddenly, joyfully, realizing I could shut myself into the bedroom and deal with the little matter of my voluminous wardrobe, which, last I looked, had been heaped in a corner with hangers akimbo. It would also be good to spend a little time with my cat, Mr. Pickles, whom I'd left yowling under the bed that morning.

I smelled him before I saw him. But kitty messes I could handle. I almost envied the little guy: if only I could express my displeasure to the rest of the family in such an easy and unambiguous fashion. They'd find the mess in the hallway, look at each other in alarm. *Uh-oh. Annie's pissed.*

I sniffed my way to the source and guffawed as I saw that Mr. Pickles clearly shared my sentiments about the Tyler household: he'd left his housewarming gift swirled atop Will's pillow. Never had I so wanted to high-five my cat. *Should I even tell Will?* I wondered wickedly as I grabbed tissues to play the responsible pet owner. *Oh, should I have changed the sheets?* I imagined myself saying innocently. *I didn't want to risk getting my dirty homewrecker cooties all over London's precious heirlooms!*

Not that I thought that Gianna had touched those sheets. I mean, she hadn't, right? *They* hadn't...in these sheets...right?

Egad. Way to be disgusting, Annie. Just in case, we'd be buying new sheets. I stripped off all the linens before disentangling my pile of clothes. At last I had everything folded and re-hung and ready to put away. I opened a drawer—the closet—another drawer—and another—then everything in the room, my mouth falling open—

Will had not made a speck of room for my things. He had told me he was going to, *promised* he was going to clear everything out before the move, give me half of the space.

But he had done nothing.

I felt the persevering little flame in my chest gutter out. It was the clearest, boldest message, the last note in a blaring symphony of unwelcomeness. I slumped to the floor, tears welling. How would a man who couldn't make room for me in his *closet* ever really make room for me in his life?

"I can't do this," I whispered. "I can't live like this."

Somewhere in the house, Josie erupted in wake-inspired wailing.

I squeezed my eyes shut, a huddled Dorothy begging for home, but this was it: a fabric-strewn room fragranced with cat shit and a screaming six-year-old just outside the door.

13

AS SOON AS Will came in, he knew.

"Oh Annie," he said, seeing me balled up and sobbing. "I'm so sorry. I just never found the time. And then it was the wedding, and the trip, and the kids were here yesterday—"

I didn't look up. He slid down next to me on the carpet.

"I didn't know you were in here or I would have warned you. I thought we could take care of the clothes tomorrow—"

"I have to work tomorrow," I said flatly.

"When you get home," he suggested hopefully.

I looked at him for a moment in exquisite pain, then burst into a garbled monologue about *respect* and *welcome*, hideous statues and missing Scrabble tiles that succeeded in conveying the depth of my wretchedness if not any coherent narrative.

"Oh, honey," Will murmured, pulling me into his arms. "I'm so sorry. This was a terrible idea. You were right about everything."

Now this was more like it. I stopped crying. "I was?" I whimpered pathetically against his chest.

"You were," he said. "And next time we move you into this house, I promise that everything will be different."

"I'm going to hold you to that," I said, sniffling my way into a smile. I sat up and looked at his face. Etched there was his own weariness, and I instantly felt indulgent and guilty for crying over a few homeless sweaters. "Oh sweetie. How are *you* doing?"

"Oh," he said with one of his vague gestures, "I pretty much want to kill them."

"Yes," I said softly. And we sat side by side against the bed, listening to the sounds of stomping and yelling, two large and exhausted adults taking this tiny refuge from the energy-onslaught of two small children.

"Okay," Will finally said. "I'll take care of this."

And he picked up the phone.

A few minutes later, Will and I were peacefully stowing wine glasses and tablecloths when the phone rang.

London answered. "Really?" came her excited voice. "Let me ask!"

She skipped into the kitchen, Josie pelting her with questions that she ignored. "Dad, it's Cousin Cammy, she wants me and Josie to go over for a sleepover, can we go?"

"Oh, what a nice idea!" Will exclaimed. "Of course you can go. Now let me talk to my cousin."

I smiled to myself as the girls jumped and screamed. Despite the late notice, Will's cousin had already agreed to watch Josie and London the next day so Will and I could go to work as planned. But taking them for a whole additional night—upon even later notice—was an act of sheer holiness. I sighed happily and bound myself in grateful slavery to this beneficent woman.

In ninety minutes, the girls were packed up and gone, Will walking back in the door laden with savory Chinese takeout. I leapt up and covered his face with kisses. *What a terrible person you are,* said a disgusted voice in the back of my mind. *What kind of mother is her happiest when the children are gone?*

14

STRIDING CONFIDENTLY THROUGH the front door of my office the next day, I felt happier than I had since the morning of my wedding.

There was something really sick about that. I had been a tourist, a honeymooner, the envy of every hunched and surly cubicle-dweller. Yet here I was alone, and in control, in a place where people liked and respected me—in a place where I knew exactly what I was doing.

Ah, competence. Self-possession. Skill! How I'd taken them for granted. How delicious it was to reclaim them now. I felt myself donning the self I remembered, sliding into my skin as though it were a beloved silk dress that had lingered too long at the cleaners.

But I faltered as I stopped at my cube. How surreal, how bittersweet it was to see *Rhiannon Delesio* there, not just a name but an identity that was no longer mine. I had left with that name, with an eagerness and optimism that already seemed childish and ill-advised. If one little week as Mrs. Tyler had so shaken twenty-eight years of aplomb, what pathetic bottom-feeder over the years could I expect to become?

"Welcome home, Annie!" came another jovial well-wisher, and I turned with a smile to make the small talk, to gush about the weather and the water and the piña coladas, to promise the photos, to show off the ring. They were all so happy for me. I wanted to protest, *no, please stop, don't you see? I think I've made a terrible mistake!* But of course I went along with it, letting them interpret my thank-God-I'm-back exuberance as the blooming joy of a new wife and mother. Some of the bitterest single women, trying hard to keep it together, even huffed out of my way.

Still, I slid my new name placard into the slot in my cube, tucking *Rhiannon Delesio* into my drawer as a keepsake. I talked to HR about updating my email address and made plans to doll up my desk with family photos.

And then I worked.

All day my coworkers came by to greet me. All day I smiled and fibbed. But when my friend Ted came by at three, trying to lure me into a furtive coffee break, I knew the jig was up.

15

AT THIS OFFICE three years before, fumbling through insurance forms and yoga-breathing my way through the new-girl jitters, I had been serenaded by a man in a sombrero and a man with a kazoo.

The man in the sombrero had been Will.

The man with the kazoo had been Ted.

They'd taken me to their favorite coffee place, quizzed me on my dating preferences, and become my first friends at Highlink Enterprises. When, a year later, Will had left the two of us behind to pursue bonnier opportunities at other firms, I had inherited his sombrero and his place at Ted's side. But in the past six months, I'd been immersed in my wedding and Ted in his prolific personal problems; we'd become the proverbial ships in the night. I'd barely even spoken to him at the wedding.

Walking down to that historical coffee shop—still our favorite—I realized just how much I'd missed Ted's goofiness and candor, his excellent ear. I smiled in the comfortable silence as we stood in line for coffee.

"So?" Ted asked finally as we secured a small table. "I'm dying here. How'd it go?"

For a moment I considered the party-line response. And then I grabbed the table and leaned toward him with sparkling eyes.

"Ted, can I tell you how happy I am to be back here?" I was giddy, cackling like a leprechaun.

He raised an eyebrow. "Okay, who gave you the drugs?"

"Oh Ted, you know I'm drug-free and proud!" I said wildly. "*Competence* is my drug! My *own*—*beautiful*—*competence!*"

Ted pushed his chair back slowly and pretended to plan an escape. "Ohhhkay, Annie..."

I grabbed his hand on the table. "You don't understand. For nearly ten days now I have felt like a pathetic, unbalanced, unlikable and clueless moron. But here I am a goddess, Ted. Here...I have power. Here...people like me. I love work and *I am never going home*."

"Holy shit, Annie. You obviously have way too many issues to cover in one coffee break."

I certainly did. But I took him through the whole trip, even scraping off the sugar coating I'd applied for Summer's critical ears. I talked without a worry about eliciting any of the three Deadly Responses: Pity, Denunciation, and Useless Advice.

"So I may be a lousy fucking mother," I ended with flourish, "but I think I have a lousy fucking husband and lousy fucking kids."

"Bravo!" Ted applauded me when I finished. "A fine monologue. Four stars." He put his hands down. "But I'm confused. Didn't you guys practically live together already? What's the big change?"

"I thought we did too," I said. "But this was so different. I guess I didn't realize how different it would be without any kind of break." Looking back, I realized I'd never been with the kids—let alone somewhat in charge of them—for anywhere near that long. Even in the months before the wedding, when I'd spent more time at Will's house than anywhere else, there had always been an afternoon's respite or a night away. There had always been the seven-day stretches when the girls lived with Gianna. There had always been my own apartment, eternally available and taken utterly, stupidly for granted.

"It won't be like this very often, I know," I conceded. "They'll be gone in a day, and then we'll be on our normal schedule. I'll get time with Will, time to put my stuff away and throw out their heinous crap. I'll get time to *like them again*—that's what I really need. Time to miss them again and like them."

"Annie, I think you're doing great," Ted said. "No, really. I think it's hard to like any kid when you're with them nonstop. I'm sure my parents didn't like us all the time. I know my friends with kids get burned out."

I nodded thoughtfully. "It's easier on Will, though. He gets frustrated too, but he loves them, you know? He *loves* them—can't imagine life without them. And I—well, it seems like I'm always waiting for them to leave so that my real life can begin."

I couldn't believe I'd said that out loud. But as we looked at each other across the table, I saw that Ted was only nodding. "I think you just need time, Annie," he said. "Just give yourself time to get used to it all."

I nodded, finishing my coffee in a final satisfied gulp. "Well, thanks for letting me go on and on. I really should pay you for this. You're a lifesaver." I thought briefly of my life's league of females, mother-sister-friends, the horror and consternation they would feel at the very *idea* of resenting a child or (worse) a doting father. Different as they all were, they now seemed a freshly formed coalition: to a one, they would understand my tumult even less than Will did.

"Oh, I'm just selfish," Ted smiled. "I was hoping we could go out again tomorrow so I can vent about Nadine."

"You've got yourself a deal," I grinned back, enjoying the pleasantly deflated feeling of fully spilled guts.

Later I found myself humming, welcoming my coworkers' good-intentioned congratulations without the morning's internal gnashing. It was funny—Will and Ted had once been so similar, clowny and teasing, to the extent that it had taken me a week to figure out which face went with which name. I remember sitting between them, looking back and forth in happy wonderment, unwilling to speak a name for fear of getting it wrong. But my internal strings thrummed for one only, and I coined the (secret) name *Yes-I-Will* as my own private memory trick.

He'd swept me off my feet. So smart. So handsome. So caring— and, *wow*, a father! It had seemed like a bonus, a testament to his character. Two blond cherubs! I saw the girls' pictures and melted. I listened sympathetically to his sad but dispassionate story of marriage and divorce. *I'll treat him so much better,* I vowed, imagining how I'd surpass Gianna, blot her out. I saw only a good man, not a haunted one; I saw only two innocents, not their mother's face.

We had talked about everything. We had laughed and laughed. Will's alluring exterior hid a comedian, a geek; he liked to play board games, to snap his fingers when inspired. The combination was lethal; I'd hug myself, giggling; I was done for. Where with others I had wondered *is this love?*—now it was obvious, a natural and inevitable swell toward commitment and marriage.

The girls—still smiles in a wallet. Gianna—still the cruel heartbreaker, unseen. *I don't want to rush things with the kids,* Will explained. Didn't matter—we saw each other every day at work. Being apart for seven nights at a stretch produced the most delirious tension; we clawed at each other in supply closets, taking lunch breaks to descend into the bowels of the parking garage and fuck, discreetly, in his family-man Subaru.

A year in, it became officially serious. Will was leaving the company, ready for bigger and better. Didn't matter—it was time to meet the girls. I sailed through the first few heart-thumping occasions, delighted by how easy it all was. We met at parks, diners, neutral locations; the kids chattered to me, clung to me. Seeing Will as a father made me swoon.

Still—we didn't live together. *It wouldn't send the right message to the girls.*

I found this noble; it was evidence of his maturity. Yet the weeks apart had begun to make me itch. Would he propose, *soon?* London had started sulking, withdrawing, but all I could think about was being with Will. *The more I'm there, the sooner things will get smoothed out.*

And then he did propose, all fireworks and flowers, with a ring that was not the family heirloom I'd wanted—that, alas, had gone to Gianna. Didn't matter—mine was dazzling. We picked a date for the coming summer, sending London into spirals of woe. I gritted my teeth and upped my family time, hoping we could work through the kinks before the wedding. I began to spend evenings, nights. But London was impenetrable and for the first time I learned I could not say just anything to Will about his children.

Then, at last: Gianna. Horrid meeting, I a tongue-tied blight; everyone chattered while I shrunk away, dismayed by my predecessor's allotment of earthly advantages. Didn't matter—Will loved *me* now—though he looked at me with a certain baffled distaste when I confessed that I hated how well he and Gianna got along.

By the time we made it to the altar, my vision of marital disclosure bore little resemblance to the early days of confessional glee. Didn't matter—real life was a series of negotiations, conscious kindnesses. *If you can't say something nice, don't say anything at all.*

Yet Will had been my priest, my diary. And now, it seemed, I had Ted alone.

16

THE NEXT AFTERNOON, I answered the phone in my prim office-voice. "Hi, this is Rhiannon."

Long pause.

"Hello?"

Finally there came a response. "*Annie.*"

"Will?" For the life of me I couldn't figure why my husband was calling from an underground bunker.

"I'm stuck in a meeting," he whispered. "I forgot I'm supposed to take the girls to find out their teachers. Can you?"

"Will, it's my second day back," I protested. "What about Linda?" Since Will's only local relative had already pitched in, London and Josie had been dumped for the day on our elderly next-door neighbor.

"She's not supposed to drive," Will said. "London's texting me in a panic."

"Yeah. Yeah, okay," I said, gathering up my purse. It wasn't a prohibitively long drive, just trafficky enough to be annoying. But at least Will had asked *me* and not Gianna—that was something! I felt suddenly elated that he trusted me to stand in for him.

"*Thank you,*" Will breathed. "I tried to get Gianna to do it, and of course she really wants to, but she wasn't sure her flight was going to land on time—"

Right. Of course. "I'll be there in thirty," I cut him off frostily.

"And then—Annie—can you keep them after that? I don't want to have to take them back to Linda's—"

I dropped my purse on the desk. "Damn it, Will! This is why you should never have said yes to Gianna in the first place! I'm going to have to come back tonight then, or on Saturday."

"I'd be sooo grateful," he whispered. "I'd owe you so many nice dinners and massages."

"Fine, Will. Fine. I will be there in thirty minutes." I hung up on my husband, left a syrupy voice mail for my supervisor, and headed out the door.

My heart sunk as soon as I saw my stepchildren. Josie was bubbling over, a volcano of perkiness. London, on the other hand, was openly sulking.

"I wanted Dad to take me," she said. "Or Mom."

"I know," I said tightly, adding—and instantly regretting—"I did too." I thanked Linda profusely and bustled the kids into the car.

At Brighton Elementary, though, I found myself carried on the collective excitement of the jabbering moms and kids. *I want to be here with them,* I realized, remembering how scary and wonderful it had always been to find out my teacher's name each year. Out of London and Josie's four parents, *I* would be the representative on this all-important day. And, well, even if I'd been appointed as a last resort, it was something, wasn't it? A memory we'd have? I proudly laid a protective hand on each girl's shoulder, guiding my kids through the crowd.

First stop was the first-grade lists, where Josie ecstatically found herself assigned to the presumed best of the four teachers. She ran off squawking with two other classmates to express her elation on the jungle gym.

Then it was London's turn. We carefully scrolled the fifth-grade rosters, surrounded by a cluster of others all doing the same thing.

"*London Tyler?*" a voice next to them cried out. "What kind of name is *London?*"

London was not about to take this kind of an insult in silence. "I was named after my mother," she shot back haughtily, causing the mocking child and her mother to look over at her, aghast. "My name is different and I love it. What's *your* boring name? Lauren? Emily?"

"I'm so sorry," the woman said, her sheepish glance bouncing between London and me. "We're new here. She never should have said that. Honey, apologize to London and her mother."

"*She's* not my mother!" London snapped back. "My mother is Gianna London, the famous model. *She's* just Annie. She's not my mom."

"Well, I'm very sorry," said the confused woman, and bustled her blundering daughter away.

I didn't know what to do. For a moment I stood paralyzed, the pain and embarrassment and anger clotting in my veins. Without even a glance at me, London had found her classroom assignment and was gabbing with a friend, suddenly as animated as her effervescent younger sister.

Then a woman tapped me on the shoulder. "Excuse me—I couldn't help but overhear. Are you by chance a stepmother?"

I looked. Smiling at me was a gracefully aging woman in her mid-forties, freckled and blond.

"Yes?" I said blankly. My mind wasn't really working.

"So am I," said the woman. "My name is Leah Michaelson. And I run a group for stepmoms that you might find helpful." She fished around in her purse, finally coming up with a battered self-printed business card. "I carry these around for stepmothers in need," she laughed, handing it to me.

Society of Stepmothers, it read. With a URL, a username, a password. And nothing else.

I looked up at Leah. "Is this for real?"

"Yes, we meet every month," Leah said encouragingly. "Tell me—how many stepmothers do you know?"

I just shook my head. Reading the news—or what passed for it online, anyway—you'd think that blended families were modern-day locusts, overrunning entire communities, reproducing lickety-split. There were something like fourteen million stepmothers in the United States alone! So where the heck were they *hiding*? Shouldn't participation in a sweeping cultural movement entitle me to some club benefits, a pride parade, a secret handshake, a nickname, *something*? I'd never felt so desperately freakish and alone.

"None, right?" Leah said. "Well there's a bunch of us in the group. You really should try to come."

"Thanks," I said, finally grasping the situation enough to smile my gratitude. "Thanks so much."

"No problem," Leah said, turning toward the parking lot at the tug of a scruffy-looking girl. And just then I heard the worst thing ever: my two stepdaughters screaming "MOM!" at the gorgeous blond strolling toward them.

They ran right past me. They would have trampled me. And then they were each grabbing a hand and pulling their mother toward the teacher lists as though it were the first time.

I couldn't even explain the shame I felt, the absolute horror of being exposed as not-their-mother to everyone in the crowd. I watched them, trying to hold back tears that I didn't even understand.

"Hey, are you okay?" came a voice. I gulped and shook myself, tearing my eyes from the girls. To my surprise, Leah was still standing there.

I just shook my head. "I—don't know," I finally stammered. "I don't...think so."

Leah tipped her head in Gianna's direction. "Is she really a famous model?"

I sighed. "Well, not famous. But yeah, she used to be a model."

Leah shook her head in commiseration. "I can tell you're going to need us," she said kindly, laying her hand on my arm. "I really hope you'll come to our next meeting. It's not a coincidence that we call our group SOS for short."

"I will," I called after her dazedly, bracing myself as Gianna and my stepdaughters turned toward me, completely unaware that anything had happened.

17

HAVING CHILDREN HAS been called the ultimate narcissistic act. Somehow, though, William Joseph Tyler and Giovanna ("Gianna") Christina London had managed to take it even one step further.

I understood why a woman who kept her maiden name would want to pass on a bit of herself. And "London" definitely had a certain trendy air to it, achieving the magical feat of being both uncommon and readily spellable.

They could have stopped there.

And yet they hadn't, partaking instead in a frenzy of cross-naming that resulted in *London Wylie* and *Josephine Christine Tyler*, two children completely smothered by their parents' identities.

"What if you'd had another child?" I'd exclaimed when I first learned of this, thinking privately that, to have a matching pair of kids, they should have named Josie "France."

But Will had just shrugged and said, "Billy Christopher? Willow…Gia? We didn't really think about it."

Obviously. Having two children co-branded by their biological parents didn't exactly make this whole stepmother gig any easier. But when I bitched about it, Will just sighed and said, "I guess it was short-sighted. But geez, Annie, no one ever *plans* to get divorced. If Gianna and I were still together, everyone would think how cute it was."

Not everyone, I thought, smiling back sweetly. I wondered what on earth Will would want to name *our* children. At least with Rhiannon Mariah we'd be getting fresh names into the mix.

As I parked at the hospital, however, I warned myself not to offer any advice to Summer if (by some uncharacteristic, grievous delay) she had not already chosen a name for her day-old daughter. I had offended enough friends in the past to realize that they only got huffy and then went on to name their offspring "Pinky" and "Cutter" anyway.

I clutched the flowers I had brought, taxiing up to Summer's floor, and then went to meet the first child of my oldest friend.

"Annie!" Summer cried as I entered the room. "Come meet Riley."

Riley would do, I thought as I gazed down at the tiny pink bundle. The name was one hundred percent Summer: a little sporty, a little girly, a little unoriginal. I couldn't help the uncomfortable feeling that Summer, however unconsciously, would blatantly fashion this child in her own image, that her ultimate reasons for procreating were as transparent as Gianna and Will's had been. Was there shame in wanting a tiny sculpted self? Or was it simply every parent's unspoken ambition?

"She's beautiful," I said, the tears filming my eyes. I couldn't help it, seeing my friend nestled on the other side of this milestone. "How are you?"

"Wonderful. Perfect. In ecstasy," Summer said. "Oh God, the *feelings*, Annie. I've never felt like this, ever. I don't want her out of my sight." She paused, gazing in wondering love at her baby. "You're next, Annie. You just *have* to have one!"

"Well, one thing at a time," I laughed. "I haven't even gotten all my books on the shelves yet."

"Don't wait," Summer said seriously. "I'm telling you, every minute you spend without a child is just...pointless. I never saw it before, but it's clear as day now. Do it now because you can never get these moments back."

"I'm actually enjoying the moments without the girls," I said, trying to keep things light.

"Oh Annie, that's not the *same*," Summer insisted. "Those aren't your *kids*! Not like Riley is mi-ine!" And she dissolved into kisses and cooing noises. "After you have a baby, you'll never want to be apart. You'll see."

"Oh, there's my baby girl and her baby girl!" came a sudden voice, and I looked up to see Summer's mother Nancy entering the room with Kevin, the brand-new father. Right behind them was none other than my own mother, Judy.

I felt the grimace on my face trying to work itself into a smile. I hadn't returned my mom's phone calls, knowing that this was an occasion not to be shared with one's grandchild-craving, perpetually disapproving mother. Yet somehow Mom had managed to corner me. This was not going to be the quick visit that I had envisioned.

"Sweetheart!" Mom cried. "Did you get my messages? I was hoping we could come together, but I didn't hear from you so I came with Nancy instead." She smiled at her next-door neighbor and best friend. "Isn't Riley just *precious?*"

"She sure is," I said. "She looks just like Summer."

This was not true at all, as Riley mostly looked like a lump of silly putty, but it seemed like the right thing to say.

It was. Summer and the two older women all squealed at once, sending the infant into fitful squalling.

Suddenly Summer was all business. "Everybody out," she insisted. "I need some time alone with my baby."

"Okay, honey," said Summer's mother, and we all bustled out into the hallway, pausing just briefly so I could lay my bouquet on a side table with the other gifts.

It was the perfect time for a getaway. "Well, I guess I'd better be getting back..." I said. "It was nice to see you, Nancy. And you, Kevin." Summer's husband looked bewildered, as though he'd no idea why he'd been brought to the hospital in the first place, let alone cast out into the hall.

"Oh, Annie, don't go yet; we haven't even seen each other," my mother said, and Nancy took up the cry. "Yes, Annie, let's just go have a bite in the cafeteria. It's really quite good. They have the *best* muffins."

"Well, just a quick bite," I conceded. Maybe if I went along with this, my mother would stop dropping such gargantuan hints about a mother-daughter luncheon or wine-tasting trip.

"I think I'll go back in there," Kevin said dazedly, jerking his thumb toward Summer's room. "Bye."

"Poor thing, he's completely shell-shocked," Nancy chortled to my mom and me as we tiptoed away from the room. "I'm not sure he's quite ready to be a dad. Good thing Summer is parent enough for the both of them!" She looked at me. "Oh, Annie, it must be *so* nice to have a husband who's already such a good father. Summer had to wait *years,* and still—look at him! But *you* can start having your own right away."

Oh God, not more of this. Not even the best muffin was worth enduring a sad menopausal ambush.

"Yes, when *are* you going to start trying, Annie?" my mother rabidly burst forth. "I want a grandchild before I'm too old. I'm already *years* older than Nancy"—Summer's mother clucked out her protest—"and she has three!"

"Mom, I just gave you *two* grandchildren a month ago," I said lightly, but my mother laughed this off as though it were not even possible that I could be serious.

"Talk to Stacia about it, not me," I said, my voice venturing toward the brusque. "I've just gotten married. I'm in no hurry to add more kids to my life when I'm still trying get used to the ones I've got."

"Tick tick tick!" Nancy warned. "You wait too long and it might not happen!"

"I'm only twenty-eight," I answered patiently. "I have plenty of time for all that."

"But do *I*?" Mom wailed morbidly, and I had to fight hard not to slug her. Somehow my every life decision struck my mother as a personal affront.

We got in the muffin-line and I made my selection, opting for a banana-nut that earned me an additional maternal frown. "Very high in fat," Mom admonished discreetly. "You just got back from your honeymoon; don't let yourself go already!"

"So how are you doing, Nancy?" I said as we sat down, hoping to shift the conversation away from my ovaries and baked-goods selections. But back it swung to me anyway as Summer's mother began lamenting her older son's failing marriage.

"She had children already and she never really committed to my son," Nancy explained of her daughter-in-law. "The little boys are really so sweet, and of course the children have to come first—but she and Anthony just weren't on the same page about a lot of things."

I nodded sympathetically. "I can imagine it was hard for Anthony to find his place in that family." This was dangerous ground to cover with two middle-aged old-schoolers, but I knew about Anthony's trials as a stepfather and tried to cut the whole family a little slack.

"Oh yes, it was so hard," Nancy agreed. "And it must be for you too. The stress of getting to know children who don't even want you there."

I probably wouldn't have put it *that* way, but... "Yeah, it's a little hard on the older one, London—"

"Terrible name," muttered Mom.

"—who seems to like me one moment and hate me the next. I can't say it doesn't put a strain on all of us, but—"

"Well, Rhiannon," my mom interrupted impatiently, "what did you expect? The children *have* a mother already. They don't need you!" Before I could comment, she had already gone on: "Now I really admire Summer for *not settling*. Young beautiful girls don't have to settle for someone's who's already lived his life with someone else."

"Now, Judy—" Nancy tried.

"I don't know why you did it, Annie," my mother went on dramatically. "You could have had anyone you wanted."

"Will's the one I wanted, Mom," I said angrily. "Will and those girls. I didn't settle for anyone but the man I love." I heard the tears in my voice despite how badly I wanted to remain calm.

"Oh *sweetheart*," my mother said, as though completely surprised by my reaction. "I didn't mean to upset you. I just want you to be *happy*, that's all. That's all."

"I'm really happy, Mom," I said dully. "Can we just drop it? Please?" I finished my fattening banana-nut muffin in simmering silence, knowing my mother was just one more person who could never handle the whole and variegated truth.

18

FOR REASONS I couldn't fully articulate, the next Sunday I snuck out. *If it's dumb I'll never have to bring it up,* I reasoned, telling Will I was having coffee with a friend.

My heart was pounding as I entered the Lazy O. It was a restaurant built for dallying, with extensive hours and meandering porch seating. Customers tucked away in here all day, downing pitchers of iced coffee and plate after plate of homemade fritters as they studied, read the paper or caught up with friends. During college it had been one of my favorite hideouts.

I'd never been nervous at the Lazy O. But now I felt too awkward to confide my intentions to the front-desk hostess. "I'm meeting someone," I said simply, motioning toward the first stretch of shady porch. "Can I…?"

And I was free to roam the place for the Society of Stepmothers.

I had waited until I knew for sure that my house was empty before typing in the URL on the business card Leah had given me. I'd been so nervous that I'd screwed up the username and password twice before finally arriving at a simple white web page that listed the meeting details for the month. When I'd seen the *Lazy O* displayed there, I actually started clapping. These ladies had good taste! My involvement had started to feel like fate.

But I was still incredibly nervous when the day actually came.

Two places within the sprawling restaurant would be perfect for a group meeting. One was the cozy indoor Parlor Room; the other was the covetable Bower Room, its knobby outdoor table set away from the others and shaded by a fragrant arbor. I thought the Bower would be too good to be true, but—

A group of women was sitting there. I approached slowly, trying to look casual in case I'd gotten it wrong. I scanned the faces as I drew nearer, hoping there was some sign. But what mark or expression could distinguish a stepmother? *We blend in with everyone,* I thought. *The invisible minority.*

And then I saw Leah Michaelson sitting on the far side of the table. Leah's face lit up in recognition. "Hey! It's the woman I met at Brighton!" Six other faces turned to gawp at me.

"Hi," I waved nervously. "I'm Annie."

And then they all came to life, offering their greetings and scooching around the table to make room for me.

"I was just telling the others how I ran into you," Leah said. "But I didn't find out anything about you. So tell us about yourself. You have two stepdaughters—?"

"Yep," I said. "They're ten and six." I gave a jittery smile. What else was I supposed to say? "That's it."

"That's enough," said a woman on the other side of the table, and with the laughter I relaxed.

"So are you married? Have any kids? Your own kids, I mean?"

I shook my head. "No kids. But I just got married, um, three weeks ago." Puzzled, I asked hesitantly, "Don't you have to be married to be a stepmom?"

"Well, technically," said another woman, "but you don't have to be married to play the stepmom role."

I nodded. That made sense.

"Okay, let's go around the table and introduce ourselves," Leah said. "As you know, I'm Leah—"

"Head Recruiter!" someone shouted out.

Leah smiled. "Yeah, I think I'm the only one who actually carries the business cards—"

"Not true!" protested a dark-skinned woman who looked impossibly young to be a stepmom. "It's just that I don't meet anyone at Berkeley who needs one. They're all bitching about *their* stepmoms—you know, the ones that their dads met when they were off at college freshman year?"

I gaped at her as the concept of dealing with stepkids as a college student officially blew my mind.

Leah told me that the scraggly girl I'd seen at Brighton Elementary was her sixth-grade stepdaughter. She also had a twenty-two-year-old stepdaughter, a fifteen-year-old stepson, and two biological kids, sixteen and fourteen, from a previous marriage. "Yeah, it's a lot," she smiled. "But we're a really happy family...except for the oldest. She's a real piece of work." She gave a little sigh but never lost her smile. "Luckily she doesn't live in my house."

I nodded through the biographies, inhaling the stories like a cocaine addict even as I knew I was jumbling the names and situations. Here were women with stepchildren only, women with biological children from previous marriages, women who had kids with their current partners; women who loved children and women who abhorred them; women who got along with their partners' exes and women who were being stalked by them. I felt so ignorant—I'd never even thought about all these combinations and variations.

"Well, I for one am *so happy* they're back in school," sighed Maggie, a woman with dark red curls and a pregnant belly still in its cute stages. "I love them, yes. But I just don't think their incompetence is tolerable in any way, you know? *I'm* the one picking up after them;

I'm the one nagging. It drives me so crazy! My fuse is shorter than Dennis's, it always has been, and it always will be. But he doesn't get that. He still doesn't get that I'm not just going to feel the exact same way he does about the kids."

"Oh geez, I had one of those too," Kim spoke up. She was a ponytailed Asian woman whose smooth face left no hint of her age. "The kids were gone for a couple of weeks with Zoey, and Nate was a total wreck. Every freaking day he asked me if I missed them. At first I was like, yeah, I do. But I really didn't. And when he asked me the last time I just blew up and was like 'NO, I don't, okay?' You should have seen the look on his face. Like I was a serial killer or something."

"Doesn't he know you're childfree?" said a pixie-haired brunette who wore confidence like a mink stole. She'd introduced herself as Regan.

"Yes, but he thinks I'm childfree because *his* kids are all I could ever want," Kim answered. She looked at me with a wry smile. "He's kind of a dimwit."

Childfree? Leah apparently saw the blank look on my face. "It means that you don't want to have any biological kids," she explained.

"It means that you can't stand the little cretins!" Regan piped up. "That you don't *like* kids, don't *want* kids—"

"It does *not!*" said June, the overloaded undergraduate. "Ignore her," she said to me, waving a dismissive hand at Regan. "Not all childfree people are black-souled goblins like this one. You can *love* kids and be childfree. It just means that, for whatever reason, you don't want or plan to have any kids."

"So what about you, Annie?" Regan asked with a piercing gaze and tiny smile. "Childfree?"

"No, sorry?" I answered, somehow feeling a bit squirmy for not earning Regan's allegiance. "I don't know when, but Will and I plan on having more. At least one." But as I said the words I felt a twinge of foreboding: how could I even think of bringing a child into this marriage when I'd already been so miserable?

"Oh well, your loss," sighed Regan, then winked at me to show she was teasing.

"No, good for you," said another woman emphatically, giving me an encouraging smile. This was Kerry, the group organizer, a thirty-something with light blond hair, blue-gray eyes, and trendy glasses. "I really believe that having your own helps take the sting out of step-parenting." She'd confessed during her introduction that she thought of little but getting pregnant, each month's taunting visitor stoking her desire and her desperation. She settled into a zenlike pose. "And I'm feeling positive this week so I'm sure it's going to happen for me too."

"I really hope it does, Kerry," said another woman gently. "But a baby isn't a cure-all. Not even close." Fran had mentioned during her introduction that her marriage was under considerable strain, the source of which had little to do with the children, step or otherwise.

"No, but it would cure the hole inside me, wouldn't it?" Kerry said softly. "I just can't imagine being happy if I can never be a mother."

"You *are* a mother," said Leah. "We're *all* mothers here." But Regan made a gagging face and Kerry looked gloomy and unconvinced.

"Well *I* had a horrible situation a couple of weeks ago," June spoke up. She'd explained earlier that she was dating an older man who had a four-year-old daughter and an even more exciting bonus prize for June: the girl's jealous nutcase of a mother. "I went to pick up Annabel from preschool as usual. She ran out and jumped into my arms and before I knew it, Samantha was there, grabbing her away from me and screaming how I was not her mother and wasn't allowed to take her home." My mouth fell open. As much as I disliked Gianna at times, spazzing in public was not a model's style. "All the parents and kids were staring at us. All the teachers came out. And once she saw that they were all there, she tried to pretend that it was her day to pick up and *I* was there trying to steal Annabel."

"No!" I gasped in spite of myself. I knew this stuff happened on daytime TV, but in my own neighborhood?

"Well, I got pissed and refused to back down. I called Ryan and they hashed it out on the phone. Eventually she gave up, shot me the dirtiest look I've ever received, spent five minutes slurping all over Annabel and telling her how much she loved and missed her, and then marched off. You wouldn't believe how hard my heart was pounding. I was shaking when I got in the car to take Annabel home.

"Ryan and I put it together later that she was hoping to talk to him, not realizing that I do the pickups on Tuesdays. Then she saw me and freaked out. She honestly believes that he's going to be in a relationship with her. Not only that, she honestly believes that they were a couple once. She tells people they were married!" June's boyfriend, she'd told me, had fallen into a drunken fling at a bachelor party that had resulted in a stunningly beautiful daughter and a stunningly poisonous vendetta.

"Adora's delusions continue too," said Leah. "She seems to think she can make me disappear as long as she refuses to acknowledge me." Adora was Leah's oldest stepdaughter, the product of a brief marriage that had ended when Adora was still an infant. Unlike Paul's two children from his second marriage, Adora had never had anything but brief visitations with her father. And when it came to sheer destructive capacity, the chunkiest tornado had nothing on this girl. "You know I like most people, but she is just so horrible and vicious. And yet Paul keeps falling for her guilt trips."

"Because she's Daddy's Little Princess?" Maggie ventured.

"More because he *is* so guilty," Leah said thoughtfully. "He doesn't like her much either, but because of that he's all full of excuses. Do you know what she did two weeks ago? She sent me an email right before she came over to our house for Paul's birthday dinner, knowing I would read it right before she arrived. In this email she told me I would never be her father's true wife and she would never care for me as long as she lived. I didn't want to spoil the evening for Paul so I told him I was sick and spent the entire time in the bathroom crying—"

"That's what I did too, on my honeymoon!" I exclaimed. "Cried in the bathroom when I couldn't take it anymore."

"That's where we always end up," Fran said. "No matter what problems we face."

"Yeah," June broke in. "I bet at every moment, somewhere in the world, there's always a stepmother crying in the bathroom."

"Because they don't love us," agreed Kim wistfully.

"Because we don't love *them*," said Kerry.

"Because," finished Maggie, "it's just too fucking hard."

After the meeting, I sailed out of the Lazy O, feeling like a new kid who'd just been invited, after months of lonesome cafeteria lunches, to join the coolest group at school. I was so happy these women existed that I couldn't even manage to care if they'd liked me.

"So, what did you think?" Leah asked me in the parking lot after the other women had gone their separate ways.

"I don't even know what to say," I said honestly. "I feel like my head's just exploded with things I never even imagined. And at the same time I feel like I've never belonged anywhere more in my life."

Leah laughed. "Yeah, that about describes it," she said. "I felt that way too. Unfortunately I had already been a stepmom years before this group existed, so I bungled along on my own. I was a mom first, of course, so you'll have a different experience, but still there's this common denominator of being incredibly naïve about what it means to be a stepmom. We think we'll be so perfect, you know? The kids will love us, our husband will support and understand us, the mom will be grateful that her kids have such a nice woman in their lives. It's just so much harder and more complicated than we ever imagine."

"God, I'm glad it's not just me," I said. "I have never felt so stupid, so incompetent. I look back even two months ago and think how little I understood about what I was getting myself into. I just feel like a total idiot for thinking I could handle it so well."

"I don't think there's a stepparent or *parent* of any kind who hasn't felt that way," Leah said kindly. "Our hopes and dreams about child-raising are so pastel and lovely." She laughed. "The reality can be like a baseball bat in the face."

I thought of Summer, my mother, my other friends with children. Alternately gushing and sanctimonious, they spoke of parenthood only as a parade of pleasures or a sacred mission. What made them so unwilling to acknowledge the struggles, the difficulties? Leah's open and humble attitude soothed me like an icy draught on a parched throat.

"I think you'll see that you can be yourself with us in a way that you can't with the rest of the world," Leah went on. "Because we get it. We won't look at you with disgust if you can't stand your stepkids. We also won't accuse you of loving them too much or trying to 'steal' them from the bio-mom. We won't think you're evil when you wish you had more time with your husband or wonder what life would be like if you'd married someone else. These are feelings we have *all the time*, and other people just don't get it. That's why SOS is here."

I looked back at her, overwhelmed. "That sounds amazing," I gulped. It was the only thing I could manage.

"It is; it really is," Leah smiled, patting my shoulder. "But enough of my sales pitch. It's been great to meet you, and I really hope we'll see you next month."

19

I SAILED HOME in a giddy haze. Before I had felt like the world's sole stepmother, an inept and conspicuous sore thumb, and now I was a valued soldier marching in noble sync with a blazing, supercool army. Just meeting these others made me feel triumphant, a sports hero aloft on a web of outspread fingers. I couldn't wait to tell Will.

But when I walked in the front door he was muttering and sulky, banging around the kitchen as he did when too irritable to sit still.

My sails sagged. "What's going on?"

"It's nothing," he said curtly. "How was coffee?"

"Fine," I said, looking at him cautiously. Maybe this wasn't the time to mention the Society of Stepmothers. Was I even *supposed* to tell Will about them? I'd forgotten to ask.

Then he shook his head and looked at me. "I'm sorry," he said, holding out his hands contritely. "I'm just pissed off. It's Ren."

Oh, no. I went to him. "What happened?"

"Oh, he's decided that it would be a 'good idea' for Josie to get tested for dyslexia," Will said sarcastically.

While I waited for the rest, sure there was some gruesome revelation to come barreling down the chute, Will stared back at me expectantly. At length I realized there was no additional bombshell.

"Well, I'm not sure that's a bad idea," I said slowly. "I mean, she does seem to have trouble with reading, and I've seen her transpose numbers—"

"No," Will interrupted. "Don't you see what he's doing? This isn't about Josie; it's about him wanting *my kids* in a private school. He's trying to convince Gianna that their public school isn't good enough, that they don't even test the kids—"

"Oh," I said. "Well, if she'd been tested, you could just explain—"

"I don't want to explain *anything* to him!" Will growled. "He has no business sticking his nose in my kids' education!"

"Well geez, Will, he *is* their stepfather—"

"He's not their father, damn it!" Will shouted. "*I am their father!*"

*W*ill had always been weird about Ren. Mocking, derisive, touchy. In our early days he'd masked his grudge with humor, sending me into fits with his impressions of drawling, fastidious Country Club Ren. I had never thought much about it, secretly enjoying the trashing of Gianna that always came with.

But now I was a stepmother. And I suddenly saw Ren through different eyes.

"Well, that doesn't mean he doesn't have their best interests in mind," I said, bristling. "When you say things like this, you leave no room for me in the kids' lives either. I'm 'just' their stepmother, not their mother. You want me to butt out too?"

"No, of course not," Will said in frustration. "I *need* you in their lives. The kids need you. But that's different."

"How is it different?"

"Because you're a woman. You're a better mother than Gianna. And you're a good person."

I stared at my husband, trying to absorb this strange concatenation of answers. Compliments, yes, and part of me wanted so much to preen in the glow of *good person* and (especially) *better mother*, but—wasn't there something deep and strange in this response? I knew Will's young life had colored his vision of surrogate parents;

he'd come to love his stepmother but had always loathed his badgering stepfather. Yet there just seemed to be something more.

"Why do you think Ren isn't a good person?" I finally asked. Ren had always seemed perfectly pleasant to me, mild-mannered and inoffensive. Yet recently I'd come to see that beneath Will's satire lay a visceral dislike of the man, a refusal to give Ren a single doubt's benefit.

For a split second Will seemed to choke. Then he said, "Oh geez, Annie, all the rich people around here are the same. He cares about money and nothing but. I don't want my kids growing up with these bad values, these boats and fancy schools and all that. He can turn his own kid into a little tycoon, but I don't want him ruining my girls."

I just nodded. "Well, don't you think we should make sure that Josie gets some tests?" I said gently. "I'm sure we can take care of it all at Brighton."

"Yeah," Will finally conceded. "Yeah, we should." And he kissed me. "Thanks, Annie. I just get so mad when—" He shook his head, brushing it off. "But it doesn't matter. You are my lifesaver, you know that?"

"That's my job, sweetie," I said softly, uneasy in the knowledge that just a few months ago I would have answered *And you're mine.*

September

20

I CALLED TO check in.

The first four times it was:

Hellooo! You've reached Summer Shepards! I'm too busy celebrating the miracle of life to come to the phone right now, but I'll call you back as soon as Riley goes down for her nappy-nap!

Summer had actually held the phone to her baby's face to jazz up her recording with some atmospheric gurgling. It really made me question my desire to leave a message.

But I had. Four times. Yet after two weeks, Summer still hadn't called back. Gee—could the *poor* woman still be waiting for her little insomniac to catch some Zs?

"This is the last time," I promised myself on try number five. But this time, Summer actually answered.

"*Oh*, Annie, I'm so sorry," she said. "It's just so crazy around here. The days just go by in a blur. You'll understand when you're a mommy."

"Well, I won't keep you," I said. "I just wanted to see how you were doing."

"I'm so happy," Summer sighed. "Or maybe I'm just delirious from lack of sleep. But *everything* has changed! I love her so much. It's like... God shining a flashlight through the chaos." Not for a second did I believe that Summer had authored that line. "It's crazy, but it's so... clarifying. All that stuff that used to matter just doesn't anymore."

Like calling your friends back? "I wish I felt that way," I confessed longingly. "I think I'm the opposite. I don't know *what* my priorities should be." I tried to laugh. "I'm a headless chicken."

"Have a baby!" Summer admonished. "I'm serious, Annie. How many times do I have to tell you? You'll be so much happier."

Maybe she was right. Still, it was not in the cards now. "We're not ready yet," I said. "Things are so messy with the girls. We're always exhausted. It feels like I do nothing but take care of them."

Summer snorted. "Well geez, Annie! What did you expect? You knew he had kids when you married him!"

I was stung. "Well, *yeah*, but I'm just saying—"

"Oh, she's crying. I gotta go."

And without saying goodbye, Summer had hung up the phone.

21

SOMETIMES IN THE evenings when Will was helping London with homework, I led Josie through her bedtime rituals. I lathered the springing curls, swathed the soft little body in terry cloth and flannel, treated the chosen storybooks to all my most animated voices. And in those moments the world receded, revealing not a troubled stepmother with a host of rickety relationships but the simplest of connections, the simplest of tableaux: woman and child.

Gianna didn't exist. Even Will, really, didn't exist. In those moments it was Rhiannon and daughter, Rhiannon and children-to-be. A future of nurturing seemed to open before my eyes, my maternal potential swelling like a womb itself.

And yet by day Josie could be such a screeching nightmare—howling, defying, terrorizing Mr. Pickles with her smothering love—that she left me near tears and pummeled with doubt that I could ever be a good mother of any sort to any child of any kind.

"That's what young kids are like," assured my friend Maryellen. "Biological or otherwise. Really, Annie, give yourself time. Most of us have years of babyhood to get our shit together. You didn't. Be patient and you'll get the hang of being a mother."

But I'm not a mother, I thought. *Or am I supposed to be? A mother like Gianna? A mother unlike Gianna? A friend? A big sister? An aunt?*

These answerless questions could gnarl me into paralysis. But I'd settle, at this point, for simply being a caretaker who wasn't piss-awful.

I will *get my shit together,* I chanted to myself on personal-inspiration mornings. *I* will *get my shit together.*

Yet it was hard to know what that meant, exactly. Obviously one *had* to avoid becoming a wicked stepmother, cruel and warty—but I wasn't even clear what mistakes led to such a dreaded downfall. Was it being too strict? Too chummy? Or were you okay as long as you avoided engineering your stepchildren's untimely devouring?

It's a matter of Resources, I remembered someone saying at the SOS meeting. *People think that a stepmother funnels away Resources from the children, either for herself or for her own kids. That because of the greedy stepmother the poor, innocent stepkids must Go Without.*

Well, in that capacity I was clean: I had scarcely purchased a haircut for myself since I'd been married, hesitant even to return to the therapist whose help I craved. And the children were certainly not Going Without. Two tiny ebullient Taylor Swifts, they'd ecstatically pranced in the house last week wearing trendy boots and sunglasses. Will had responded with token praise, slipping into the kitchen where he made a pan-bashing show of the dinner preparations.

"I'm thinking of going back to school," he'd told me later that night. He was trying to sound casual, excited, but there was something grim about the set of his jaw.

"Now?" I'd asked in surprise. Law school had always been his dream—a dream abandoned when Gianna got pregnant—but how could we possibly afford it?

"It's as good a time as any, isn't it?" he'd said. "Sure, we'll have to scrape for a few years, but then I'll be making much more money." He paused, casually tossing out what he thought was the glinting lure. "You might even be able to stop working."

Oh, Will. "I like working," I'd finally answered kindly, wrapping my arms around his waist. "We're doing just fine, sweetie. You don't have to become a lawyer." And God, that was the last thing I wanted—a husband constantly working, leaving me a single parent half the month and a widow all the rest.

"I want to," he'd said stubbornly. "It's what I've always wanted." Yet still his voice rang with hardness, not passion.

I didn't know how to say what I had to say.

"Sweetheart, you shouldn't try to compete with him," I'd finally murmured. "You know that, don't you?"

He didn't answer.

"And you don't need to," I went on. "It's not what any of us want. We love you for who you are. We don't need any more money."

But he'd only struggled out of my grasp and gone out for a midnight run. And we hadn't talked about it since.

I wasn't surprised. Will never talked about his real issues with Ren, making it clear when I pried that it was a nerve too electric to touch. It left me sad for him, sad for myself, for I could relate so profoundly to Will's fruitless rivalry: commiseration might have brought us closer. But instead I tried to keep quiet when Gianna's face or name sent me off engulfed by that raw competitive loathing, so human and destructive, that routinely shredded my guts to liquid and never did a modicum of good.

Of course, neither of us breathed a word of our respective irritations to the kids. It was always *your mom* this and *how's Ren* that, light and friendly and aren't-we-so-congenial-and-well-adjusted. Will's efforts at perfect suppression were, admittedly, hit and miss. But when I felt the worst I spoke the best of Gianna, giving myself a virtual cookie every time I said *your mother* or lavished the woman with praise. It rankled some justice-loving part of me to be so dishonest. But I was learning that, even in the best of scenarios, parenting was a series of careful choices—a mash of truth and fabrication, simplification and omission—each made on the fly for the benefit of the children. Honesty, with kids, could be the worst policy of all.

So I lied. And I gave praise where praise was not due. Yet none of it was selfless: for if my honey-drenched words could lull London out of her loyalty bind (this term bestowed upon me, of course, by the stepmoms), she might realize that I was no threat to Gianna, that it was beneficial and not traitorous to love us both.

Well, a girl could dream.

But no gesture or offering, not even the frequent kissing of her mummy's model-perfect bum, seemed to earn me any points. No one had ever rebuffed me with such constancy as London Tyler.

And then.

There had been the magical moment, the right flick of the wrist to land the dial on the right radio station, the right Sara Bareilles song wafting through the living room just in time for both London and me to exclaim, "I *love* this song!" We had laughed and begun to dance—not like mother and daughter perhaps, but like friends, like aunt and niece, like people who liked or at least chose each other. Like people with something good and healthy sprouting between them.

And London had been sweet and charming for the rest of the evening, funny even, and in fact a good deal less annoying than Josie—who'd been at her baby-me worst. Distantly I remembered meeting this girl, a precocious and well-spoken nine-year-old who had disappeared as soon as she'd learned that I was a girlfriend, not just her father's friendly colleague. In her place she'd posted a bodyguard who deflected attempts at closeness with moodiness and silence, a defense that had proved so effective that I had nearly forgotten that the bodyguard was not the real girl at all.

So the emergence of London Authentic had been something like a triumph. And I had felt so good, *so* good, all the next day, free even of the apprehensive gloom that inevitably settled upon me as I pulled into the driveway each evening. *I'm getting home to my family*, I would think, bolstering myself to go inside. *This is supposed to be the best part of my day.* And yet it had never felt that way, not until London had stepped out from behind the shield.

So I had gone in the house, half-skipping, half-whistling, fully excited to fling off the friction and, finally, *belong*. But as anyone could have told me—as I could have told myself, really—conflicted kids did not so readily accept their own progress.

"Mm," London had grunted from the couch at my greeting, not offering, as she had the night before, a genial hug. *She's absorbed in homework,* I had told myself decisively, heading into the kitchen to see about dinner.

But the girl was sullen during the meal, smearing Alfredo noodles through a garden of uneaten peas while ignoring all attempts at engagement. *Something bad happened at school,* I imagined. *I'll have Will ask her later.*

Later, though, was playtime with Josie as London listlessly watched television on the other side of the living room. "I am the Sugarplum Baby," Josie was chattering, adjusting the pink tutu that was currently functioning as my Afro-inspired headdress. "And you are my Sugarplum Mommy..."

"She's not your mommy!" London suddenly cried in a rage, leaping up from the couch to stare lividly at us, the offending pair. I gaped back; I would have bet serious cash that London was in preteen dreamland, unaware of any life forms around her. "Don't call her your mommy!"

Josie stood her ground, face twisting in defiance. "I didn't say MOMMY; I said SUGARPLUM MOMMY!" she screamed back.

"She's not any kind of mommy," London snarled. "We only have one mother, and it's *not her*."

I was still too shocked, too conspicuously tutu-laden, to speak. How could such vitriol fly from the lips of this girl who'd, just last night, held my hand and spun me silly? Then Will blazed in from his office, my bespectacled hero, looking every inch the dreamed-of lawyer. "Annie is your step*mother* and you are not allowed to speak that way," he said to London. "If I hear you say anything like that again, you're going to be grounded for a week."

"But it's *true*," London said, crumpling into tears. "Josie's calling her *Mommy*, and she's not our mother."

"Josie can call Annie what she wants," Will said. "Just as you can."

"But it's not fair to *Mom*," London wailed. "It's not right to *Mom*."

"What you call Annie is between you and Annie," Will said. "It's not up to Mom. You know I call my stepmother 'Mom.'"

"Well I'll start calling Ren *Daddy* then!" London screamed, and ran out of the room to slam her door. I wished I hadn't seen this threat stab so baldly into my husband's heart. He stood staring after his oldest child, jaw working, as Josie and I looked on.

Josie climbed into my lap, sweet and stubborn. "Sugarplum Mommy," she whispered to me, patting my thigh.

22

"I'D SAY SHE'S feeling guilty because she's really starting to like you," Ted said the next day at a lunchtime stroll. "You guys had this great time and she started feeling disloyal to her mom, so she had to lash out." He shrugged. "Not much to it. It's pretty textbook."

"I know," I said. "I *know*. I even know the *name* for it—a 'loyalty bind.'"

"Fancy pants," Ted said admiringly.

"I should have been prepared," I went on. "But I just wanted to believe that things had changed. I just wanted to be comfortable and happy for once." In truth I'd been utterly crushed by London's outburst, crying brokenly in the shower after I'd extracted both Josie and the tutu from my person.

"Don't be dumb," Ted said. "You're stepmother to a drama queen. Count on this for ages. But what *I* want to know is who is putting London up to this? Is it Gianna telling her she can't like you, or does she just have some weird kid ideas about what she's supposed to do?"

"Will says that Gianna would never say anything bad about him or me," I sighed. "I'm not sure, myself. He thinks way too highly of her, if you ask me."

Ted gave a little knowing sigh. "He always did," he said.

I stopped and looked at him. "You didn't?" I normally tried to avoid discussing the years before I'd come along, when Ted and Will were fresh out of college, my husband as yet untainted by marriage and babies and the whole getup that seemed bent on dragging my life into the toilet.

"I've never been taken in by Gianna's kind," Ted said finally. "All aloof and calculating. Will, of course, thought I was jealous. He was absolutely smitten from day one."

I gulped back the pain. *He's mine now*, I reminded myself forcefully. *Mine forever. Gianna didn't last, can't have him now.* But another part of me whispered: *He's only yours because she decided she didn't want him.*

"Even when she left he never really saw her for what she was," Ted went on. "There was always some blindness there." He looked at me and smiled. "But that's all in the past now," he said cheerily. "Now he has a wife who treats him like a king. If I know Will, though, he wants to believe Gianna's doing right by the kids because he doesn't want to deal with it if she's not."

"Oh yes," I agreed. "I'm sure that's part of it. He will come up with *any* excuse to convince himself everything's fine and he doesn't have to do anything." I paused thoughtfully. "But on the other hand, he told me the other day that I'm a better mother than Gianna, so that has to count for something."

"I'm glad he sees that," Ted said. "She loved to play the dutiful wife and mother, but I think it was an act. And you know why she was always a bit cool to me? Because I saw right through it."

I grabbed my friend's arm, suddenly grateful that he'd known Will for so long. Yes, he remembered things I'd soon forget; but here was someone—one of the few, really—who knew both Gianna and me and was decidedly on my side.

"I'm so glad to have you, Ted," I said. "Besides you and"—I was going to say *my stepmom group* but bit back the words—"well, *you*, it feels like I don't have any friends at all. Not real ones, anymore." Days later, Summer's brush-off still hurt.

"Aww, Annie," Ted smiled. "I've missed you too."

Funny, I thought as we walked on in comfortable silence, how by increasing my family by so many I'd reduced my support by so much.

Of course, there were always the voices.

Where once there had been nothing but real voices, concerned voices, friendly voices on the phone or across a table, now there were mostly the sibilants of phantom advice-givers. *You are PATHETIC for putting up with this,* one might insist. Then: *You are a HORRIBLE PER-SON for not loving them enough.*

It was the proverbial duo on the shoulders. Xena, the tough and sultry Warrior Princess herself, sported the devil's hot pants; a warped and hyperbolic Angelina Jolie pursed her lips under the glinting halo. And so the grand battle played out near my earlobes: independent (selfish) woman versus abnegating (tedious) mother, each prickly and self-righteous, agreeing only when it came to my total insufficiency in either respect.

Kiss her, cradle her, directed Angelina when Josie cried over something stupid. *Call a sitter and go out for falafel,* instructed Xena, flexing her muscles. Rarely did I fully heed the counsel of either daemon, instead carving out a middle course that seemed reasonable yet managed to eliminate neither my resentment nor my guilt.

But they're not my kids! I railed at Angelina.

But they're my kids! I slapped at Xena.

And neither was really true.

I knew that if I could just become Angelina—if I could just stop fighting, stop whining, stop asking Will and life for *more, more, more*—

that both voices would disappear. I'd be that perfect stepmother, giving all, asking for nothing, waiting patiently but never pushily for my unconditional love to be returned. *Please help me be less selfish,* I prayed helplessly (to whom? Angelina?) as I lay in bed racked by my failures.

But during moments of stress and conflict, it was always Xena's words that curled like smoke into my ears. *Your husband should be doing more for you,* she nudged. *You're newlyweds, and he treats you like a babysitter! He's taking advantage.*

Angelina countered silkily. *You should be doing more for the kids. How do you ever expect them to love you if you don't give them everything?*

I could not please them. I could not silence them. There were voices, but they weren't friends.

23

GREELY'S GABLES PROCLAIMED the plaque gleaming on the side of Ren and Gianna's ginormous manor.

Great. As if I didn't have enough issues roiling in my guts, I now had to compete with a woman whose house had a fucking *name*.

Resignedly I rang the bell. Even the *ding-dong* sounded snooty.

Oh, I'd been here before—morbidly curious, back then, to see how the wealthy lived and particularly this new member of the nouveau riche. Amidst the finery I'd hoped to find suggestions of unrest, disgruntlement, outright misery.

But there'd been nothing but smiles and clean carpets, not even a holey sock or mysterious stain to blow entirely out of proportion. I'd stood uncomfortably in the upstairs hallway as Will had helped Josie find her ballet slippers, wanting to denounce the extravagance around me yet half-wishing they'd invite me to housesit.

Somehow, though, I'd never noticed this plaque on the side of the house. Perhaps it was brand new; certainly it was a relatively recent arrival, for it declared all the current residents' names in chronological order: Ren, Gianna, London, Josie, and Clint. Nosily I peered closer to the bronze plate, looking for the old holes or faded paint that would indicate a first-life cover-up: a older plaque that featured only Ren, Clint, and the mother who no longer lived there.

But before I could come to a conclusion, I heard footsteps and jumped away from the potential palimpsest, straightening my skirt. Gianna opened the door, greeting me in a hushed voice. She looked fresh and sun-kissed, gold hair tumbling; a sleepy, rosy-cheeked Clint sprawled in her arms. Amazing how Gianna always managed to look simultaneously like the Virgin Mary and Helen of Troy: both holy and irresistible, she was the devoted mother, the succulent wife—and now, cradling Clint, the selfless stepmother too. I didn't know how many more one-ups I could really be expected to take.

"Did you talk to Will?" I managed, stepping into the foyer. "He said he would call—he had a meeting he couldn't get out of—"

"Oh, it's no problem," Gianna said. "Let me just put him down and I'll go get the girls."

I followed Gianna deeper into the house and up the stairs, noting the updated artwork, a new set of furniture. I hadn't been here in what—a few months?—and they'd already redecorated. Must be nice.

Thinking of my long absence made me cringe with guilt. Of course I'd intended to come with Will to every pickup, staking my claim as the new wife and stepmother, mitigating for Will the weekly indignity of walking into the radiant mansion of the woman who'd left him. My constant presence, see, would show Gianna that Will and I were a team now, and happy; we didn't need *money*. We didn't need *bling*. We had *each other*, a concept Gianna clearly hadn't known how to appreciate when Will had been hers.

Yet London had started sneering at me like a territorial dog, leaving me flushing and tongue-tied, humiliated in front of the very woman I'd hoped to impress. And as the demands of a mortgage and two growing girls started sucking at the chubby hoard I'd accumulated while single, immersion in Gianna's endless resources started to feel unwise and finally just masochistic.

So I'd stopped coming. And Will never said anything about it, simply asking if I planned to join him and then stopping even that as it grew apparent that I would no longer be darkening the majestic doorstep of Greely's Gables.

I'd felt awful. But being there only made me self-conscious and catty, and if Will didn't need me, well—didn't it make more sense just to greet the girls at home? What that said about my own personal courage—let alone my commitment to supporting my husband under trying circumstances—I tried not to contemplate.

"Okay, hopefully he'll sleep for a bit," Gianna said as she returned to me, shutting Clint's door behind her. "I think he's coming down with something. Did he look feverish to you?"

"I don't know," I stammered, feeling like the world's lamest stepmother, a dolt about to be gonged off the stage. Meet Rhiannon, the ridiculous clodhopper! She raises two kids half the month, but doesn't know *anything* about children! Look at her stammer and blush!

"Hopefully it's nothing serious," Gianna said, leading me down the hall to the upstairs family room. I couldn't help noticing her perfect ass, the cheeks a holy trinity of tight and high and round, unmarred by panty lines, gravity or justice. Did stay-at-home moms now wear *thongs* on a regular basis? I nervously tugged at my bunching Hanes, vowing to keep my behind from Gianna's sight for the duration of the visit. At least I happened to be wearing a push-up bra.

"Okay, girls, time to go to Dad's," Gianna said as we entered the family room where London was reading, Josie playing with scattered Legos.

"Yay!" Josie cheered, but London only looked at me and demanded, "Where's my dad?"

"He'll be back before dinner," I said lightly, my heart starting to pound in anticipation of being exposed, once again, as hopelessly inept with my own pseudo-child.

"Come on, get your stuff," Gianna prompted, and London grumbled to her feet, padding down the hall after Josie. As the girls came back out with their bags, Clint burst from his room. He saw the luggage and began screaming, "Bacation! Bacation!"

"It's not vacation, dummy; we're going to my dad's house," Josie said sourly. "And *you* don't get to come!"

"Knock it off, Josie," Gianna snapped as Clint burst into tears. "It's okay, angel. We'll do something special tonight, you and your dad and I."

"What are you going to do?" London asked, her face screwing up. "Why do you always do the special things when I'm not here?"

For the slightest moment Gianna shot a look at me—one exasperated stepmother to another—and then heaved Clint into her arms, telling London, "Yes, darling, you're *deeply* mistreated. I'll be sure to recount the full plot of *Curious George* for you after we watch it tonight."

I like her, sometimes, I thought. And though I was instantly shocked by my self-treachery, at that moment I was also grateful that I didn't have children of my own, always bickering and jockeying for position with the stepkids.

Still, that was no reason to expose my second-place ass. I stayed in back of the group as we tromped down the stairs. "Mommy," Clint asked, "when do my sissies come back?"

"Soon, sweetheart," Gianna murmured.

"Don't call her Mommy," London mumbled sullenly, and I couldn't help a small smile. At least the kid was consistent.

24

"YOU SHOULD GO," Will was encouraging me as I looked doubtfully at my reflection in the mirror. "Give them a chance. It's just a dinner, time to catch up."

I sighed. "I know. But I just want to spend the night with you." Each month we only had two Saturday nights to ourselves, and I hated devoting one of them to a group of people I no longer felt I could trust.

"I'll be here waiting for you, naked, with a rose between my teeth," Will said lasciviously. "And then we can spend the whole night together, if you know what I mean…"

I jumped into his arms and pressed my body against him, the anticipation of returning suddenly worth the brief separation. It seemed that every time the kids headed off to Gianna's, Will and I inched towards coupledom again, rediscovering a passion and intimacy that always seemed to reach its peak on the weekends—just in time for Josie and London to come back. I never told Will, but I inevitably grew depressed on our kid-free Sunday mornings, the dwindling hours signaling the imminent reallocation of all Will's attention and time. He called our weeks alone "off weeks," but for me they were very much *on*.

"I won't be too long," I said, and—with one last kiss for my husband and peek at my reflection ("you look *amazing*," Will promised)—headed out the door to meet my friends.

I do like how I look, I thought as I entered the restaurant, and that was good. The emerald top set off my near-black hair and light complexion; the black pants made me look tall and sleek. I was a decent advertisement for young stepmotherhood, a woman who'd acquired children without missing a beat or gaining a pound—a figure of certain envy to my sleepless and bedraggled friends still lugging around their baby weight like aquaphobics sporting precautionary inner tubes.

But as I sat down beside Kelly and Maryellen, I felt all the tension and ambition skitter away. Kelly was still single; Maryellen had a toddler. So what? This wasn't a competition, a social media PR campaign, a battle for who'd done best. We were friends. We all had problems. No one was a poster child. I felt my guard crumbling down.

"So how are you?" Maryellen asked. "How's the stepmom life?" She seemed genuinely interested, curious. Though I hadn't been that close to Maryellen in recent years—she was busy with her baby—I knew I could count on her genuine kindness.

Still I hesitated. Even if you wanted to be honest, where did you begin? *It's such a mess of emotions*, I wanted to say. *I was so unprepared. I'm a total wreck.* But instead I said, "Up and down, I guess. I'm still adjusting."

"I can imagine—" Maryellen started to say. And then Summer walked in.

So it was all squeals and lip-biting, passing Riley around the table like a stack of vacation photos. I imagined the proceedings devolving into Hot Potato, the pink bundle tossed hurriedly from hand to hand, and couldn't help giggling at the thought of Summer heaving her precious papoose across the room to avoid getting eliminated from the game.

"What? What's so funny?" Summer asked.

I just shook my head. "Oh, nothing. Just spacing out. How are you?"

Summer needed no more encouragement. She launched into a detailed chronicle of product reviews and poopy schedules, mommy groups and extreme laundry obligations. "Every moment is something *new*," Summer gushed, her eyes rolling around in pleasure. "She's like the best TV show and movie I've ever seen, times a million. I mean, I could just watch her *all day*."

"So how's Kevin doing?" Maryellen asked.

Summer blinked for a moment, as though it were the name of a distant classmate whose face she struggled to conjure. "Oh, he's such a *guy*," she said finally. "All awkward. Doesn't know how to hold her. Afraid to drop her. But he's so cute though. He's loving it."

"I bet Will's loving having a wife again," Kelly said to me. "I mean, to go from being a single dad to having a whole family again!"

"Yes, he really is so happy," I said truthfully. The way he bopped around the house, the way he whistled—it was clear to me that his life had come together in some deep and soul-healing fashion that made me ever guiltier for feeling so conflicted and unfulfilled.

"And what about you?" They were all looking at me. But where before I had seen concern and openness, now I saw canines glinting for the kill.

"I'm—happy too," I answered slowly. "I mean, it's a lot harder for me, getting used to having kids and everything, but we're hacking our way through I guess."

"What about Gianna?" Kelly asked eagerly. "Is she jealous?"

I blinked. Had Gianna been jealous of anyone, ever? "Oh, I doubt it," I said. "She's rich and beautiful and remarried herself. She's got a *yacht*."

Kelly sat back in her chair. "So *you're* jealous of *her*!"

I gave an embarrassed laugh. "It's hard not to be, a little," I said sheepishly. "I mean, she's the mother of Will's kids, his first love. I don't really care about the money. But I wish I didn't have to see her all the time."

"I *never* let Kevin see any of his exes," Summer declared loudly.

"Well, that's not really an option for us," I said, trying not to sound annoyed. "And it's funny, because Will gets all pissy when I just *talk* about old boyfriends, yet he doesn't understand why I get irritated having to see Gianna."

"You think he still has feelings for her?" Kelly asked breathlessly. I saw the others' eyes widen, exchange glances, as though they'd all been wondering.

"No! No, of course not," I said at once. "Nothing like that. She's just the kids' mom now." And that was all it was, no question. Right?

"Does it bother you? That she's the mom?"

What the hell was this? They should appoint legal counsel for stepmothers having to answer these kinds of questions to the general public! How could I possibly describe the constant overturning of my emotions, the way I ricocheted between strident jealousy and boundless relief, the way I wanted desperately to be the girls' mother in principle even as I couldn't wait for them to go back to Gianna's? How could I describe how simultaneously wonderful and bereft it made me feel to stay bundled in bed those nights when the girls awoke sick or frightened? They were not really my responsibility—they were not really mine. Who here could understand how freeing and agonizing that combination could be?

"Sometimes it does," I said simply, not even hoping to translate. "But sometimes it doesn't."

"Well, I think you're really courageous, Annie," Maryellen said. "Having kids is hard enough, but you have so much more to deal with.

It's tough for me to imagine. At least when Claudia starts mouthing off I have scary-mom leverage."

"Thank you, Maryellen," I said, touched. "I don't feel very courageous, but I'm doing my best. It's definitely a lot harder than I thought it would be."

"At least you got to skip the labor pains!" Summer guffawed, as though unable to endure another moment on the sidelines. "Now that's one thing I really envy you for!"

I looked tiredly at the woman I'd known for so long, wanting to give her something else to cry about. But Summer had swept Riley back into everyone's view and was cooing loudly into her daughter's face.

"But you were worth it, weren't you, my pretty baby? Anything would be worth it to have my own precious girl! Wouldn't it, my pretty little baby? Oh yes it would! Oh yes it would!"

25

WILL WAS NOT completely naked when I got home, the only thing between his teeth a strand of floss as he finished up his nighttime routine, but he was lounging on our bed in his silk boxers and looking unbearably strapping and edible. Sometimes—when we were alone and I was at my most confident, when the issues with Gianna and the girls seemed like mere flea-bite annoyances—I felt wobbly, weepy with gratitude to have this man as my husband, panicked at the thought that he might somehow slip through my fingers.

"You look so good," I sighed, pulling my shirt over my head. Yes-I-*Will!*

"I told you I'd be waiting," he grinned. "How was your evening?"

"Later," I said, snapping off the television and crawling to him.

And later he asked again, drawing me unwillingly from the drowsy drifting that only seemed to come easily in his arms. "Ugh," I groaned, not wanting to relive the dinner. "Summer is so *annoying*." I told him the whole story.

"Hmmm," Will mused when I was done. "*Somebody* sounds a little...I don't know...jealous?"

"I am *not!*" I protested, slapping his chest. "Summer has really lost it. I get that it's an exciting time, but she's *so* over the top."

"Yeah, I know," Will said. "But try to cut her some slack. This is once-in-a-lifetime stuff. For most people, having a child is probably the greatest experience of their whole life."

I was stung, suddenly wondering. *Have all our moments together paled in comparison to that?*

"I'll never forget the feeling of knowing that I was a father," he went on nostalgically. "That I had a daughter. A *daughter*, a little tiny child that was part of me, that belonged to me."

I fought hard not to heave up my crème brûlée. It was so disgusting to think of this—not of London's infancy, exactly, but Gianna's unforgettable participation, a proud and tender Will watching over the baby suckling Gianna's bountiful teats. Will could never understand that to me such stories were as painful as reminiscences about past blowjobs and wedding nights; he might as well be recounting the feel of Gianna's inner sanctum as he plowed his way toward conceiving his children.

"It still doesn't give her the right to be *rude*," I managed to say. "It really doesn't."

"No, but I'm just saying you should be the better, wiser person here," Will counseled. "You know how Summer is; she's got that selfish side—"

"So why does she deserve all this fanfare?" I exploded, sitting up in bed. "You know what? I'm sick of being the better, wiser person. I really am. I always just shut up and take it, every single thing, because I'm supposed to be so much better and wiser than all these ignorant creeps who say they love me."

"It's the plight of the mature," Will said, trying to lighten the mood, but I was not to be derailed.

"You know, I have kids now. Did anybody think to throw me a shower or give me a gift or acknowledge that my life is changing just as much as any other mother's? No, of course not. I decided to do something weird, so I guess I deserve what I get, some second-class citizen, swept under the rug—"

"Annie, don't you think you're being just a tad—"

"No I fucking don't," I hissed, pointing at him. "And you're just as bad, you know that? You are. My wedding was ruined by *your* daughter and you didn't do a damn thing about it."

He threw up his hands, shieldlike. This was not his idea of post-coital bliss. "Annie, we *talked* about that—"

"No, you basically said I was a horrible person for even thinking it," I retorted. "You said 'she's just a child' and I guess that means I'm supposed to 'be the better person' and accept that she's allowed to do anything she wants, including *come on our honeymoon*—"

"Annie—"

"And then there's Gianna, beautiful little mother-of-the-year *Gianna,* who gets to fuck with our schedule whenever she wants—"

He sat up and grabbed my arms. "Annie, what the hell?" His face was unsettled, almost suspicious. "Where's all this coming from?"

I just shook my head. I hadn't meant to spew like this, and I dreaded the look of disappointment that always pervaded his features whenever I dared to express discontent with our life or his children.

"You didn't want the kids to come with us on our honeymoon?"

I swallowed. "I thought I did," I gulped, and burst into tears.

He released my arms and ran his hands through his hair, as though he couldn't be expected to deal with someone so patently ridiculous. "Annie, I don't know what to tell you," he said, baffled. "You know the kids *are* just kids. And Gianna is the way she is too. And we're all kind of this package deal. I can't change that."

"I know," I whimpered.

He continued to shake his head. "I don't get it. What's changed? You knew I had kids when you married me—" He blinked, the word triggering a memory. "Oh, God."

"What?"

He looked at me in horror. "I can't believe it. This is just what Gianna said would happen."

Wait, *what?* I blinked, sputtered. But he was going on:

"You want me to be something I'm not, someone without kids, someone without a past—"

"No, I don't," I protested desperately. But didn't I? If I had the power to rewrite history, would those children even exist?

"Well if you're so miserable with me, with this horrible life I've landed you in, maybe you should just—"

But he didn't say it.

"I should just what?" I whispered.

"My kids aren't just going to disappear, Annie!" he said, profoundly agitated. "Neither is Gianna. So if all this is too much for you, you'd better just step away now. I won't have my kids hurt again." He was staring at me, arms crossed, jaw working: protecting his children from their wicked stepmother. If there had been any question of his ultimate allegiance, the names on the trophy had now been clearly etched.

I stared at him, dumbfounded. *He loves them more than me.* Though I had always suspected that, took it as an unspoken *fait accompli*, the pain of hearing it whipped my breath from my throat. And how quickly he'd turned on me—he said nothing of our *marriage*, of his own feelings for me, as though he had married me just to mother his children, as though any woman could fill that same curvaceous gap.

"So these are my two choices?" I spat. "Leaving you, or getting stepped on? You're right, it *would* be impossible for you to do anything to make me happier. You're right, Will—*I'm* the problem." And I threw on my robe and stalked from the room.

✧✧

The night was cold and endless and I sat, unmoving, in the dark, occasionally reaching up to palpate my icy nose or mop its steady trickle.

Finally there was a stirring, a shadow in the doorway.

"Annie, can we talk?"

I didn't answer. But he came to me, groping for the couch, sitting down next to me. "Please?"

I swallowed wetly. I really couldn't do this without opening the floodgates.

"Before you say anything else, I have to know something," I finally said.

He didn't answer at first. Then he cleared his throat. "Okay."

"What did you mean when you said 'this is just what Gianna said would happen'? Do you talk to her about our relationship? Because *I'm* your wife, Will, and that's just a complete betrayal—" I sat there shaking, unable to finish.

The couch squeaked as he shifted his weight. "No," he finally answered. "I don't talk to her about our relationship. But I did tell her we were getting married, and she had some concerns."

"What business is it of hers?" I said at once through gritted teeth. "How could you even *listen* to what she had to say?"

"Every mother wants her kids taken care of, Annie," Will said. "She was afraid you would grow to resent them, and me because of them, and, well, since you're not a mother yourself—"

"I don't want to hear any more," I spat. "God, I can't believe you would talk about me behind my back." I stopped, trying to control my pounding heart, knowing I had to ask the very worst thing, the ghastly unmentionable. I opened my mouth seconds before the words would come. "Tell me the truth, Will. Do you still love her?"

There was a long pause, nothing but held breath and dripping tears in the silence.

"Annie," he finally said, "I love you. But the relationship with the mother of your children is complicated."

I let the words float over me and settle. My feelings seemed suspended, unable to land and bloom. Was it true, this maxim of Will's? How could I know? I only had ex-boyfriends I rarely saw. I'd never married someone else. I'd never given up a lifelong dream in order to have a baby with that person, never looked at a child and saw another's face mingled with my own. Was that relationship always complicated? Were the parents as perpetually interlaced as their carried-on genes?

I didn't know. But I realized with dread, as I absorbed Will's words, that Gianna was a permanent specter, not just a friendly co-parent who'd disappear on the stroke of midnight when Josie turned eighteen.

"Annie, I'm sorry I was harsh with you," Will said, fumbling for my hand in the dark. "I just feel so helpless when you're unhappy. I can't stand that my life is so full of failures. I never thought I'd be divorced. I never thought I'd be sharing my kids. And it's not good for anyone, you know? Not me, not them, not you. I want to believe it can all work and that we can all be happy. And then this stuff comes up and it makes me so hopeless and exhausted—"

"I guess it's kind of like your package deal," I said gently. "Just like the kids and Gianna come along with you, these feelings come along with me. You can't expect me to love everything, to be used to everything. It's only been two months."

"I know," Will said. "I really know. I just want everything to start working. I feel like I've been struggling nonstop for years, and now that we're married—"

"Now that we're married we have to work even harder," I finished, more bluntly than I'd intended, but not about to let this one go. "So I'll quote you. If this is all too much for you, you'd better step away now. I need someone who's going to be on my side, not someone who's going to blame me for not being some kind of Stepford Wife doormat."

"I'm sorry, Annie," he groaned, pulling me into his arms. "I really don't blame you. I just want it all to go away. I'll talk to London about the wedding. I'll do better with Gianna. Hell, I'll beat up Summer if you want me to."

I couldn't help but laugh through the sniffles. "I just might take you up on that."

He took my face in his hands and kissed me. "I love you, Annie. Things are going to change, I promise."

26

"I HAVE A new hero," said June as the Society of Stepmothers sat around the Bower Room's craggy table. She slapped down her hands in excitement. "Tevye!"

She was greeted with blank looks.

"Tevye?" Leah finally asked. "As in *if I were a rich man, deedle deedle* Tevye?"

"I thought that was Gwen Stefani," Kim said.

"No, it's from *Fiddler on the Roof!*" June beamed. "Just listen to this!" And she pulled out her phone. "'A fiddler on the roof,'" she read. "'Sounds crazy, no? But here in our little village of Anatevka, every one of us is a fiddler on the roof, trying to scratch out a pleasant, simple tune without breaking his neck.'" She looked around the group. "Those are the opening words of the play. Don't you get it?"

"Are you saying that we're like the persecuted Jews who were driven out of their homes in Russia?" asked Maggie skeptically.

"Well *no*, I mean—well, kind of. Not the persecuted part. But I mean we have the same problem of living in a place where we're not wanted, where people are suspicious of us and we have to keep out of people's way if we don't want trouble. Just trying to live our lives too, you know? Make some music of our own? But we're always in danger of falling off the roof."

"I see what you're saying," Leah nodded. "But wasn't that play all about tradition? We don't have tradition to tell us what to do."

June considered this. "Well, ultimately, neither did Tevye—"

"God, I hate musicals," Regan griped. "Will you ladies *please* explain what the hell you're talking about?"

"It's a metaphor, Regan," June said dryly. "The characters use tradition to navigate their way through a difficult life. The fiddler on the roof is their symbol, their metaphor for what it's like to try to live in a world that doesn't want them." She paused thoughtfully. "Ultimately, though, Tevye loses both his tradition *and* his home..."

"So *why* is this like us again?" Regan broke in, exasperated. "Don't tell me you're getting evicted!"

"Agh!" June sighed, sitting back in her seat. "Never mind!"

"I'm just teasing, sweetie," Regan smiled. "I'm Jewish. You think even those of us with good musical taste can avoid *Fiddler on the Roof?* Never. I get the reference."

So did I. I smiled to myself, thinking the Tyler house had just been awarded its own special name: Anatevka.

"*Where* is Frannie?" Kerry suddenly spoke out. I looked around the table. I couldn't quite remember what Fran looked like, but I did notice one face that hadn't been present last month.

"I saw her yesterday, and she didn't tell me she wasn't coming," Kerry groused. "You'd think everyone could make it once a month! But no, there's always something." She pointed at us accusingly. "I've read all the stepmom books and they *all* have meetings and *all* the members are always at every meeting."

"Yeah, well this is real life, okay?" Maggie said. "It happens. We all have work and kids and husbands to juggle. When you get pregnant, you'll start skipping a few meetings too."

"I hope so," Kim whispered to Regan as she popped a savory appetizer. "We don't need her puking on our crab cakes."

The look on Kerry's face was impossible to read. And then her eyes filled with tears as her mouth stretched in a valiant smile. "Well, you're stuck with me for now," she said, unable to stifle the telltale tremor.

Apologies and encouragement flooded the table. "It's fine," she said bravely. "I'm still thinking very, very positive. I know it's going to happen soon. So? Who has a story to tell?"

"ME!" said Kim, waving her hand in the air. "*I* spotted Alison Calliope!"

Everybody groaned.

"Who's Alison Calliope?" I asked.

"Oh, she's like this holy, saintly stepmother that we basically all hate," Kim explained. "She has one stepson, one son with her ex-husband, and a daughter with her current husband. And not only do all the kids get along, but so do all the parents and kids. And I mean *all* of them. Get this—last summer, they all went on vacation to the Bahamas together—not just Alison's family, but her ex *and* his wife, *and* her husband's ex too!"

"*No,*" I gawped.

"*Yes,*" Maggie said. "She's beautiful, and nice, and *thin,* and does free legal work for non-profits. And that's why we all hate her guts."

"Her kids go to school with my stepsons," Kim explained. "She's not one of those no-life mombies, so I don't run into her that much, but this time—oh my God." She clutched her stomach as though the story churned nauseously, extra-terrestrially, within. "I went to pick up Marty after soccer practice on a weekend and Alison and her family were all there in the south field having a picnic and flying kites." She looked at them all, letting this sink in. "Yes, *kites,* my friends, even her big butch husband skipping through the fuckin' field like it was some *Sound of Music* sing-along." She closed her eyes wearily. "I *so* wanted to barf."

"See, yet another link between musical theater and evil," Regan smirked. "But don't worry, I bet there's something really fucked up going on—you know, they probably have some sicko Utah compound where all the parents are banging each other or something. Normal people just don't act like that."

"Well, most of us don't have it that easy, but Alison *is* very nice," Leah said to me. "I met her once at a fundraiser and she was very friendly."

"...and that's why we all hate her, Pollyanna," Maggie emphasized, shaking her head at Leah.

"But she's a stepmother, right?" I asked. "So what if she wanted to join this group?"

"She wouldn't, believe me," Maggie said. "SOS is for people who need *support*. People who actually have *problems*. You know, bratty kids, delinquent mothers, Disney dads, no money? We don't get a whole lot of women fretting over the perfect pie crust." She paused. "Anyway, we wouldn't let her in if we didn't want to. Just like we wouldn't let in any of our husbands' exes. Lots of them are stepmothers too, but we have to give priority to the people who find us first."

"God, I didn't even *think* of that," I realized, imagining Gianna sauntering up to the table. "That would be *awful*."

"So how are things going for you?" Kim asked me. "We didn't get to hear much about your family last time."

I summarized the general dynamics at home, my abiding self-doubt and the undulations with London. "But right now I'm mostly worried about Will's ex."

"The model," Leah remembered. A collective groan rose from the table.

"Well, she's not anymore," I clarified. "But yeah, she was. And she's still beautiful. And"—I took a deep breath—"sometimes I think he's still in love with her."

"Oh, that's just your insecurity talking," Kim said.

"Yeah, it totally is," Maggie chimed in. "Because have you looked at yourself? There's no chance the ex looks better than you."

Damn, she was blunt. I almost spit out my coffee in my rush to turn crimson.

"Guys usually aren't interested in their exes at all," June said. "I mean, they make movies about people getting remarried to each other and stuff, but no way is that the norm. Trust me, it's all in the research."

"The *research?*" I asked. Who *was* this odd little sprite of a stepmom?

June exchanged glances with several women at the table and they all started laughing.

"Maybe we should tell you how we all met," Kim said. "I mean initially."

"Prison?" I ventured.

They laughed. "No, but I hope we'll all get to share a cell someday," said Maggie. "Actually it was just a support group for stepmoms. But the cool thing was that we didn't all used to live here. We all met online."

"Just Regan and I were in the Bay Area back then," Kim said. "She and I met in person soon after. But Maggie was out in Sacramento, and June—get this—was a high school student. In Ohio."

"I started doing this research about stepmoms for a project," June explained. "It was this cool cross-curricular class, and we had to look into some aspect of literature and get research data and stuff. I picked the evil stepmom in all the fairy tales, because I actually had one. A stepmom, not a fairy tale. So anyway, I found their online group. At first I was just lurking, trying to see what they were like. And then I started to really *like* them, and I came out and told them what I was really doing, and they were all super nice and we became friends. A year later it was time to apply to college and it turns out that my dad and evil stepmom live here, in California, so I could apply to Berkeley as a resident. Freshman year I met Ryan at the restaurant where I work. He had a kid. And bam, here I am."

"And she is just as fabulous as a real-life stepmom as she was as an online spy," finished Maggie. June took a bow, flinging up her right hand in a Miss America wave.

Was my mouth hanging open? All I wanted to scream was *WHEN CAN I JOIN THE ONLINE GROUP?*

As I pondered whether there was a polite way to demand access to their virtual haven, Maggie went on, "God I miss that group. Don't you guys?" It came out that their tiny community had been abruptly disbanded a few years back after some kind of security breach. Now some of them dabbled on sites here and there, but Society of Stepmothers had no official online venue.

Damn.

Leah turned to me. "Anyway, Annie, you'll hear all our stories eventually. But to get back to your comment, it's totally normal to feel worried and insecure about your husband's ex. Every second wife does."

"I don't!" Regan interjected. "I have nothing to worry about from that lumpy old bag."

I laughed. "Well, Gianna is far from lumpy. And I know he loved her once. I try really hard not to be jealous or jump to conclusions. I know I can't change the past. But she's the one who left him, and I can't help but wonder if he's ever really moved on."

"Ask him," Leah encouraged. "Give him a chance to put your fears to rest."

"I did," I said. "We had this huge fight, and afterwards I asked him and he said that he loved me. But then he said——" I paused, hating to repeat his words. "He said, 'The relationship with the mother of your children is complicated.'" I looked at their faces, cringing. "Is that true? Is that true with your husbands?"

"Nope," said Kim.

"No way," said Maggie.

"He pretty much hates her guts," said June. "Can't really get less complicated than that."

I swallowed painfully. "So then..."

"Well, I know this won't be a popular thing to say," Leah broke in, "but my feelings for *my* ex are complicated."

"Really?" I asked hopefully.

"I'm not sure if it's because he's the father of my kids or just because we were married for a long time, but of course there are feelings there," Leah said. "I feel bad about the way we separated. I feel bad that I hurt him. I feel bad that he sees the kids less than I do. And I do remember that I really loved him once. I love Paul now, but—I'll always love Curt in some way. I really will."

"That's all very nice and sweet, Leah, but we're talking about a *guy* here," said Maggie. "When he says his relationship with the ex is complicated, it sounds like he still has a thing for her." She turned to me. "You said she's the one who left Will?"

I nodded numbly.

"Maybe he has a thing for her, but maybe not," Leah argued. "Look, these are blended families we're talking about. We all have histories and pasts. Feelings don't always turn on and off that easily, do they? You can't tell me that none of you feel *anything* for other people you've dated."

A few of the women nodded grudgingly.

"But what about him saying it's because she's the mother of his children?" I ventured. "Do you think that if—when—we have our own kids, all that stuff will go away? Then *I'll* be the mother of his children. At least one or two of them."

Nobody seemed to know what to say.

"I hope so, Annie," Maggie finally said. "But it just sounds to me like he's making excuses."

"And I'm not sure we should have kids to get our husbands' attention," June said gently.

"Well, no, I mean—I wouldn't," I said quickly. "I mean, that wouldn't be the reason." I was taken aback that someone so young would challenge me, but then I remembered that June was a more experienced stepmother than I was, not to mention confident and wise far beyond her years. Respect in this group was earned.

"To me it would be about actions more than feelings," Leah said. "If he's putting you first, not crossing boundaries with her, and making it clear in every way that you're his wife and priority now, I think that's all you can ask of someone who's been through a painful divorce."

I absorbed this. Like everything else in the stepfamily arena, I had no idea how to judge what was normal and reasonable: I was always groping for a light switch, trying to read a code without a cipher.

"I think he does put me first," I said slowly. "At least most of the time. But boundaries? I really don't know. He doesn't seem to be able to say no to her," I confessed. "He never wants to upset her."

The group burst out laughing.

"Well *that*," Kerry said, "is something different entirely."

"Yeah!" added Kim. "None of our husbands *ever* wants to upset the ex. I swear, Nate would rather set fire to his pubic hair than dare to unsettle the saintly Mother Superior."

"Why *is* it that the men are always so afraid of the women?" pondered Maggie. "You hardly ever see an ex-wife bowing to her ex-husband's every wish, always the reverse."

"They're afraid they'll lose custody," Regan suggested. "That if the ex gets pissed she'll take him to court and win. We all know the courts still favor moms."

"Men just want to live their lives without a bunch of drama," Kim said. "Nate simply views it as keeping the peace. He'd rather be inconvenienced than have a fight with her. I get that, but when's he going to learn that it's better to have a fight with her than a fight with *me?*"

"I think moms feel more entitled than dads," June said thoughtfully. "I know my mom did. Even though she valued my dad's role in my life, deep down I think she saw herself as the primary parent and thought that he should honor what she wanted. And, as angry as my dad used to get about it, he seemed to agree because he almost always deferred to her." She paused. "They had a lot of fights about visitation and stuff. I'd hear her on the phone with him, always pretty calm, but she'd definitely say what she wanted to say. She never seemed afraid of upsetting my dad or stepmom." She looked at us, cringing. "Was that wrong? Was she taking advantage of a weenie?"

"I think we all just want a situation that's fair," Leah said. "I think both the parents should be able to speak up when something bothers them, and both should also try to keep the peace as much as possible. I guess I'm more like a dad, because I always try to give Curt the benefit of the doubt and let things pass."

"All I know is that it hurts to see a man let himself be stepped on constantly," Maggie said. "Fatherhood isn't supposed to be emasculating. These dads need to grow a pair already."

"It's never going to happen," Kerry said sadly. "Never, never, never."

"Okay, I have another question," I spoke up. "Are we supposed to tell our husbands about this group?"

Kim shrugged. "That's up to you. Most of them know and are very supportive."

"Dennis admits this group has more or less saved our marriage," Maggie said. "He's always in a good mood when I get back because he knows *I* will be."

"Derek wasn't happy about it at first," Kerry said. "He thought I was just spilling all our 'family secrets' and complaining about him. But then he realized that being able to talk to other stepmoms took a lot of the burden off of him, so he's come around."

A woman named Hester looked around the group, then back at me. She hadn't been at the first meeting I'd attended and she'd hardly spoken a word during this one. Furtive and reserved, she looked at me as though she wasn't quite ready to trust a newcomer. "My husband doesn't know. He wouldn't like it and he wouldn't understand." And that was all she said.

"So you haven't told Will then?" Regan asked.

I shook my head. "I was about to, after the first meeting, and then something came up and I never did. Then I wasn't sure if I was supposed to."

"From what you've said about your relationship, I think I'd tell him," June said. "It doesn't sound like you have a reason to keep secrets. And telling him could open up some good conversations."

She paused, then grinned. "Plus, if he knows about us, you can all come to our annual family picnic!"

They all laughed.

I raised my eyebrows. "You have an annual family picnic?" I could just see it: surly kids of all ages and a bunch of uncomfortable dads talking about their ex-wives and strapped wallets. *So...I hear you've been divorced?*

"Well, not really. But we always talk about having one. So someday it might happen...and then you could come!"

"Actually, we really do get together with each other's families sometimes," Maggie said. "My husband works with Leah's, so we've known each other a long time."

"And Kerry and I go to the same church," said Fran.

"Nobody hangs with me, though," Kim joked. "They can barely tolerate me for a couple hours a month, so playdates are out."

I laughed. How much better could this get? A support group, maybe an online group someday, and even the potential for *family friends?* One of these amazing ladies would probably have to pry my fingers off her leg at the end of the meeting.

"I'd like to tell Will," I said. "I just hope he'll take it well."

October

27

"COULD SOMEONE GET that?" Will called from the bathroom as the phone began to shrill.

I didn't budge. I hadn't even had a landline in my apartment; my friends had always just called my cell. But Josie rose to the occasion, sprinting from her room over to the yellowed, wall-mounted number that—judging from the fine plastic craftsmanship and the profusion of grubby fingerprints—had probably been one of Will and Gianna's first joint purchases. "Hello, Tyler residence, Josephine Tyler speaking," she recited in one tumbling breath. "Oh! Mommy! I have *so* much to tell you!" And she began twirling herself around the distended cord, off on another spill-all marathon whose details I tried, as ever, to tune out.

I sat at the kitchen table with my laptop, scrolling through the latest batch of uploaded photos. There were a handful from our hike a few weekends back, some random ones of Mr. Pickles, and an endless stream of London's selfies. Then I came across a set of shots that Will had taken of Josie, adrift in dreams on the futon one warm afternoon. The instincts inside me clashed: scroll past them uncomfortably; post the cutest one on Facebook and earn the world's approval. I'd get more oohs and aahs from a single shot of this six-year-old than I'd gotten from my entire wedding album.

I lingered on the photos. I had never understood why parents drooled over their children's somnolent limbs as if they were marzipan dainties. Yet even I had to acknowledge Josie's beautiful little features, the dew on the lip, the sweet rise and fall of untroubled breath. This wasn't the first time that Will had taken such tender close-ups of his youngest.

But I didn't remember seeing similar shots of London, sleeping or otherwise. Then again, she was less likely to fall unconscious in convenient settings. She was older and more inhibited; perhaps Will couldn't get past the posing to something more authentic. Perhaps—like me—he was not at all enamored with adolescing features that grew more to resemble Gianna's with every passing day. (Okay, even I couldn't pretend to believe this reason was a real possibility.) Or perhaps—well perhaps he just preferred Josie ever so slightly, she a little freckled scamp that managed through her monstrousness to remain irresistible.

"There were boogers," I heard Josie recounting quite seriously to Gianna. "It was a problem."

Inwardly I chastised Will for even the smallest bias: I knew how it felt to be the unfavored daughter. Then again, could I blame him? It was just so much *easier* to love an adorable, affectionate child—and London, for her part, had done little of late to drum up a fan base.

"Um, Annie? Can you help me with something?"

I blinked. As though summoned by my unfavorable thoughts, the girl herself stood in the archway. London looked supplicating, almost shy.

"Yeah!" I said, shaking myself to life. "Yeah, of course. What is it?"

"Oh, are those pictures of us?" London asked, sitting down excitedly next to me once she realized what I was doing.

"Yeah. Aren't these ones funny?" We started flipping through the pictures, putting together a slideshow of the family's best shots.

In the living room, Josie was ending the call with a string of noisy kisses that surely weren't doing anything for the phone's germ content. I heard Will take over the conversation.

"What are you doing?" Josie ran up to us. "I want to help!" I settled her on the other side of the computer. *No, that's not going to work out for us,* I heard Will saying to Gianna. *Let's just stick to the schedule.*

I fought back a smile. His first test since our Big Conversation and he seemed to be getting it right! My heart surged with triumph: *He loves me! He really loves me!*

And yet Xena wondered whether he'd be talking quite so firmly had he been out of earshot.

Moments later Will peeked into the kitchen, holding up the phone. "London? Want to talk to Mom?"

The girl swept off to her room to pick up her own handset as Will and Josie admired the completed family collage. It was only an hour later that I remembered what had brought my older stepdaughter to the kitchen in the first place.

Nervously—hating the nerves—I knocked.

"Yeah?"

Did that count as preteen consent? Cautiously I opened the door. London was lying on her bed, ignoring her open textbook in favor of her text messages. I cleared my throat. "Um, hey London, I was just wondering if you still needed my help with—with something?"

"What?" London put down the cell phone and looked at me blankly. "Oh, no, never mind. My mom helped me."

Of course she did. I forced my face not to fall. "Oh, okay. Well I'll be out here if you need anything else." And, slinking back to my place, I shut the door.

It's not a big deal, I told myself, fighting feebly against the disproportionately crushing disappointment. *We made the slideshow, right?* And if London had come to me once, London would come to me again. It was a good sign. These were all good signs. *Patience, Rhiannon. Patience.*

But patience was a bitch. It had been the lesson of my lifetime and I still couldn't get it. How I'd yearned as a child to be older, free to wear makeup and hairless legs. How I'd struggled through my incarceration at my parents' house, counting the days until high school graduation. The wait for Will's proposal—for my promotion—for my wedding day—each of these had felt interminable, the minutes stretched and distorted like victims of a medieval torture device.

Yet nothing in my life had compared to this. Nothing had been harder than waiting for a child to love me—or waiting for my own home to feel like one.

28

THE GIRLS WERE gone, the plates scraped, the bread basket empty. Between Will and me lay a demolished fettuccine platter, two nearly-drained glasses of ruddy warming wine. It was Saturday date night, and for the first time in ages I felt nothing but affectionate marital confidence when I looked across the table at my husband.

People could change—he was proving it. His efforts bolstered me. It was as good a night as any.

I knocked back the last gulp of wine, trying not to look too anxious. "So. I've been meaning to tell you something."

Will smiled at me with a receptive little shrug. "Shoot."

"Well, remember the other day when I met Kelly for coffee?" I began to craft an elaborate *well-wouldn't-you-know?* story about stumbling onto the stepmom meeting, wondering exactly how many lies I could spin before completely devaluing the underlying honesty.

"It's kind of like a mommy group for stepmoms," I kept on before he could react. "You know, parenting tips for those of us who are still getting our feet wet." This was, of course, only fractionally true, but how could I tell him about Kerry's disgust for her bratty stepkids, or Regan, who'd referred to all children as *revolting money-chugging soul-suckers?*

I waited, heart pounding, for the shake of head or furrowed brow that meant certain disapproval. But Will only sat back and smiled.

"Annie, you amaze me," Will said. "That's great of you to think of things like that. But you're doing *just fine*. You don't need any help." His eyes flicked toward the center of the dining room.

I looked at him blankly, trying to make sense of this surprising interpretation. Finally he caught the waiter's eye and then turned back to me. I smiled patiently. "That's nice of you to say," I said slowly, "but I feel like I do. It would give me more confidence, I think. I don't quite feel that I'm doing as, uh, swimmingly as you say."

"There's my perfectionist," Will sighed. Then his face lit up as he pulled out the famous snap. "You know, there's a woman at work who has a mommy group. I think her name's Rachel, something like that? No—I think it's Rachelle. Anyway, they take the kids on outings and things. Maybe you could do that with Josie? I'm sure she'd love it."

Wow. He *really* wasn't getting it. "That's a good idea," I nodded supportively, shamming interest, "but I'm not sure that would be the right type of thing." I paused, leaning forward as though offering a little-known fact. "You know, some mothers wouldn't feel comfortable with a stepmother joining the group, especially when the biological mother is in the picture."

I'd seen it myself. When I'd told other mothers that I was the stepmom, they'd literally taken steps back from me as though divorce were contagious—as though the slightest social interaction might sweep their own children up into my sinister vortex. They heard *stepmother* and saw divorce and adultery, shattered homes and stolen children, the clawing-at-the-heart horror of watching their flesh and blood loved and raised by an interloper. Clearly, embracing any stepmother as a peer felt like tempting fate, like inviting one into their *own* lives. How many women would dare?

But Will had never believed me before, and he wasn't buying it now. "In this day and age? Come on, a mother is a mother," he insisted, looking up to thank the waiter for bringing the dessert menus.

I forced a smile, marveling at his delusions as I weighed the relative merits of bread pudding and chocolate mousse. "Well, I feel a good connection with this group," I braved on. "And it would really make me feel better." I hated sounding like I was wheedling and fluttering, asking his permission—but I desperately wanted the spousal blessing.

And then I caved, afraid it wasn't coming. "I'd love to do both, though," I added quickly. "Can you ask your coworker about the group?"

He looked so happy and relieved.

Later, during our bedtime rituals, Will had news.

"Oh, I forgot to tell you," he said casually as he walked into the bathroom. "I talked to London about the wedding."

He FORGOT to tell me? My pulse began to sprint. "You did?"

"Yep," Will said, clearly very pleased with himself. "And you have nothing to worry about. She said it was her phone and she felt really bad that it went off."

I nodded to myself. "Okay, that's good to know. What about the other stuff?"

He answered through his toothpaste. "What do you mean?"

"Well, there was more than the phone," I explained, trying not to sound irritated. "What about the talking during the ceremony? The fight with Josie? What did she say about those?"

No answer came. Then: "She didn't mean to be distracting, Annie. She said she was sorry about everything."

I lay in silence as he finished up. "I'm glad I talked to her, though, I really am," Will said thoughtfully as he climbed in bed beside me.

"I don't spend enough time just talking to her about important things. So thanks, sweetie." He leaned over to kiss me, then lay back against his pillow, a distant smile playing on his lips.

He looked so lovely when he was wistful. I reached over to stroke his cheek. "What are you smiling about?"

He shook himself. "Oh, nothing. She's just a really good kid, that's all." There was something of the lovesick in his sigh as he settled into the pillows and flicked off the light.

There was something of the Warrior Princess in mine.

29

"CAN I GO get her?" London asked breathlessly from the back seat as we pulled up Evie's driveway. She was straining at her seatbelt, haloed with a certain shimmer of spontaneous combustion.

"Sure," I laughed as I parked the car. London bolted, not even ringing the doorbell as she busted into the house. I followed, lingering in the entryway. "Hi there," I called out. "I'm here to pick up Evie."

"Be right there!" screamed an approaching voice from around the corner, followed shortly by a woman.

"Oh—hi." The woman stared at me, comically blinking.

I pasted on my toothiest smile. "I'm Annie Tyler," I said, holding out my hand.

"Carly Winston," she stammered, then shook her head. "Sorry. I just was expecting—when Evie said she was invited to London's house, I just assumed she meant Gianna's."

Exactly the reason we have to start getting more involved, I thought, pleased with myself for suggesting this to Will. "No, it's our week," I smiled, trying to look convivial, non-threatening, user-friendly. "We didn't have any plans this weekend, and we haven't seen Evie since our wedding, so we thought it would be fun to have a sleepover."

"Well, she's thrilled," said the other woman, relaxing. Thankfully she seemed to be picking up on my warmth and not my desperation. "Thanks again. Just let me know when I should pick her up tomorrow."

We all headed back to the car, London and her friend giggling nonstop in the back seat as we drove back to Anatevka. *This might really be fun,* I thought excitedly. After Will's proclamation of his daughter's innocence, I had pledged to turn over a new leaf with London and leave it there—stapled to the floor if needed. No more of the roller coaster, the endlessly revolving leaf: I was going to banish my suspicions and make good happen. *One step closer,* I thought determinedly, *to becoming Angelina.*

The girls scampered off and I went to find Will. "It's a good look for you," I laughed as I entered Josie's bedroom, finding my husband in a tiara and pink netted wings.

"He's the king of the fairies!" Josie proclaimed proudly.

"He certainly is," I agreed, trying to keep a straight face. "Well, are you ready to get started?"

"I don't think the king of the fairies should have to do manual labor," Will said hopefully, adjusting his tiara, but I pointed sternly to the office. Will begrudgingly removed his costume and followed me to the worst room of the house.

We had never fully completed my move. Three months after that nightmarish day, box after box was stacked along the sides of the office, leaving Will a tiny space for his desk and a few books. To his credit, he rarely complained about the trespassing clutter—hoping, perhaps, that if he ignored the matter I would tackle the project on my own. But I couldn't put anything away without his help: the house was stuffed. It was going to have to be a joint effort.

We began to paw through the remnants, making slow but satisfying progress. *You did good,* I thought to myself: the whole trajectory of the afternoon had been my idea. The ointment-fly was Josie, whose scheduled playdate had fallen through. But London had actually *hugged* me when I'd suggested the slumber party. Even Will—always afraid to imply that he didn't want to spend time with his children—

looked thoughtful and pleased when he saw that London craved her friend's companionship more than his own.

Still, there was something mildly sinister about Evie. Even when she smiled sweetly there seemed to be something flickering beneath the surface, a little devil-in-residence that took control when the adults vanished. I could see her whirling teachers 'round her fingers after spending recess pushing dorky girls into mud puddles. London, by contrast, seemed positively innocent and good-natured.

Maybe that's the secret to liking one's stepkids, I smiled to myself. *Surround yourself with children you REALLY can't stand!*

Yet London was clearly awestruck, adoring; I had never seen her more enamored with anyone—even Gianna. The realization inspired a mixed reaction: delight that Gianna was not paramount after all; concern about the other girl's impish influence. *You don't even know the kid,* I scolded myself sagely. *Don't jump to conclusions.*

Yet our guest's magnetic pull was not lost on Josie, either, who hounded the older girls until they resorted to insults and torment. "DA*DDDYYYY*!" Josie screamed in hysterics, sobbing across the house in a manner all too evocative of my wedding reception. *Maybe it had been Evie's fault, not London's,* I thought suddenly, surprised and guilty that I'd never considered that possibility before. *See?* simpered Angelina triumphantly. *I told you you're a wicked stepmother! Any good mother would have automatically suspected the other child first.*

"Dad, we want to be *alone*!" shouted London as she stormed into the office after her sister. "Can you keep her *away* from us?"

"JoJo," Will said calmly, "you know what it means when your sister's door is closed. You need to let London and Evie have their time together."

Josie began to stamp and howl in a manner signaling total meltdown.

"Why don't you go play with Mr. Pickles?" Will suggested.

"No, Mr. Pickles needs this time to rest," I said hastily. No matter how many times I explained it to Will, he couldn't get it into his head that my cat was not a toy suitable for Josie's manhandling.

Will shot me a look. "Well, I'll tell you what," he said, gathering his younger daughter onto his lap. "How about you and me and Annie go out for sugarplums?"

The transformation was instant: Josie's face was a jubilant sun. "*Can* we?"

"I don't see why not," Will said, kissing her nose. He turned to the older kids. "You girls will be okay here for an hour or so, won't you?"

London and Evie exchanged glances and nodded eagerly. "Sure," Evie said. "When London comes to my house my mom always leaves us alone."

I wondered if that was true. I wondered if it was a good idea to bribe Josie with candy when she behaved like a hellion. But when Will was here, Will was in charge. Besides, I could use a break, too.

At the confectionery, we settled at a table with mugs of hot cocoa and a dozen glittering candies. I couldn't begrudge Josie her enthusiasm: the chewy sugared treats were delicious. "Sugarplum Daddy," Josie declared happily as she smacked away. "Sugarplum Mommy. And Sugarplum Baby!"

Will and I shared a smile. Neither of us had any idea why Josie had extended her love of candy to her family tree, or what exactly the *Sugarplum* designation meant to her. With a child as imaginative as Josie, you didn't need all the details. But in London's absence, Josie was free to be her most fanciful, to call me what she wished. *I'm the Sugarplum Mommy,* I thought, smiling back proudly at the woman who walked past our table and declared Josie *an adorable child.* It was so easy to pretend to be what everyone saw: a lovely young couple with a lovely young daughter. It was so easy to pretend that there was no Gianna, no London, no insecurity, no angst, just love and love and love, mom-dad-baby, the sweet and simple story that everyone envies and craves.

Yet the sugarplum-glaze wore off as soon as I returned home, walking in to find London and Evie in the master bathroom, elbow-deep in my makeup. "Annie—" London stuttered, a fright in heavy blue eyeshadow and brick-red lipstick that had transferred in large part to her teeth. "We were just—"

As if there were any explanation for a makeup raid. I had been a teenager once, too. And so I stifled my bark and listened to Angelina. *See the humor in this! Now's your chance to shine.*

"Makeovers! What a great idea!" I said brightly, trying not to cringe as I saw my makeup strewn across the counter, expensive lipsticks left disfigured and uncapped. "But I don't think those are the right colors for you." We spent the next hour giggling through new faces and hairstyles—Josie, of course, demanding to be renovated too—and modeling them for an enthusiastic Will.

"Such beautiful women in my life!" he swooned. And when we'd finished the family movie we'd rented and sent the kids off to brush their teeth, I sat alone on the couch feeling as though everything, despite the fights and sugarplums and unfinished unpacking, had gone exactly as it should have.

See? said Angelina, actually sounding proud of me for once. *You're getting the hang of it! Sometimes the most wonderful moments spring from the things you can't control.*

"Um, Annie?"

"What is it, sweetheart?" I answered absentmindedly, still relishing the moment.

"I, um, want to tell you something?"

I blinked myself back to the present. This was London standing there in the doorway, looking intensely uncomfortable. I straightened up, snapped to. "What is it?"

London opened her mouth, but nothing came. "I—" she finally managed. "I just wanted to say thanks." She swallowed. "For the makeovers."

"Oh, sure," I said lightly, walking over to her. "You too! They were fun, weren't they?" I grinned and patted my gel-laden pompadour.

"Yeah," London said slowly, then smiled. "Well—goodnight!"

"Goodnight," I smiled back, allowing my hand to venture out, for just a moment, to rub London's shoulder before she turned and padded to her room. I stood there watching until the door clicked behind her, then released the breath I didn't know I was holding. *I made it,* I thought. That was it—the day was over. And maybe we were making some progress after all.

30

THE VERY NEXT morning I was up and at 'em with Josie, our butts in the car promptly at 8:30. *It's Happy Happy Fun Time!* I kept chanting insanely to myself, which was the only way I could stave off the terror of what I was about to do.

Josie launched herself from the car as soon as I parked, bolting for the biggest play structure and abandoning me to my quivering entrails.

I looked across the park. There they were with their Starbucks and yoga pants: the Moms of the Mommy Group. My husband could never say I didn't love him: only for him was I willingly walking into this death trap.

No! Angelina argued. *Not a death trap! It's Happy Happy Fun Time!*

But Xena just mimed hanging herself.

I managed to slide one ballet flat toward the direction of the group. Just a simple shift in weight and—bam!—I was on my way, mastering the art of bipedal motion and everything.

When I joined the circle, the Moms were in mid-laugh over a punch line I hadn't heard. I stood there awkwardly chuckling until my kamikaze instinct grabbed the controls and tipped me into a nose-dive. "I feel naked!" I blurted out. Seven Mom heads all turned to me with blank looks.

"Without my coffee!" I added in desperation, smiling too broadly. "No coffee!" I was pointing fanatically at my empty hand.

Then the Moms smiled. "Oh, tell me about it," one of them said, the only other one without a cup cemented to her palm. "You must be Annie. I'm Rachelle." As we shook hands, she introduced me to the Moms, but I was too petrified to remember a single name. "I work with Annie's husband," Rachelle told them, pointing at Josie's head bobbing on the playground. "It's Josie, right? How old?"

"She's six."

Everyone smiled and nodded and went back to their conversation. I took a deep breath, delighted that my entrails were relaxing. Maybe this could really be fun.

They talked about Mom Things and I tried to look cool while hiding the fact that I didn't speak the language. They were all looking to me for opinions about organic foods and pediatric dentists. My alarm bells were clamoring: *Don't they know I'm the stepmom? Did Will not tell them?*

I didn't know what to do.

Should I say something? I couldn't. How could I bring attention to myself; how could I invite the suspicion or pity or even surprise into their eyes?

Should I pretend to be their mom? I couldn't. What if they found out? What if they knew Gianna?

Should I keep quiet and let them think whatever they wanted? Well—

"Annie, where do yours go?"

I blinked to attention. Now *that* I could answer. A Mom got very excited in a Jack Russell kind of way. "Oooh! Mine too. *Love* Brighton. Absolutely love it. Have your kids had Mr. Peccolini, for second?"

"Ummm..." I said, instantly filmed with sweat. That would have been three years ago; I didn't even know London then. "I'm not...I, uh..."

Ah, to hell with it.

"Josie's only in first this year. London might have had him, but she's my stepdaughter, so I wasn't in her life back then."

I dared to glance up. Every face was frozen. *Sorry, Josie,* I thought, muscles tensing in advance. *If I have to sprint for it, you're just going to have to be left behind.*

But a moment later they looked normal. Well, most of them. A dark-haired Mom seemed to be glowering into her coffee.

"So you're a *stepmom*," a different one said, a blond. She looked intrigued, like she'd seen pictures of such creatures on Instagram (#homewrecker #kidstealer #whore).

"Y-ep," I said faintly.

"Did I not tell you guys that?" Rachelle broke in. "Sorry. Annie and Will just got married, is that right?"

I nodded, still unsure how any of this was going to go. At least I knew that Will had prepped Rachelle, even if she hadn't passed on the message to the others.

"Well, tell me this," said the sullen dark-haired Mom. "Is it *really* so hard to figure out what areas of the kid's life should be for the mom only?"

Wha—? I just stared back at her.

"My husband's *wife*, I mean ex-husband—I swear to God it's like she has absolutely no sense about her role," the woman went on. "She's completely ridiculous, always up in their business. She's wanting to take them to doctor's appointments and tell them what to wear and get copied on the emails I send to my husband. Oh, and get this: SHE GAVE MY KID A HAIRCUT!"

"No way!" someone else gasped.

"Yes! I get him back after the weekend and his fucking *hair* is shorter! And now of course he always wants to go to *that* barber.

It's like, God, woman, get a life and stop trying to steal my kids! She's pathetic."

My panic button was blaring. *Abort! Abort!* But I was paralyzed.

"She's just jealous," Rachelle soothed. "She's trying to steal your thunder because she doesn't have kids and it's the only way she can feel better about herself."

"Well, it's pathetic," said Dark Hair, turning back to me. "I mean, you understand that between you and Josie, certain things are sacred, right? You wouldn't do them with your stepdaughter, would you?"

Oh dear dear dear God what do I do

And then I stepped boldly into the wet cement of cowardice, leaving my shameful footprint for all time. "No, definitely not," I said, trying to look appalled by the crimes she'd just enumerated. "Wow. Your kids' stepmom sounds like a *real* piece of work."

They went on talking, eventually turning to other things, eventually disbanding the chat to join the kids in the playground enclosure. I sighed, so relieved to have made it through. Now for *Happy Happy Fun Time!* I could romp with the best of them.

But as soon as I walked through the tiny gate, Josie screamed out at me and frantically waved. "ANNIE! HI! ANNIE! I'm up here!" She was at the top of the tallest slide.

I cringed and waved back. Why hadn't I thought she would use my name? Several of the Moms turned to give me puzzled looks. I was praying that Dark Hair hadn't noticed.

But she had. "Wait, what?" She looked at me incredulously. "You're *her* stepmom too? Why are you bringing her *here*?"

I felt like I had been sent to the principal's office. I couldn't speak.

"This is a MOMMY GROUP," the Mom insisted. "It's for *MOMS*. Not wannabes."

"Hey, Monica, let's not do this," one of the blonds said. "She hasn't done anything."

"*Unbelievable*," Monica hissed, turning her back to me.

The other women looked uncomfortable and embarrassed. But whose side were they going to take? I looked up at Josie. "Jo, we gotta go, okay? I think Daddy's making pancakes."

It wasn't enough. Josie just shrugged at me and kept playing.

"Come on, Jo, really, playtime's over. Please slide down now and come with me."

She ignored me.

I was on the precipice of tears. "Please, JoJo, *please*," I begged her. "We gotta go. We'll stop by the toy store on the way home. I'll get you a toy."

Josie looked down at me. "Two toys!" she haggled.

What could I do? There was no way I was going to lay my hands on the child; Mommy Dark Hair would surely file a report with CPS. "Yes, two toys, fine," I said. "Come on now."

And Josie happily slid down the slide and ran to me.

Oh the *shame*. At this plain bribery even the women embarrassed by Monica were recoiling from me. I was not only just a pathetic childless wannabe, I also had to resort to my wallet to win a child's obedience and affection. The Moms looked at each other awkwardly as Josie and I walked back out to the parking lot. I tried to keep my head high.

Then I heard footsteps behind me. It was Rachelle. "God, I'm so sorry," she said. "Monica's had a rough time since her divorce, but it never crossed my mind that this would be an issue. I should have told her before, but I didn't even think about it."

"It's fine, it's okay," I was babbling. "Not a good fit. I understand. Thanks anyway." I turned away again before my tears started flowing. "Tell Will I said hello!" she said hopefully to my retreating back.

But I wasn't sure what I'd be saying to Will. I hated him for not understanding anything about mom culture and pushing this disaster on me, for not making it very clear to Rachelle that *neither* of the girls was mine. I hated Monica for being a crazy bitch and her husband/ex-husband for turning her into one. I hated Rachelle for *trusting* the crazy bitch. And I hated myself for being so chickenshit and insecure that I'd lied to these women about simple facts that should not have been shameful or embarrassing in the first place.

In the backseat Josie was salivating for information. "Annie, why are you crying? Annie? What's wrong? Are you sad? Annie!"

"They were mean to me, Jo," I finally said.

My tears had stopped by the time we returned from the toy store. But, as usual, Josie took my breakdown as big news to share.

"Daddy, we're home! But Annie is so sad. They were mean to her. Daddy, where are you? I got two toys!"

"What?" Will stepped out of his office in perplexity.

"THEY WERE MEAN TO HER," Josie repeated with her usual subtlety. "But see, I got a Barbie and this dress-up outfit!"

Will looked at me, stricken. "What happened?"

"We'll talk later," I said wearily. "I'm going to go lie down."

Being a stepmother had a few priceless benefits, and this was one: the all-out abdication of responsibility that was only possible when your name was nowhere to be found on the child's birth certificate. But of course I wouldn't have needed such a benefit at this moment if I'd been anyone's mother.

I couldn't shake all the gross feelings. I felt like a fur-wearer doused in Monica's red paint. Yet even to think of that metaphor... did it mean that somewhere inside me I thought that the crazy bitch was *right,* that she'd caught me in the dirty act of parading around in another's skin?

I lay down on the bed, hoping that Will would be too busy juggling three kids (were London and Evie still here? I had no idea) to check up on me anytime soon. I didn't know what to say to him. I didn't want to blame him; I was far too exhausted to fight. But his delusions had a real cost, didn't they? On the other hand, mine must too, an even greater one. I didn't want to think about it.

After a few minutes I grabbed my laptop and logged in to Facebook, avoiding the news feed where I was sure to be bombarded with the kind of schmaltz that scientists would soon link conclusively to suicidal ideation. On my own Timeline I looked for the chat window, praying that one of my friends would be online.

I yelped when I saw her name. It was *Maggie,* dear wonderful Maggie who had given me her email address at the end of the last stepmom meeting and had accepted my Facebook friend request soon after.

We'd never chatted yet, though. Nervously I sent a message. For a minute there was nothing. But then the words appeared.

Hey, sorry I was doing crack

Um, what? I was still thinking of something clever to say when she wrote again.

You know. games. addicted to effing candy crush
saga.
what's up?

Hooray! She asked! And her lack of capitalization gave me license
to mutilate the English language. I told her the whole dreadful story
in one great belch of a reply.

After offering condolences, she wrote:

so why did you go to this horrorfest again?

Because I love my husband. Because I wanted him to be right.
Because I am a coward. But I wrote:

Felt like I should.

There was a pause.

Have you thought of disengaging?

Dis-en-what-now?

What does that mean?

Oh it's when you stop trying to be a parent and leave
it all to the dad
'not my kid, not my problem' kind of thing

Wait, what? This was a Thing? A stepmom Thing? But—

What if I want to be a parent

Well good luck with that!
I kid, I kid. I consider myself a parent. :)
But you can still disengage from certain things. Good
example is discipline. Lots of people don't go there

What else?

Homework, chores, driving the kids, buying them stuff
- anything really
It's just a matter of what will save your sanity.
You just kind of plug your ears and pretend it's not
happening
It takes some practice, esp. if you're a control freak
like most of us

I thought for a long time before I answered. I was nervous to hit
the return button.

That sounds like giving up (?)

But Maggie's reply was instant.

Sometimes you have to if you want to save your sanity

I inhaled audibly. It wasn't an answer I could bear to believe.

31

"SHIT SHIT SHIT!" I screeched to myself repeatedly as I screamed around corners, laying on the horn. "Learn to drive, nutball!" I shouted out the window, catching just a glimpse of the old lady's mystified reaction before hunching over the wheel again and stomping the gas pedal.

I was afraid of karma and radar detectors, yes—but ultimately far more terrified of being late to this momentous appointment.

But I *was* late. Five minutes, at least. And as I walked across the campus—the adrenaline giving way to shaky dread—I knew exactly what I'd find as I pushed open the door to Mrs. Medrin's classroom.

Will and Gianna perched next to each other across from an earnestly head-bobbing Mrs. Medrin, their quiet voices stopping mid-syllable when the hinges squeaked. The three heads swiveled in my direction.

"May I help you?" Mrs. Medrin squinted at me.

Will shook himself to life. "Oh, I'm sorry. This is my wife, Annie."

"I'm so sorry I'm late," I said breathlessly, coming across the room to shake the teacher's hand. "I'm Annie Tyler."

From the corner of my eye I saw Gianna glance at Will and smile.

"Have a seat," Mrs. Medrin said, then realized there were only two chairs in front of the desk. "You can just take one from the classroom," she said, motioning to the sea of shrunken furniture. I loudly wrestled a diminutive chair from the embrace of its mini-desk, excruciatingly aware of the others' silent endurance as I finally sat down beside Will. My chair placed me a full six inches shorter than the others: some junior parent observing the Real Deal.

"Now, as I was saying, London is performing well in all subjects," the teacher said. "She seems to be very hard on herself, though. In the few instances she's lost points on an assignment, she's both cried and tried to argue with me about the grade. In general, we try to encourage the students to learn from their mistakes and move on, since perfectionism can be quite damaging, and we're working with London on that. But the good side is that she is extremely bright and driven."

Like her father, I thought proudly.

"She's got good genes," Will said with a nod to Gianna. I felt my chair shrink six more inches.

"And what about socially?" Will asked. "Behaviorally?"

The teacher thought for a moment. "She can be emotional," she finally answered. "She tries so hard to be older—sophisticated, you know—but that doesn't mean that her emotions are always up to the challenge. Hormones, relationships, personal issues all come into play at this age. I haven't noticed anything in particular related to the remarriage, but I do appreciate you notifying me about it," she said to Will and Gianna, offering a sympathetic smile to me.

This was a new one. *Fucking Gianna,* I thought bitterly as I forced a smile back at the teacher. *Just couldn't wait to tell London's teachers how much damage her new stepmother is doing.*

"Well, family transitions can be hard on kids, so we thought you should know," Will said with all the confidence of a caring father. Good God, had *he* notified the teacher? I felt myself swaying on the tiny chair, blindsided and humiliated. I'd come to take my stand as a loving parent, not to serve as the explanation for all of London's problems.

"I'm remarried as well," Gianna mentioned then. "But you shouldn't have any difficulty there—we're pretty well adjusted."

"It's been a few years for them," Will said, ever so slightly irritated.

"Yes," Gianna said. "Ren's a very involved stepfather. But he figured today that Will and I could probably handle it." She glanced at me and then Mrs. Medrin, sharing an amused smile with the teacher that made me want to bash their heads together.

"We all care very much for London," I said. "If anything, we err on the side of being too involved," I laughed, proud of my graceful comeback. But then Mrs. Medrin's face turned grave.

"I know it sounds silly, but over-involvement *can* be a problem," she said. "With the older kids, we try to encourage parents to step back a little, avoid coddling and solving all their problems."

"Well, I didn't mean it like—" I tried to protest.

"Just be careful," warned Mrs. Medrin. "Children need to be loved, not over-parented and over-protected."

I nodded mutely. The message could not be clearer: butt out, stepmother. Whatever you're doing, it's probably wrong. The kid has parents and neither of them is you.

We all shook hands then, but I felt numb as we said our goodbyes and left the classroom. What had happened here? I'd come to show what a *good* stepmother I was, how involved and agreeable and un-wicked. Yet somehow I'd come off as an unnecessary meddler, spoiling the upbringing of a child who'd be better off without me.

We began to walk toward the parking lot, Will and Gianna obliviously chatting about London and upcoming art lessons as I followed them dazedly. *Why am I here?* I thought miserably. *Why am I doing this to myself?*

You deserve it, said Angelina smugly. *Because you were here to show off. You didn't really come because you thought London needed you here. You wanted to show Gianna and the teacher that you exist. You wanted to stake a claim you have no right to. And every one of them put you in your place.*

It was true. I'd wanted to be a Force: a confident and capable bundle of brilliance that inarguably counted just as much as a mother. I'd wanted everyone to gasp and rethink and recognize my equal standing with Will and Gianna. And I'd even wanted, by *engaging* my ass off, to prove to myself that Maggie was wrong.

In short, I'd tried to impose another one of my gauzy daydreams on real life. But instead I'd been late, clumsy, and painfully superfluous. Worst of all, Gianna had seen right through my pathetic motives.

"What?" I asked. Lost in dreary contemplation, I hadn't realized Gianna was talking to me.

"I was just saying I'm surprised you changed your name," Gianna repeated. "Considering you already have a career."

Ah, yes. *That.* I shifted uncomfortably. In truth I agreed with Gianna's reasoning: I'd never planned to take my husband's name. But that was before I'd known I was to become a second wife. How could I tell Gianna that I'd taken Tyler as my name simply because *she* hadn't—because I wanted, however foolishly, to be Will's *first* at something? Because, lacking first-wife cachet and children of my own, I didn't know how else to show the world that I was the real, true love?

God, Rhiannon, you are so insecure and pathetic, Angelina dismissed me in disgust.

"Oh, yeah, well my job isn't that important," I stammered. "I guess I just liked the sound of it. And all of us having the same name."

Even this last didn't seem to ruffle Gianna. "But isn't it a problem? I mean, you know...Anne Tyler, Annie Tyler?" At my blank look, she added, "The author?"

Oh. Yeah, now that she'd mentioned it, the name did sound familiar. "I guess I just read different books," I said, too weary now to care how illiterate I sounded. The truth was that I wasn't reading anything these days, though Amazon.com had recently delivered a truckload of goodies—*A Career Girl's Guide to Becoming a Stepmom, The Enlightened Stepmother, Keys to Successful Stepmothering,* and the most deliciously titled *Stepmonster*—that I'd stashed out of Will's sight. If today was any indication, it was time to get reading.

32

HOME AT LAST. And no cars in the driveway.

I collapsed gratefully against the steering wheel. I'd worked late, making up for the hour and a half I'd spent at London's teacher conference. My boss, even so, had bitched me out for leaving and turning off my cell phone, a rare event that had just happened to coincide with a pissy client's quarterly meltdown.

"I have to be able to count on you, Rhiannon," she'd lectured, sounding all too much like my prime nagger, mother Judy. "Your promotion came with additional responsibilities, and I expect you to step down if you can no longer handle them."

"It won't happen again," I had answered calmly. *Believe me, lady, I ain't going to another school conference.* But it was an unsettling reminder that—in my supervisor's eyes, at least—I was slipping in the only area I'd always felt beyond reproach. I just wanted to crawl into my pajamas and hide.

Hastily shedding my work clothes, I ran a hot bath, praying for a few precious private minutes before Will got home. I had just settled in and closed my eyes when the front door banged open.

"Annie? Annie, are you here?" He was shouting. Irritated, I sank lower in the tub, submerging my ears. *Oops! Can't hear you!*

But as his voice got closer to the bathroom, I could. Grudgingly I slid back up to the surface. "I'm in the bath, Will."

A second later the door busted open. "Did you wash the girls' sheets?" Will demanded.

Um, what? "No, not yet—"

"Where are the clean ones? We have to get everything cleaned up!"

He was approaching frantic. I sat up in the bath. "What's going on?"

"Gianna's father just had a stroke," he said, stepping back into the hall to open the linen closet. "She's dropping the girls off on the way to the airport."

Oh, God. Damn you, Yes-I-Will—I did *not* need the kids around tonight! "Why can't they stay with Ren?"

He popped his head back in the bathroom. "Geez, Annie! Because their grandfather is sick and they need to be with their father!"

I closed my eyes. "I'm sorry, I just had a really bad day—"

"A really bad day is when your father has a stroke," he said bluntly, already back out in the hall and rummaging around. "This is an emergency and not everything can always follow your perfect little plan."

Ouch. I sank my bruised ego back in the bathwater and considered my husband's point. It was true; life did intrude. I really couldn't have expected him to ask my permission first. Yet I couldn't help feeling invaded—ignored—irrelevant. He hadn't even asked about my bad day. And how could I be considered an equal partner if I made virtually no decisions about our lives together?

Tell him you're going to go out tonight, said Xena. I could go to a restaurant, to a coffee shop, and have the time alone I needed. Hell, I could go to the local spa and have an uninterrupted bath! *This wasn't your decision, so you don't have to abide by it. Do what you need to do.*

Yes, that was exactly right, I told myself decisively, removing the stopper and stepping out. I'd just help Will clean up and then head out for a few hours alone. And when I came back, I'd be feeling much better and ready to take on the family again. It was a win-win.

The house wasn't that bad, I thought as I dressed in jeans and started picking up. And why did Will have such a bug up his butt about cleaning? These were our kids, not photographers for *Architectural Digest*. Besides, from what I could tell, frolicking in clutter was their preferred lifestyle anyway.

"Need any help with that?" I asked Will when I found him in London's room, caught in the timeless struggle of man-against-bedsheet.

He grunted. "No. I'm done." He began tossing heart-shaped pillows back onto the bedspread.

"Well, we're looking pretty good here, so I think I might—" I started, and then the doorbell pealed. Will bustled to open the door. I briefly considered a slip out the back before I followed him.

Both girls, bulked up with jackets and bags, fell into Will's arms.

"It's okay," Will soothed, holding them tight. I hovered around the trio, my hands a pair of birds fluttering futilely for a perch. Wasn't the fourth wheel supposed to *complete* the set? I should have listened to Xena and made a run for it after all.

Finally there was nowhere to look but Gianna's face. "I'm sorry," I said helplessly. Gianna nodded her thanks. This was not the same woman who'd so effortlessly outshone me just hours before. Yet even with swimming eyes and swollen nose Gianna managed to look vulnerable rather than revolting; she wept the pretty crystal tears of an ingénue.

"Okay, I'll call," Gianna said to Will; to her children, "I love you." And she bent down to embrace her daughters, give one last kiss.

We called out our goodbyes. And Gianna hurried to the car as we shut the door.

Okay, I decided. *Now is the time to go.*

But in the end, I couldn't do it. Their confusion, my justifications—I couldn't say the words. Instead I put on a brave face. "Who wants hot chocolate?"

Maybe, I told myself, if I did my best to temper my family's grief, I could bury my bad day in theirs.

33

"THE WEIRD THING was," I said to Ted the next day, "it kind of *worked.*" To take the girls' minds off their ailing grandfather, Will had gone wacky—the sombrero-wearing wacky he'd been when I'd first met him—and the whole family had kooked it up in a game of charades. I had laughed until the tears came, thinking that this was the sort of *wholesome* that I'd once hoped would be my stepmotherly inheritance. I'd forgotten all about my chiding boss.

"Well, isn't that cute," Ted said wryly. "Home and motherhood save woman from the wrath of miserable, soulless career girl."

I rolled my eyes. "Don't make it sound like *that.* Usually the kids are worse than Brenda. It was just nice for a change."

"I'm kidding," Ted said. "Everyone knows that Brenda is a total bitch, and it may or may not have anything to do with the fact that she hasn't been laid in sixteen years."

"You know, it's funny," I mused. "I think she really has gotten worse since I got married—"

"—you mean since you started leaving randomly in the middle of the day? Gee, I wonder why?"

"Well, yeah, okay," I conceded. "But it's not just Brenda. Other single women have gotten a little less…inclusive. And at the same time, a lot of the moms have too. I guess no one wants me in their club."

"Well don't look at *me,*" Ted said. "I'm only hanging out with you because you tend to buy me coffee."

I smacked him. "I'm serious! I feel like a pariah."

Ted looked at me for a moment. "Don't take this the wrong way, Annie, but I think you sometimes take things a little too personally. Believe me, most people are just trying to get their shit done. They really don't care if you're married or single or a mom or stepmom or whatever."

"You just don't understand how women are," I huffed, but I wondered. Was I the true author of these subtle conspiracies?

"You won't get any argument from me on that point," Ted sighed. "Nadine is still raking me over the coals. She remembers *everything*, and if I forget the slightest little anything, I'm the worst boyfriend in the world who doesn't love her and takes her for granted and blah, blah, blah."

"Geez, maybe I should switch teams," I said. "I could fill a book with the stuff Will 'just forgot to mention.' What is it with men? Is it that hard to remember to tell me things?"

"But she can see I'm honestly trying," Ted went on. "I'm not trying to be insensitive."

"It's not that much to remember!" I continued my parallel rant. "Like, 'hey, I agreed we'd take the kids early next weekend.' Or even better, 'Gianna asked us to take the kids early next weekend. Would that be okay with you?'"

"The other night she honestly cried because I couldn't remember if she liked peanut or almond M&Ms. This, apparently, meant I didn't love her. Is it just me or are we crossing into whack job territory here?"

"He couldn't even remember to tell me that he had this pivotal conversation with London about her trying to ruin our wedding—"

"Wait, what?" Ted snapped back into the conversation. "You never told me about this." His eyes widened. "Wait, are you talking about the phone thing?"

I felt the chills slide up my vertebrae. "I thought you missed the ceremony?" I said faintly. Ted had warned me before the wedding that he wouldn't be there until dinner.

"No, I got an earlier flight," he said. "I thought you saw me. I was sitting a few rows behind London and her friend."

My heart was thudding. "And you saw her do something?"

"Well, she was definitely playing with the phone, because the reflection blinded me. I looked over and she was pushing buttons. It was a few minutes later when it went off."

I absorbed this tensely. It wasn't conclusive: London could simply have been thoughtless, not malicious. Yet Xena purred, *She lied to Will. Now you can prove it.*

"She said it was an accident," I sighed, not willing to admit the existence of my daemon voices to anyone, not even Ted. "I should probably just let it go." *Yes,* said Angelina, suddenly busting into the Disney song like my stepdaughters did every freaking afternoon. *Let it go! Let it go! Focus on the future with London. It doesn't matter what she did, and you'll never really prove it. Be the adult here! Be a mother!*

"So," said Ted, hoping to nudge me back in his direction. "What do you think? Nadine? Crazy?"

"Oh, absolutely," I said without hesitation, giving Ted a commiserating look. "But aren't they always, Ted? Why is it you can't ever get a normal girlfriend?"

His answer was instant and glib. "Serious slim pickings. Most women my age have *kids.*" He made a big show of shuddering. "That's way worse than mental illness."

I didn't know if he was joking or not, but I laughed anyway. "Good point, O wise one. Why couldn't Will just have a sweet little phobia or something? *So* much easier than offspring."

34

I WAITED IN the bath, poised under the water like an amphibious jack-in-the-box, until I heard Will come into our room and close the door. The kids were in bed at last! Grinning, I burst from the water and wrapped the towel around me, making sure to leave a little cleavage above the fold. Then I sidled into the room, fingering my hair with an air of studied absentmindedness.

Will was already in bed with the TV going. He didn't even look at me as I let the towel drop.

Okay, fine. I shook my head and climbed into bed beside him. "You know, they say that couples that have a TV in the bedroom have half as much sex as those who don't," I teased, curling my fingers in his hair.

"Ha, ha," Will said. He didn't move his eyes from the screen.

Now *this* was a newly married man in the prime of his life. I tried another tactic. "I was hoping we could spend a little time together tonight," I said hopefully. "Maybe talk a little?" With the girls' unexpected arrival the previous evening, Will and I hadn't even discussed the teacher conference.

But the groan in his eyes made it clear that Will was not in the mood for any sort of intercourse. "Like clockwork," he muttered to himself.

I was mystified. "What's that supposed to mean?"

He sighed and turned off the television. "It just means that every time there's some little change in our plans, you have a crisis."

That could not possibly be true. "I'm not having a crisis," I protested, hurt. "I just wanted to spend some time with you. I miss you."

His face softened. "I'm sorry. I know things have been crazy. And I still don't know what's going to happen—Lou's up and down. No one can say."

Had he talked to Gianna that day? How did I keep missing these things, these calls and texts and emails? *Check his phone!* Xena barked. I considered it. But I knew he had a passcode.

"Should I send the girls out there?" he mused on. "Should I go? I can't afford to miss too much work, and I hate taking the girls out of school. And what if he recovers?"

I was confused. "But why would you go?" Surely this was an assignment Ren could handle.

"Someone would have to take the kids out there," Will said, clearly coming to a different conclusion about Ren's fitness for the task. "And—well honestly, Annie, Lou was like a father to me. For many years."

Oh. *Well.* I knew my own detached, bumbling father wasn't exactly the touchy-feely type, but I hadn't realized that Lou London was so freaking fantastic.

"We're also supposed to have Josie's conference next week," Will mused on. "But maybe you could go to that?"

I laughed nervously. "Oh, I don't know, Will. London's teacher didn't seem to think too much of me being there. I think I'd better bow out."

Will looked at me blankly. "What are you talking about?"

"I think she made it pretty clear that stepmothers aren't wanted," I said, but Will still looked confused. "With her comments about over-parenting?"

"Oh, that? I'm sure that's not what she meant," Will said. "That comment was directed at all of us."

I couldn't keep the sarcasm out of my voice. "Was it? And do you think Gianna's comment was directed at all of us when she made that snide remark about you two being able to handle the meeting without me?"

Will shook his head. "I don't even remember that."

"Well, she said it," I said. "Just like you wouldn't stop chit-chatting and kissing her ass. For your information I felt really shitty after that conference. And I got reamed out by Brenda afterwards for leaving work. So if you don't mind, I think you two should just go at another time when you can have your little love-fest without me."

"Whatever, Annie," Will snapped. "You know, I really don't know what you want from me. I don't include you in things, and you say I don't respect you. I try to include you, and you can't stand that I get along with Gianna. Nothing makes you happy. It's like you're constantly dissecting the world for evidence that it's against you. And guess what? People find what they're looking for. Surprise."

I was enraged. "A bunch of cliquey bitches humiliated me in public because I was stupid enough to listen to you and join a mommy group! You think that was in my fucking head? Just ask Rachelle what happened. Ask your *daughter*."

"I *told* you I was sorry about that. But it was an isolated incident."

"It was not!" I screeched, too loudly. "Since we got married I've been trying to tell you how things are for me and you just don't want to listen! And I get it—it's so much easier for you to think everything is my problem so you don't have to do anything. I'm too sensitive, I'm paranoid, and you're such a *hero*. So great at including me! You sure made a real effort to *include* me by defending me to London's teacher. You sure made a real effort by telling the world about poor London and how she's suffering because we got married. Oh, and speaking of London? You sure made a real effort to get to the bottom of what happened at our wedding. I talked to Ted today and he said that he *saw* London playing with her phone. It wasn't an accident. She lied to you!"

"Oh, so now you're grilling our wedding guests for evidence?" Will said in disgust. "I don't know what you've got against my kid, but you need to drop it. It's *over*. Nothing *happened*."

"Nothing that mattered to *you*, anyway! I get that your real wedding was with Gianna and everything with me is just old news. But it meant quite a lot to me. Silly me, I was actually thinking it would be my only one! But now I'm not so sure."

"You know what, Annie? Fuck you. I'm done." He hauled himself out of bed and wrestled open the door, only to fall instantly to his knees.

"Daddy?" Josie said, rubbing her eyes. "Daddy are you fighting?"

"Oh no, sweetheart, we're just having a talk," Will soothed, pulling her into his arms. "C'mon JoJo, let's go back to bed." He stood and heaved the little girl to his hip, closing the door behind him. He didn't return that night.

35

WHEN I ARRIVED at Anatevka the next evening, weary and stingy-eyed, it was business as usual. London: door closed. Josie: door open, holding animated discourse with model trains. Will: in his office, door open. No greeting when he heard me come in.

I sighed, changed clothes, and went into the kitchen to start dinner. One thing was sure: kids kept you going through the motions.

Will came up to me as I sautéed. "I'm sorry about last night," he murmured against my ear. "I know we both said things we didn't mean. Can we just pretend the whole thing never happened?"

I took a deep breath, wishing I could do more than that: I would wipe the fight from history, memory. It had lurked like a malignant bulge all day, impossible to stop fingering and prodding. I'd been angry, sure—but the threat of divorce crossing my lips had shocked and unsettled me. Was I really that unhappy? Or had it been, as Will said, something I hadn't meant? I wanted to claim *I was provoked!* But I hadn't been, not really. I'd been more like a land mine waiting for the slightest pressure.

But.

If I agreed to drop it, it meant dropping everything: no more sleuthing and crime-fighting when it came to London or the wedding. *I don't know what you've got against my kid,* Will had said last night. And I honestly didn't know either. What *was* it that kept me poking at this one thing? The wedding was months gone. Was it a matter of truth, of principle—I didn't like London getting away with a lie? Or was I hard on London simply because she didn't love me—because she repeatedly spoiled that vision of the happy stepfamily that I thought I was owed?

Families forgive each other, Angelina said slowly, as though speaking to an imbecile. *You're never going to be part of this one until you learn how.*

"Yes," I said, dropping my spatula and turning to throw my arms around Will. "I'm sorry."

"I'm sorry, too," Will murmured, kissing me. "Let's just try to get through the next couple of days and I'm sure everything will be back to normal."

I nodded gratefully. But some things were already normal—particularly London's mood swings. *If there is anyone in this family who works like clockwork,* Xena noted snarkily, *it's Gianna's Mini-Me.* London had been fine the day before, caught up in charades and her father's doting attention, but at dinner today she'd gone icy, refusing even to look me in the eye. Knowing the pattern, I had tried to brace myself for backlash from the fun we'd had the previous weekend. But no matter what I told myself, no matter how I breathed and visualized and filled my mind with positive aphorisms, the rejection—when it inevitably came—still stung. I wondered dismally if the highs were even worth the lows: maybe it would be better to stop trying entirely, to remain neutral and disconnected. But a family life of polite tolerance was hardly the path I'd envisioned for myself.

"London, will you *please* get in here and do the dishes?" I asked for the third time, finally stepping into the living room where the ten-year-old sat reading and ignoring me. Josie had done her part, carting the plates to the sink; it was London's job to rinse and load.

No response. Not even a glance. I stormed across the room and grabbed the book out of London's hand. "Hello? The dishes aren't going away and neither am I. You have a job to do—get in there and do it."

London looked back at me murderously. "I don't have to listen to you," she hissed, breaking the lethal eye contact only when Will walked in the room.

Oh, thank God, I thought. I hated needing Will to enforce my ineffectual attempts at discipline—but I would rather he fix the problem than get myself into a screaming match with London or, worse, lose the battle.

"I'm not feeling well, Daddy," London said plaintively, turning up her big mournful eyes to her father. I had to fight not to laugh. Oh, what *bullshit!* As if Will were that stupid!

"I'll take care of it tonight, sweetie," Will said lovingly to his daughter. "Okay? Why don't you go take your shower?"

"Thanks, Daddy," London simpered, clinging to him for a moment before practically skipping off to her room. I stood watching the scene in dumbfounded outrage.

"What are you doing?" I demanded, following Will into the kitchen. "There's nothing wrong with her. Don't you realize she only calls you 'Daddy' when she's trying to get away with something?"

"It's been a hard few days for them, Annie," Will said. "I don't mind helping out. What's the big deal? I'm not asking you to do anything."

He just didn't get it. He never wanted to enforce chores, worried that the girls would want to spend more time with Gianna if he made life at our house less fun.

"No, but you completely undermined me!" I said furiously. "How do you expect London to listen to me if you come in and show her that she doesn't have to?"

"Annie, they're my kids, okay?" he answered curtly. "I know what's best for them. I appreciate you trying to teach them life skills, but I don't think this is the time to demand a bunch of extra work from them. They're *grieving*."

"They're *slacking*," I snapped. "They're taking advantage of the situation, and they're taking advantage of you." The pronoun was all wrong here—Josie didn't appear to be grieving *or* slacking—but "they" obscured the fact that, a mere hour after promising otherwise, I was already harping on London. Over a new offense, yes—but it still didn't do much for my image.

"Even if they are, we all need a break once in a while," said Yes-I-Will with an air of finality. "And as their father I reserve the right to give it to them." With that, he rolled up his sleeves and turned the water on. I could only stomp out of the room to seethe.

36

"CONGRATULATIONS, ANNIE!" KERRY said in a singsong voice, clapping her hands. "You've made it to the spreadsheet!" Kerry was the official organizer of the stepmom group, looking quite the secretary-librarian in a gray cardigan and tortoiseshell glasses, her blond hair clipped up on both sides. She explained that each member's contact information and collection of names—her own, her partner's, the children—got recorded on the group spreadsheet for everyone's easy reference. "But you have to come to three meetings before we put you down."

"Screw that rule," Regan said. "I make it a personal priority to start putting people down immediately."

Kerry groaned and went on. "We want to make sure people are committed to the group before we put them on the roster, because as I was telling you last week, it's not like in the books where everybody always comes back." She sighed.

"No…we do have a few attrition issues," Kim said diplomatically.

I couldn't imagine why. Membership fees? Hazing? I shook my head. "Why don't people come back?"

"Too busy, mostly," Kerry said. "And the ones with little kids are too guilty to take time for themselves."

"And then a lot of people just find us too late," Maggie added. "By the time they seek out a support group, they are so full of resentment and their relationships are so bad. They get divorced and then it's sayonara, stepmoms."

"Yeah. They're like totally *leveled*, you know?" Kim said. "They had every fantasy under the sun about being stepmoms. They thought it was cute that their husbands were dads. They didn't live together before marriage or talk about any of the issues. They just thought it would work out somehow."

"Idiots," Regan declared. "What? I don't say that to their faces."

"—and then they end up depressed and miserable, with husbands who feed them all the typical bullshit about how they are failures because they should love the kids as their own. It's disaster. So they either get divorced or they can't deal with us telling them that they deserve better. And they leave us. Sob."

"Oh, God," I groaned. "That's me, isn't it?" I had always thought myself so smart, so wise. And here I was, fitting too uncannily into the mold of a stepmother with a doomed marriage.

"Aw, I didn't mean you," Kim said consolingly. "And sometimes it does work. It's just that I think people should deal with these issues *before* they get married, you know? A stepfamily is nothing like a marriage between two single…carefree…joyously unencumbered people." Grinning, she wiped her theatrically misty eyes. "It's not just gonna magically work out because the people are so in loooove."

"Yeah," said June. "I do love Ryan and Annabel. I *think* we're headed in that direction. But I'm not ready to commit yet. It's scary, not knowing what Samantha is going to do next. And Annabel loves me now—but what about when she's older? How will she feel if her mom keeps feeding her lies about me?"

"Exactly!" Kim said. "When it comes to marrying someone with kids, it's more complicated than just you and him. There's you and him, and her, and her, and *her*…"

"Yeah, and speaking of *her*," Regan smiled, "how are things with Will's ex?"

"He stood up to her!" I said proudly. The group broke out in applause. "Well, until last week." They stopped applauding. I explained the situation with Gianna's father. "Now we're just waiting to hear. Is he going to live? Is he going to die? Will Annie and Will *ever* get to be alone again?" I sighed. "It's exhausting, not knowing. We're bickering, we're fighting. And in the meantime, there's London." I told them about the ups and downs, the slumber party, the teacher conference, the ongoing squabble over potential wedding sabotage. "I just don't know what I'm supposed to be to this kid. Am I a parent or not? If I am, where's the respect? If I'm not, why am I doing so much for her? Am I supposed to do that thing you told me about, the plugging your ears thing?"

Maggie smiled at me, amused. "Disengaging."

I knew the word now...I just didn't like to say it. "Right," I said. "Do you all do that?"

There was a mix of head movements all around the table. Leah and Hester shook their heads; Maggie and June and Kim offered variations on *kinda*; Regan and Kerry nodded enthusiastically.

"Best thing I ever did!" Kerry said.

"I try to with Adora," Leah said, "even though she always sucks me in. With my other kids? No, I can't imagine that working. I think it's much harder to be disengaged if you have your own kids in the household. Parenting some and not others just gets weird. In my family, Paul and I act as full parents of all the kids. Although, with particularly sensitive stuff, the biological parent usually takes the lead."

"My stepkids only see their bio-mom a few times a year, so everything falls to me," said Hester. "I'm the real mom to them and that's how I want it. Disengaging from them would be like disengaging from life itself."

Wow, that was unexpectedly serious. I paused respectfully before asking the group: "So how do I know what I should do?"

"I think most of us started out pretty engaged," Kim said. "Mainly because we think that we should be. We want to be. Then we start getting hurt and disrespected. So we step back, leave certain things to the dad. And we see how it goes." She paused. "This might sound out of nowhere and super obvious, but before you can really decide what you want to be—well, the thing you have to confront is that you are not their mom, and you are never going to be their mom."

I knew this. Of course I did. Why, then, did it still bring tears to my eyes?

"That doesn't mean you can't be extremely important to those kids," Maggie jumped in sympathetically. "It just means that there are things you can't do and things you don't have to do. You can't take her place, but you also don't have to play by the mommy rules. If you don't feel like doing mom stuff, don't. If you don't like going to teacher conferences, don't go. The responsibility for those kids lies with Will and his ex. Whatever you do for them is your choice, not your obligation."

I tried to absorb this. "I always thought that being a stepmom just meant being a second mom. Not that I would replace Gianna or be the same as her, but that I would be equally important, somehow. And that I would feel just like Will does. I hear these voices"—oh God, was I really admitting this?—"whenever I start feeling resentful, telling me I'm a bad mother, I'm a terrible mother for wanting time with Will, for wanting time alone—"

"Oh, I could talk all day about mom-guilt," Leah agreed. "Believe me. When my kids were young, I had to fight it every time I did something for myself. It'll be bad enough for you, Annie, if you have your own kids someday. But don't do this to yourself now. You're a stepmom, yes. But you're also a wife, a friend, a *person*—"

"But I just feel like I *should* be in love with them the way Will is."

"Look, no one expects those kids to love you as their mother," Maggie said. "So why do you expect yourself to love them as your kids?"

"Because that's what I want to feel!" I exclaimed. "That's what I thought I was getting! And some women do. Don't you?" I asked Hester. "And you?" I asked Leah.

The two women nodded. "Yes, I do," said Hester. "But I've raised them since they were toddlers. And Leah—well, Leah's just that kind."

"My stepkids are great," Leah said. "Anyone would love them. And you might feel that way about yours someday. Or you might not. But you can't force it, Annie. You have to give yourself a break. And more time."

I sighed. It was a reasonable answer, but not the answer my heart wanted to hear.

"Well, I've started financially disengaging," said Kerry with a smile. "Between the child support and all the extras, there's no way we're going to have money for a baby unless I start saving. So I got my own bank account and that's where my paychecks are going as of next week."

"Oh my God, did Derek flip?" asked June.

"He was a little miffed," said Kerry impishly. "But he finally admitted it's not fair that I should have to pay for everything just because

Belinda won't. If he can't help himself to my money whenever he wants, maybe it'll help him say no once in a while!"

The women were all nodding supportively. I started feeling sick again. Faintly I asked, "Do you *all* have separate bank accounts?"

Everyone but Hester nodded.

"I saw right away that he spoiled them," Kim said. "There was no *way* I was jumping into that sinkhole. So we have a joint account for the household expenses, but we keep the rest of our money separate."

Leah said, "We do that too. I'll admit it—I was really hurt when Paul didn't want to combine our money. I felt like he didn't trust me, like making such a big deal about money was just cold and petty. But just practically speaking I came to see it made sense. We both have different financial arrangements with our exes, for one. Anyway, I'm a convert. I can confidently say that having separate accounts does *not* mean we are any less committed to each other."

Hester groaned. "I wish you girls had been around when I first got married. I would have done so many things differently. You know I'd spend my last penny on the kids. But having all of our assets entangled makes things very tricky." The others were nodding empathetically. I kept quiet.

"So I take it you combined all your money?" Kerry asked me.

"Yep," I nodded weakly. In fact it had been such a happy moment, going to the bank and seeing our same last name on the paperwork. I'd thought, *This is it! I'm married!* "I just thought that's what you did when you got married."

"Well, some do and it works just fine," Leah said. "It really depends on your situation." She pointed across the table. "Kerry here has been working full-time so that Derek's ex could stay at home."

"More than that, my *dear* husband told me that we couldn't have a child together at all because we had to support Belinda," Kerry said. "You can imagine what I said to that."

"Did you give him the Stepmother Salute?" Kim asked, raising both middle fingers.

Kerry wrinkled her nose at the vulgar gesture but then smiled. "Something like that," she said. "I just got to a point that I was so resentful I couldn't keep quiet. I couldn't keep settling for something that was so unfair."

"But what *is* fair?" I asked. "I just always thought 'all for one and one for all' was how it was supposed to be."

"There's no 'supposed to' in stepparenting," Regan said. "It's just like we said before—you aren't *obligated* to do anything for kids that aren't yours. You do what you are comfortable with and what works for your family."

"Which, in your case, is nothing," Kim teased.

"Ah, but you'd be wrong there," Regan said triumphantly. "I pay the kids' tuition. And I pay Blane's fuck-tax, I mean alimony."

Every mouth at the table dropped open. "*No,*" June gasped.

"Yep," Regan said. "I make way too much money to hoard it for myself. I could tell Blane that he has to work two jobs to support his ex and kids, and I could make them go to public school, but then I would have an unhappy, stressed, broke husband. I don't want that. It also keeps Martha happy and out of our hair, which is great. And—" She paused. "This is the one way I can help that doesn't change who I am. I know I'm not a great stepmother. I don't *want* to be an anything-mother to anyone, which is patently obvious to the kids. But this is the one place I can make their lives better."

Kim's eyes widened and she pointed at her friend. "You *love* them!"

"No," Regan protested at once. "That's *not* what I said." But her cheeks were turning red.

"Yes, yes it is! You *love* them!" Kim danced around in her chair. "Regan loves her stepkids, Regan loves her stepkids!"

Regan clapped a hand over Kim's face. "Shut *up!* I do *not!*"

But the rest of the stepmoms took up the chant.

"Last time I share anything with you jerks," Regan muttered huffily, but she couldn't hide a tiny smile.

"That's the other reason people sometimes don't come back to our group," Kim laughed, turning to me. "We're jerks."

"We like to think we give a kick in the ass with every hug," June said cheerily.

"I like jerks," I grinned. "So where do I fill out this form?"

37

I RETURNED TO Anatevka more confused than ever. If I was a fiddler on the roof, trying to keep my balance amidst buffeting winds, the gale was now whipping twice as fast.

True, I hadn't been happy—or successful, for that matter—trying to mold myself in Angelina's image. But to have so many options was as daunting and baffling as my previous course had been exhausting and guilt-inducing.

If being a stepmom *wasn't* necessarily being a second mom—where did that leave me?

Anywhere I wanted. It meant, in fact, that Xena was sometimes right. And Angelina was sometimes wrong. And only I could set the terms.

I groaned. Certainly the notion was positive, freeing—but embracing it meant cremating my long-held vision of cozy familial bliss, obliterating the fantasy that stepparenting was really no different from its conventional cousin. Before marriage I'd always gravely told people *I know it will be challenging*, as if to assure them I knew what I was doing. But what had I imagined, in those moments of fabricated wisdom? A few howled "you're not my mother"s? A tantrum or two? A pine cone in the seat, as modeled by the ornery but gold-hearted Von Trapps? I'd vaguely imagined the inevitable tears and trouble followed by kisses and love, every snag shifting into a valuable teaching moment accepted willingly by grateful children.

I had never imagined how quickly I would be worn down. I had never imagined I would greet these difficulties with anything but superlative grace.

But I wasn't ready to kill the dream yet. Not now. Not fully. I took a deep breath and got out of the car, affixing a smile to my face as I prepared to go inside.

But I could hear the fighting even before I opened the door. I stopped on the stoop, listening.

"I told you already," Will was saying sharply. "The answer is no."

"But it's not *fair!*" London screamed back, bursting into tears. "Everybody's going to do it but me!"

"Well, it's better to be an original than a copycat anyway," Will said without sympathy. "You can find something here or I can take you out to get a regular costume, but I'm not spending hundreds of dollars on some elaborate gown. It's out of the question."

Ah—Halloween was this Friday. As I understood it, normally Gianna took care of the costumes. But Gianna, of course, was gone.

"Ren will buy it for me," London pleaded. I let my fingers fall from the doorknob. I didn't need to see Will's face to know I should cringe.

"This is a matter of principle, not money," Will said tightly, and I could hear the fury in his voice. "You will absolutely *not* ask Ren to buy you this costume."

"You're the worst dad ever!" London yelled, sobbing. "I hate you! I HATE YOU!" And I waited on the front step until I heard my step-daughter's door shake the walls.

Then silence. Gingerly I opened the door.

Will stood alone in the living room, trying to get his feelings under control. "Hi," I said softly, coming up behind him to rub his back. "I overheard. Are you okay?"

"I'm fine," Will said brusquely, though I could see he was not. How could London be so cruel to keep flinging Ren at her father like so many ninja stars, seeing how deeply and predictably her barbs tore?

"She'll get over it," I said confidently. "All you can do is stand firm. It's not your fault that she's spoiled."

"I know," Will said, but looked uncomfortable with the adjective. "I don't think she's spoiled, though. Just used to having things."

In other words...spoiled. But I didn't belabor the point. I gave Will a squeeze and went to change clothes.

Later, we sat on the living room floor with Josie, deep in a game of Candyland, when London emerged from her room, face blotched from crying. "Can I play?" she asked, still a bit too poutily for my taste.

"Of course you can," Will said, standing up. "But first let me give you a hug."

For what? I thought, but I didn't say a word.

"I'm sorry, Daddy," London said tearfully, falling into his arms.

"I'll tell you what," Will said. "If you do some extra chores around the house this week, I'll buy you the costume. How's that sound?"

London squealed with joy, jumping into her father's arms. "Yes! Yes!" she cried. "Whatever you want! Anything!"

I couldn't believe it. *How* could Will continue to give in to London's tantrums and manipulations, knowing that his acquiescence only encouraged more of the same? It was all well and good for Yes-I-Will, who got to play the heroic, adoring father for a glittering moment—but that much worse for Josie and me, who had to endure London's snowballing entitlement sprees. I stood and left the room, too disgusted and furious to speak. How could he be so cowardly and short-sighted?

You just don't understand what's it's like to love a child, Angelina said loftily as I fumed alone in the dark hallway. *It's only selfish, miserly stepmothers who think it's wrong to give in sometimes.*

But I couldn't buy it. Constancy was a facet of love itself. Will wasn't being a good parent; he was caving to his deepest fears. He simply couldn't endure the possibility that London would somehow get the coveted costume from Ren.

It was ridiculous. But there was nothing I could do.

Standing in the hallway, I could hear London excitedly describing the dress to Will. Grimly I forced myself past the pair and into the kitchen. "Why don't you take over my game while I start dinner?" I suggested to London, trying to keep my voice normal. I hoped to lose myself in the preparation of a meal that, with any luck, my stepdaughters wouldn't immediately spit out.

The cooking calmed me. But when I saw Will and London grinning at each other across the dinner table, in love again, it made my stomach turn. I suddenly felt drained of all energy. Why should I cook and clean for these ingrates?

That proves it! Angelina crowed triumphantly. *You're not cut out to be a parent. Just like all the other women in your group! The problem isn't stepparenting—it's YOU. Parenting is giving, and giving, and giving. YOU just want to take.*

But I knew, watching Will and London giggle, that the issue could not be entirely personal. Perhaps I was not cut out to be a parent; perhaps I was weak, selfish, and greedy. These were possibilities I couldn't discount.

But it wasn't so simple.

Everyone knew that much of parenting was thankless. Will's cooking and cleaning and spending and schlepping got no more explicit appreciation than mine. But in return Will felt and got something of infinite worth: unconditional adoration. How many parents would endure the screaming, the tedium, the teary solipsism of their children, if they did not feel beneath their annoyance a relentless undercurrent of naked, breathtaking love? And how many stepparents were forced through the same draining motions without that all-important catalyst—then found themselves berated for their weariness and discouragement, their inability to experience many of the much-belabored rewards of child-rearing?

It was suddenly so obvious. Love was the magic ingredient that made parenting fulfilling. Love supplied the stamina: it was cheerleader, inspiration and aegis. And without it, a stepparent was just a nanny without a paycheck.

Of course, for me it wasn't *quite* that simple either. (Was it ever?) My relationship with the girls couldn't be called loveless. But that love was an unpredictable river, swelling and shrinking with maddening irregularity. It was not—and might never be—the unchanging wide sea of a lifelong connection.

And at the moment it was a runnel in a drought.

I rose from the table before the others had even finished, taking my dishes to the sink. "I'm going to lie down for a moment. I have a headache."

They murmured *okay* and *feel better,* mostly focused on their own conversation, and I slipped away to the bedroom and lay down.

Who the fuck am I? I thought miserably. *Too irritable to be a mother. Too needy to give up.* All I knew was that I had to be sequestered from my family like a beast in the dark, or I would say something I'd regret.

I waited until I heard the dishwasher churn to life, then rose guiltily to finish the cleaning up.

Will was on the phone. "Oh—no, not tonight," he was saying. "They're already in bed." I looked quizzically into the living room. In fact "they" were in front of the television, scarfing down cookies.

"I will," Will said, and hung up.

"Who was that?" I asked.

He didn't answer. But it didn't matter—I knew.

"Are you feeling better?" Will asked.

I nodded, reaching for a sponge and starting on the counters. "Yes. Thanks."

"So, Josie's teacher conference is tomorrow afternoon," Will said conversationally. "Would you come?"

Hadn't we covered this already? "I really can't, Will," I said. "I promised Brenda I wouldn't leave during the day."

"Please, Annie. I need you."

Had he suddenly developed a chalk allergy? A fear of macaroni artwork? I was missing something. "What's the big deal?"

Will swallowed. "Since Gianna is gone, Ren is going to be there instead." He looked at me imploringly. "Please, Annie," he said quietly. "I can't do it."

I looked into my husband's defeated, pleading eyes. I could still refuse: I knew that now. But this time it wasn't about me proving anything; if I agreed, I would be there for my husband alone. And wasn't that my job, as a wife?

I nodded resignedly, forcing a smile. "If it means that much to you, I'll be there."

Will's relief was palpable as he smiled and kissed me. "Thanks, Annie. It's just this one time, I promise. And if the teacher says anything bad about you, I'll break her knees."

I laughed, returning the kiss. Maybe it would all be okay. Will would stand up for me; Gianna wouldn't be there; and I'd be prepared this time—prepared to keep my mouth glued.

I'd just have to take the chance that Brenda wouldn't find out.

38

"I'M VERY PLEASED to have Josie in my class this year," began Ms. Gerber with a luminous smile, speaking with the unnecessary loudness usually foisted upon the foreign-born. Was the tension that palpable? I could only imagine what the teacher was thinking as Will and Ren stared back at her rigidly, I myself perched awkwardly in between.

"She's a wonderful child, very loving and sweet and full of life," Ms. Gerber went on with the same jovial force. "But I'm sure you know that. My only concerns at this point are behavioral. Her school work is generally good, but when she gets distracted it can be quite poor. And unfortunately she is easily distracted. Does she do her homework in a quiet, dedicated place?"

"Yes, of course," Will answered at once. I bit my tongue. While Josie did have a desk in her room, more often she did her homework in the living room, half-watching TV. She was only supposed to do that with coloring assignments, but Will never checked.

"At our house she usually works at the kitchen table," Ren said. "She likes the company. But if it's a problem, we'll move her to a quieter space."

"I think that would be wise," said Ms. Gerber. "Even for a first-grader, it's important to reinforce good study habits so she'll be ready when the work gets harder."

I nodded. Will hadn't come clean, but hopefully he was listening.

Then Ren spoke up. "Another possibility is—I believe my wife had called to request testing for dyslexia?" Next to me, I felt the air grow icy. "Do we have those results yet?"

"Yeees," Ms. Gerber said, rooting around in her papers. "I just got them. I haven't had a chance to read the report in detail yet, but it looks like the results aren't conclusive. Josie may have mild dyslexia, but it's equally likely that she doesn't. Many children her age do the same things as they learn to read and write, the transposing letters and such."

"So what are the next steps?" Ren persevered. "Is there another round of testing we can do?"

"Unfortunately, we've done what we can do here," answered Ms. Gerber. Will tensed up and I reached for his hand reassuringly. "Generally with the mild cases it's advised just to pay close attention and see if there's any need to retest in a few years down the road." She paused. "Of course, private testing is also available."

"Do you have any recommendations? On the private testing?"

Will's stature began to approach rigor mortis.

The teacher looked ever so mildly annoyed, but she flashed her profligate teeth at Ren. "Not offhand, but I can check with the office and let you know."

"Thank you," Ren said. "I'm sorry to be so persistent. It's just that I myself have a learning disability—"

"What's that got to do with anything?" Will snapped, unable to contain himself any longer.

Ren turned patiently to Will. "A diagnosis as early as this would have saved me years of struggle." He paused, seeming to address all of us. "I just want what's best for Josie."

My heart went out to Ren. He'd probably never been to the girls' conferences; he surely didn't realize that stepparents were preferred to be mute if not invisible. I, this time around, was the model of perfect supportive silence, my hand crushed to pulp in Will's viselike grip.

"Of course," Ms. Gerber said with more warmth, seeming to understand. "I do too, Mr. Greely. I will keep a close watch on Josie and let you know if I have any concerns."

Ren nodded his thanks.

"Now as for the matter of the new marriage," the teacher went on with a gesture to Will. Oh God, not *this* again. I had to fight not to squeeze my eyes shut and cover my ears. "I have seen no evidence that Josie sees this as anything but a positive."

Had I heard right? *Really?* I giggled before I could help myself. "Sorry," I whispered.

"I thought you might want to see this," Ms. Gerber said with a smile, pulling a drawing out of Josie's file. I peered closer. At the top, Josie had scrawled "My Famlys" over a bisected page. On the left were a dark-haired "Daddy" and "Mommy," a light-haired "London" and "Josie." On the right, a light-haired "Mommy" and "Daddy," the same two daughters and even the vexing "Clint."

"This is quite remarkable for a child of Josie's age," Ms. Gerber went on. "Most will continue to draw themselves clustered with their parents and siblings, their stepparents and stepsiblings drawn smaller and in the corner, if at all. It is clear from this picture that Josie sees herself as a member of both families, the child of two sets of parents. To me, this shows that Josie is extremely well-adjusted and happy in her family arrangement."

"That's great news," Will said, but I was too choked up to speak. I could only nod, trying discreetly to wipe away my welling tears. I wondered if Ren felt the same.

"She's just a really lovable kid and I'm glad to have her in my class," Ms. Gerber finished. "Let's all work with her on the behavior and focus issues, and I see no reason why Josie can't become a very good student."

I was soaring as we left the classroom. Score! I was not totally warping Josie for life! *You were the missing piece in my world,* I imagined Josie saying to me one day, reaching sweetly for my hand. *When you came along, my family was finally complete.*

Then Ren's voice intruded on the daydream.

"Since Gianna's still gone, I was just wondering if it might be possible to spend a little time with the girls," he asked. I blinked myself back to the real world just in time to see the stony look on Will's face. "Clint really misses them and would love to see them," Ren added.

The man was no dummy. He knew Will was less likely to disappoint a child than a man he mistrusted.

I could see Will trying to work up a way to refuse without looking like an asshole. Eventually, he gave up. "Well, sure, that should be fine," he said. "How about tonight? You could take them out to dinner, give Annie and me a chance to spend some time together." He walked over and put his arm around me. I appreciated the affection—and the thought even more—but why did I suddenly feel like a pawn in some dark masculine game, the piss in a pissing contest?

Ren's smile was jubilant. "Okay, great!" he said. "Clint will really like that. Thanks, Will."

"No problem," said my husband, trying to smile.

When I got back to my desk, my voicemail light was blinking.
Oh, God.

I'd checked my messages as soon as I started the drive back to work, and there had been nothing.

It's probably just Ted, I tried to convince myself as I sat down and typed in my code. But my palms were sweating. Then the message played.

Annie, I'd like to meet with you as soon as possible. I'm out at a client site the rest of the week, but can you set up a time with Blythe for Monday?

There was no anger or accusation in the voice. But, still, it was Brenda.

39

I ARRIVED HOME to a quiet Anatevka. "Are the girls already at dinner?" I asked Will, coming up behind him in his office chair to kiss his ear.

"Yep," Will said, turning to kiss me.

"So do you want to go out?"

Will didn't answer right away, but I could see he was reluctant. "Well—I want to be sure we're home when they get back," he finally said.

I could have expected that. But I wasn't going to let it ruin the evening; we could just as easily have a romantic dinner at home. "Fine!" I said brightly. "We can just make the chicken the way we like it." As opposed to the only way the girls would eat it. I was already looking forward to a nugget-free plate.

We began the chopping and cooking. "So what did you think of the conference?" I asked, deciding not to asphyxiate this pleasant adult hour with my fears, unsettling though they were, about Brenda's potential wrath.

"Pretty good," Will said. "But I can't believe that drawing Josie did."

"I know!" I gushed. "I can't wait to tell my stepmom friends about it. She's so—mature for her age. She's amazing." I didn't note what a difference it was from London, who seemed to think it her duty to nourish and exploit parental rivalries.

But Will stopped slicing and stared back at me uncomprehendingly. "She put *Ren* down as Daddy."

"Yes, but she put *me* down as Mommy," I said. "That's a *good* thing. It means that she's comfortable and happy with all of us. It's not like she doesn't know that you're Dad and Gianna's Mom—"

"I'm not sure she knows that!" Will said, a little hysterically. "I don't know *what* they tell her in that house."

"Will, I really think it's harmless," I said softly, my enthusiasm guttering. Didn't Will care at all what a triumph this was for me? "Josie loves you. You're her father. But she has stepparents she loves too."

Will muttered something incomprehensible and went silent.

The vegetables fell under our knives. I began to panic, hearing phantom footsteps and slammed doors, the sand spitting relentlessly through the hourglass. The girls would be back any minute, *any minute,* and we were wasting and bungling our precious privacy! I felt hysteria bubbling, wanting to be miles away from Will yet extend our couple-time indefinitely. I gritted my teeth and chopped on, hoping the boiling in my brain would subside in time to have a relaxing meal.

But when finally we sat down together, Will was the one to take the first step. "Look. I'm sorry, Annie. I know I've been irritable." He paused. "I just feel like I can't do anything right. I feel like you're always mad at me."

I sighed. "I'm sorry I've given you that impression. Honestly, right now I'm just exhausted." It had been fourteen days with the kids with only a thirty-six-hour break in the middle—fourteen days of fighting, teacher conferences, work conflict, and very little sex. "And yeah, I'm a little frustrated. We're not communicating well. And the stuff with London..." I trailed off, not sure it was a good idea to elaborate.

But he was looking at me receptively. "What exactly is bothering you?"

I struggled with the words. "I know she's upset right now, but it seems like she's using the situation to manipulate you. The dishes, and now the costume…"

"I don't want her to miss out on the group costume," Will said. "That's not fair to her."

I didn't know how to argue. He'd spoken with such moral certainty, as though getting a cheaper costume were akin to denying his daughter food and shelter.

"It's just a lot of money with Christmas coming up," I finally said. *My money,* I didn't add, though I was excruciatingly aware of that now.

"Well, we don't have to get her as many presents this year," Will said with a shrug. But I knew that was about as likely to happen as the "extra chores" London had promised to do.

"Okay. I just think we should both try to be more consistent," I said diplomatically. "So the girls know what our expectations are, and what to expect from us."

Will stared at me for a thoughtful moment. "Honey, I don't want you take this the wrong way, because you're *so* great with the girls, and I know this is all still new to you, but—"

I grimaced, bracing myself.

"—parenting isn't just a big rulebook that you have to follow 24/7. It's a lot more, you know, *organic* than all that." He hesitated, not wanting to be unkind, but it was far too late. "You have to use your *heart* sometimes. You know?" He reached for my hand, trying to soften the blow.

But what he'd just said was *You're not a real mother and you don't know what you're doing.* It was Angelina's relentless message coming through my husband's lips and reinforcing my every insecurity.

My eyes filled with tears. "Wow," I said, trying to gather myself. I blotted my eyes. "Is this your way of saying you want to have a baby?"

Will looked confused. "What?"

"Well isn't that the only answer?" I said with a brittle smile. "So I'll be a real mom and have access to these magical emotions that you have? So I'll stop being a cold hard bitch who relies on a rulebook rather than a heart?"

"I didn't mean—"

"Yeah, you did," I said. "And I'm with you, Will—I'm tired of being on the outside and feeling all the wrong things. I want to be a real mom. I want to think entirely with my womb and look at all children like they're precious fucking snowflakes. So bring it on. Let's have a baby."

Will laughed nervously. "Annie, you know this isn't the time—"

"Why not? It's as good as time as any, isn't it?" These were the words he'd spoken about law school. "I'm never going to get any of this until I have my own child. You know that as well as I do. So let's just get a move on, shall we?"

I could tell he didn't quite know if I was serious. "I really think we should wait," he said.

I didn't quite know if I was serious, either. But I didn't let up. "Why?"

"Well, we're not fully adjusted yet," Will answered. "To our new life. And the house. I mean, we only have the three bedrooms."

"So someone can share. That's what siblings do," I answered. "What's your solution, then? Waiting until London goes to college?"

I brayed with laughter, expecting him to appreciate the ludicrousness of the statement, but the look on Will's face made it obvious that was exactly what he wanted.

"You're *joking*," I said incredulously. "London is ten years old. We can't wait until I'm thirty-six to start trying for a baby!"

"Lots of women have babies when they're older," Will said lamely. "And it's not just you and me, Annie. We have to think about the needs of the whole family."

"Oh, so it's three against one, is that it?" I hissed. "How convenient. Funny you didn't mention this before we got married." I shook my head in disgust, my every indignant emotion jumping to the defense of the baby I wasn't even sure I wanted. "Well I've always been straight with you, so let me make myself perfectly clear: I'm not waiting that long."

And then Josie tumbled through the front door, laughing and shrieking. "Daddy! Annie! Save us!" came Josie's squeals as Ren growled after her. "Daddy!" She ran circles in the living room before spotting her father at the kitchen table and flinging herself upon his mercy.

Ren was there a second later, panting, his strawberry-blond shag swept away from his face. "Oh!" he said at our stunned expressions. "I'm so sorry—we were just goofing around."

I shook myself to life. "It's no problem," I said, standing to carry the dishes to the sink. "We're finished. Did you have a nice dinner?" I addressed Josie.

"Yes, it was yummy," said Josie. "We were Indians!"

"No, we had Indian *food*," corrected London, who had joined the congregation in the kitchen, Clint's hand in hers.

Damn! I gawped at Ren, impressed. Anyone who could get the girls to eat something as inadvisable-looking as curry deserved some props. "Well, that sounds nice," I said, vamping, as Will continued to sit shell-shocked at the dining room table. "Thanks again for taking them out."

"It was my pleasure," Ren said, and I could see that it was. His obvious love for his stepdaughters gave me hope: in a few years, that could be me!

"C'mon, Clint, let's go to my room," Josie said, happy to play hostess to her little stepbrother on her own turf. London had already disappeared into hers.

"Don't get involved in anything, Clint—we're leaving in just a minute," Ren called. Then he turned back to Will and me. "Good news—it looks like Lou is going to recover," he said. "Gianna should be home tomorrow."

"Oh, that's great!" I said, my heart clamping down on the impending kid-free time like a guard dog on a thief's retreating buttock. "Isn't that great, Will?" I prompted loudly, half a second away from poking him vigorously in the shoulder.

"What a relief," Will agreed, finally rising from his chair. "Just have her call me to discuss plans."

Ren was about to speak when Josie and Clint stormed back into the kitchen. "Daddy!" Josie demanded. "Clint's being a brat!"

"She won't tell me where the playroom is," Clint groused to Ren, cranking into a whiny cry.

"I *told* him we don't have one. *Tell* him we don't have one, Daddy!"

Will turned his gaze matter-of-factly to the sulky four-year-old. "We don't have a playroom, Clint," he said without emotion. "In this house we have to make do with our bedrooms. It's quite sad."

Ren had the good sense to look exquisitely embarrassed. "Okay, well, we'd better head out," he said awkwardly, heaving his son into his arms. "Thanks again, guys. See you later."

As soon as the door closed, Will and I looked at each other and burst out laughing. "Oh my god, the look on his *face*!" I wheezed.

Will did his Country Club Ren impression, modified to show knock-kneed mortification and backwards shuffling.

"What's so funny?" Josie asked, mystified, looking from Will to me. "Dad? Annie? Tell me! What's funny? I don't get it! Tell me!"

"Nothing, Jo," Will said as he pulled Josie close to him and gave her a squeeze. "You'll understand when you're older."

She broke away from him and put her hands on her hips. "Don't you underestimate me!"

We only laughed harder, making the child depart in a shrieking tizzy. But before parting ways into our evening tasks, Will and I held each other's eyes for a moment. "I'm sorry," we both blurted out at once.

Despite the ongoing tension, the fourteen days of stress, the brand-new elephant that had lumbered into the room just minutes before, I had to believe that if we were still laughing, there was hope.

40

GIANNA PICKED UP the girls from school the next day, dropping by only briefly to collect a few precious items.

And with that, my house was once again mine. I stood in the middle of the living room dancing giddily in place. Silence! Solitude! Sex! All these could and would be mine!

I checked my watch. Will would be home in moments with our favorite wine and special-occasion takeout. I sprinted to the bedroom to fling off the sheets, sliding our satin set into place. Now what had I done with that garter belt?

You know, if you have a child, you'll never get nights like this, warned Xena, who seemed to be taking over for Angelina as primary mood-killer. *Everything will be just as loud and busy, but shit-scented as well—every single bloody day of the week! Do you really want that? REALLY?*

"I'm not thinking about that right now," I said aloud. Tonight was about Will and me reconnecting, rebooting our relationship. Everything else could wait.

Still, I couldn't deny how much more alive I felt without the children around, how much younger and lighter, how much more *myself.* If my marriage and sanity were suffering now, how could I think an eight-pound spigot with constant needs was going to make things any better?

Because, I argued, sliding the stockings over my newly shaved legs, I would feel differently about my own child. Because it would give me the instinct and the imperative—biological and emotional—to be a good mother to *all* the kids. Because all the exhaustion would be worth it to create a new life that belonged to Will and me alone.

I looked at myself in the mirror. *Because I'm running out of options,* I thought.

Oh, please, Xena scoffed. *That is a despicable reason to bring a child into this world.*

"I'm not *thinking* about this right now!" I reminded myself more forcefully. I closed my eyes, conjuring Will's naked body. Tonight was about one thing only.

You know, some people might say the two are somewhat related, Angelina simpered, amusedly patting her perpetual bump.

Not tonight they're not, I shot back. One thing was now obvious: raising kids exacerbated relationship weaknesses. There was soon, and then there was *now.* I wanted my marriage back to bedrock before baby made five.

And I would do it, starting with a little dose of lingerie.

At last I heard Will fumbling with the door. I appraised my reflection, gave my bra one last upward heave, and went to pull my husband into my arms.

41

THREE NIGHTS LATER, just before dusk, two kids materialized on my front stoop like donations. They grinned up at me, bedecked in pink and blue, babies too big for a basket.

"Wow, you guys look amazing!" I exclaimed. London was glowing in a luxurious teal gown and rhinestone crown, frosted eyelids and satin gloves. Josie wore the dime-store version but was none the wiser, giddily stepping off the stoop and onto the front lawn to twirl and twirl her shiny skirts.

I waved to Gianna as the car backed out of the driveway. The girls would go back to their mother's house that evening, but it was Will's year for Halloween custody.

"Will, come quick! Two princesses have honored us with their presence!" I shouted into the house as we went inside.

"*She's* a princess," London hurried to differentiate, "but *I'm* a queen."

Oh, I'm pretty sure you're the princess, I smiled to myself, but I really was warmed to see how poised and graceful London was in her costume. Her posture, the lift of her chin, the way she clutched her skirts all betrayed a radiant contentment that I had never before seen in my stepdaughter. I had a vision of a grown, mature London, brilliant and successful, emotions under control. She really was going to be as beautiful as her mother.

I didn't know how to feel about that.

Will came out of his office, gasping and fussing over his girls. "Your Majesties!" he exclaimed, bowing and glove-kissing. "Ah, to what do we owe this honor?"

"Daddy, we won first prize for group costume!" London shrieked, her ten-year-old self peeking out of the sophisticated façade as she threw her arms around her father. "Thank you, thank you, thank you!"

"You're so welcome, sweetheart," Will said, holding her. And though part of me niggled at the affection and the price tag, mostly at that moment I didn't mind the money at all.

Josie, however, cared nothing for these tender moments. She was at the window, watching the sun go down. "Can we go now? Is it time? Is it? Can we go?" She caught my eye. "I really *need* candy."

"Just a few minutes," Will said. "Do you have your buckets?"

Both girls pointed at the plastic pumpkins they'd discarded by the door.

"Okay, well, I guess there's no reason to wait," Will shrugged. He looked at me. "So. One of us will stay here and hand out candy, and one of us will go with you girls."

"Daddy," London said with the same haste usually reserved for *not it*.

I kept my cool. "Couldn't we both go?" For days I'd been picturing us strolling along with the other parents, appreciating the latest in fake spiderweb technology. The girls' faces wouldbeam brighter than the jack-o-lanterns as they returned from each driveway with a full treat report.

But the other three Tylers looked aghast. "Then who would give out the candy?" Josie asked.

"Well—we all would," I said. "When we get back."

"We *have* to give out the candy the whole time," London insisted. "People always come to our house for our Cream Pops." Ah. Perhaps that explained the giant bag of mysterious lollipops that

YOU KNEW HE HAD KIDS...

had been dropped off, special delivery, two days before. A previous apartment-dweller with no trick-or-treat obligations, I hadn't given it much thought.

"Maybe Mommy could come like last year?" Josie asked hopefully, looking up at Will.

"No, Mommy has plans," Will said quickly, looking embarrassed. "Annie—"

"It's fine," I said. "I'll stay here. I didn't realize what an important house we have." Nor had I realized that Will and Gianna had continued to share the holiday as recently as last year. Josie *had* explained that Ren's neighborhood was "too nice for trick-or-treating"—the estates too large and spread out to yield much in the way of a full candy–sack—but had neglected to mention that Gianna still came *here* as an alternative. How had Ren allowed—stomached—that?

Because he knows what's best for the children—

Shut the fuck up, I silenced Angelina in mid-sentence. *Just. Shut. The. Fuck. Up.*

And she did.

I smiled. "Well, you'd better get going!" I said brightly. "Let's just take a few pictures before you go." Maybe it was better this way—a warm house, a heaping bowl of candy, and a whole parade of cute kiddies coming right to me.

So off they went, and I oohed and ahhed for a steady half-hour, pouring lollipops in the outstretched sacks of pirates, princesses, and *Hunger Games* ensembles. While I was in the thick of Cream Pop distribution the phone began to peal, shrilling obnoxiously for ten rings before pausing for a few seconds and starting again. God, wasn't the answering machine plugged in? I looked toward the kitchen, but down the driveway swarmed another flock of ballerinas and vampires. It wasn't really my phone anyway. I let it go.

I didn't notice that the phone had quieted until it started up again a few minutes later. *Oh my GOD!* Stubbornly I ignored it: I was no slave to an insistent caller. But then I heard my cell phone's distant music. I sprinted for the bedroom, annoyance turning to concern.

"Will?" I picked up, plugging my available ear against the cascade of knocks on the front door. "Are you okay?"

"I need you to pack a bag for each of us," Will said frantically. "Carry-ons. We'll be home in ten minutes and we have to leave immediately for the airport."

I struggled to make sense of his instructions. "Are you okay? What's going on?"

"It's another stroke. Lou's going. We have to get the kids out there to say goodbye."

42

TEN MINUTES LATER the door flung open to emit two teary girls and their frenzied father. "We're back!" Will shouted.

"I'll be right there," I called from the bedroom, where I was still trying to find a warm sweater for Josie, who (despite her menopause-grade toastiness) would require something more than a t-shirt on this Midwestern journey. I zipped up the final bag and brought them all out to the living room.

"Oh, thank you," Will sighed gratefully, taking two of them off my hands. "No time now, girls—you can change in the car." He turned to me. "Will you take us to the airport?"

"Sure, I can drive if you want," I said, puzzled. Will generally liked to be behind the wheel.

"Oh, but maybe you shouldn't," Will realized. "I don't know when we'll be back and you might not be able to come get us."

I stared at my husband, dumbfounded. "Will, I'm *coming*." I held up the larger duffel and garment bag in which I'd stowed my and Will's things.

He blinked at me dumbly. "You're what?"

Oh, God. "You didn't get me a ticket," I stated dully.

"Annie, I just thought—with work and all—" he stammered. He was right, of course. He knew I was supposed to meet with Brenda next week; he knew I felt watched, judged for my every bathroom break and water-cooler indulgence.

But it was Friday night. I could come back Sunday if needed. And this was a family emergency! Surely I deserved some managerial leeway. *Your husband's ex-wife's father is not your family,* I could hear Brenda saying sarcastically, stripping me of my promotion with cold menace. And though I could hardly argue—I didn't consider *Gianna* my family, let alone some dying old coot I'd never met—the prospect of Will traveling with his beautiful ex and their kids was sure as hell a family emergency to me. Brenda never had to know the details.

I stared at Will in mute frustration, wondering why he didn't understand the horror in what he was proposing. At least—at *least*—he could have asked me what I wanted to do.

"Come on, let's get in the car," I said gruffly. "You can call and try to get me a ticket on the way."

Hours later, we crowded into the dull fluorescence of a dying man's room. I hovered by the doorway as the others rushed the bed, Gianna pausing to give her waiting mother a weary embrace.

The girls were sobbing, tongue-tied. They'd been distractible on the plane, charmed by all the fuss made over the flouncy costumes they'd elected to keep on. But confronted with goodbye, they were overwhelmed.

"Lou?" Will asked, grabbing the man's hand. "It's me, Will. Your son-in-law. Former. Remember? Can you hear me? I just wanted to say thank you for being such a wonderful man. A father. To me and Gianna. And grandfather to my kids." His voice broke. "We love you. Have a safe journey, Lou. I know you'll be watching over us." He released the semi-conscious hand and put either arm around his daughters, blinking as the tears fell. "Give him a kiss, girls, and say goodbye."

The sobbing broke out anew. "Goodbye, Grandpa," the pink and blue princesses choked as they gently touched their lips to Lou's, slicking his cheek with their tears.

I blotted my own face, my heart throbbing with conflicting emotions. Their grief was unbearable; I wanted to shelter and soothe them. Yet I stood alone, nothing more than a witness, the sole stranger to this fading man—an intruder who cried only for the grieving and not for the nearly-gone. How could I belong here when my sorrow, genuine though it was, was marred by a sinking, resentful awareness that Will and these children would never weep over my own father's deathbed, that Gianna's family would forever be preferred?

"Let's go, girls," Will sniffed, leading his daughters toward me. "Let's give your mom and grandma some time." Together, we stepped out into the hall.

The first thing I saw was Ren hurrying toward us. I had to fight not to fling my arms around the anxious arrival and shout *thank God you're here!* I'd despaired when Ren wasn't at the airport; but Gianna had explained, pacing at the gate, that her husband was across the country on business and would have to meet them separately. So the trip itself remained awkward—but knowing Ren would be coming gave me the courage to sit alone in my tacked-on seat while the four original family members sat two-by-two a few rows ahead. I had chanted my positive aphorisms, forcing myself to turn on my iPod and close my eyes rather than stare resentfully at the backs of their heads.

"Am I too late?" Ren asked breathlessly. He slipped into the hospital room as the rest of us sank wearily to a padded bench.

The exhausted girls sat morosely, Josie curled in Will's arms. I gently stroked London's hair. "I'm so sorry, sweetheart," I whispered, gulping with a little thrill as London leaned against me and closed her eyes.

I was just drifting off when Ren rejoined them. "Gianna wants to stay here," he reported softly. "Should we go to the hotel? I can take the kids if you want."

"No, that's fine," Will said, adjusting the conked Josie as he rose to his feet. "We should have two beds in our room."

Without speaking we trudged to the parking lot and out into the bitter night.

November

43

THE FUNERAL WAS brief and simple—a minister, a casket, a hole in the earth. Friends spoke their praises. The eyes all around were wet, or glassy, or closed.

After two days the intimacy was still uncomfortable. I felt like a spy, some kind of sleazebag funeral-critic, as I sized up the black velvet that Gianna had chosen for herself and the girls. *Surviving daughter Gianna London may have retired from modeling,* the review would read, *but she hasn't abandoned her flair for the dramatic. Having spent the previous day scouring the neighborhood for designer clothing, Gianna and her two daughters made quite a splash, casket-side, as the three blond beauties in black.*

God, I was such an asshole. I couldn't imagine how I would feel if the situations were reversed and Gianna was there, constantly, watching my family bury our patriarch. Yes—Gianna *had* decided that the nice outfits I'd packed for London and Josie weren't somber enough for the funeral. But come on, it wasn't a personal slight. I had to cut the woman a little slack.

Will, at least, was wearing the suit I had chosen for him. I reached for him, tucking myself against his body, as Lou London was lowered into the earth.

Later, at the reception, I found myself grazing alone at the snack table when Gianna came over to check on the quantities.

Of course, I had just shoved a giant cracker in my mouth. "Can I help with anything?" I asked anyway, hand shooting out to screen Gianna from the spraying crumbs.

Gianna shook her head. "Thanks, but the cousins sliced enough celery to feed the state," she said with a smile, as strikingly beautiful as ever. But up close, I could see the exhaustion etched through Gianna's face, the telltale raw nostrils of Kleenex-burn.

"I'm so sorry, Gianna," I said in a sudden flood of sympathy. "You know if there's anything Will or I can do, just ask."

"I appreciate that," Gianna said. Were her eyes filming? "I really appreciate it."

We paused awkwardly. "How's your mom doing?" I finally asked.

"As well as can be expected, I guess," Gianna answered. "She'll probably come live with us for a time."

Heck, they could probably lodge a dozen widows in that place. "That's great," I said. "I'm sure that will be good for all of you."

"Yeah, it will be especially nice for the girls, I think," Gianna said. "It was hard on them when my parents moved. They were around constantly when we were—when I was working," she finished diplomatically. In other words, when she and Will had been married. I just nodded, wondering what had prompted the grandparents' departure. Will had never mentioned it.

"You know, I just wanted to apologize for the whole plane thing," Gianna said then, looking embarrassed. "I was perfectly happy to take the single seat, and—"

"It's fine," I assured her. When we'd discovered the seating arrangements, Gianna had offered to take the solo spot. But London had wailed and I was not about to insist. "London was clearly upset and needed to be with—with you." I couldn't quite bring myself to say *her mother*.

"Well, I'm sure it'll be different on the flight home."

"Yes," I agreed, carefully slipping away as a couple approached Gianna with their condolences.

The things that brought people together were so strange, I thought as I looked idly around Gianna's mother's living room. You get married and divorced—you need never see your former spouse again. You get married and have *kids* and get divorced—you spend the next twenty years of your life planning and arguing and compromising with a person who belongs in the past. Everyone forced together in a box, bobbing and grinning for the sake of the children, new wives and husbands obliged to share space and moments with the people they feel least comfortable with in all the world.

Yet Gianna wasn't so bad. In fact she had been nothing but friendly to me for quite some time. I sighed, wondering if I would ever be able to look at the woman without picking, comparing and obsessing. Gianna seemed to have no such issues with *me*.

I drifted toward the hallway, unsure where Will and the girls had gone. Hearing pattering feet upstairs, I slipped unnoticed into the corridor, stopping in my tracks to peer at a cluster of framed photos on the wall. *This is more like it,* Xena glinted, and I couldn't help a small evil laugh. There she was: Gianna with a perm and sky-high bangs. Gianna with shoulder-pads. Gianna with braces. It was good to know that even the ravishing had their ungainly years.

Then the smile withered on my lips. There was Gianna, breathtaking bride, an impossibly young and innocent Will gazing at her with mingled joy and reverence.

I gulped. *Stop looking,* insisted a voice, one too concerned to be either Angelina or Xena. But I couldn't.

Gianna, glowingly pregnant. Gianna looking up at Will, a swaddled infant in her arms. Gianna and Will with both their girls, posing on the very couch where I now did my crossword puzzles and cuddled my cat.

"A little stuck in the past, huh?" came a sudden voice, and I screeched. I turned, a hand on my pounding heart. It was Ren.

"Sorry," he said. "Didn't mean to scare you."

"That's okay," I answered, turning back to the wall. "I was just—" I motioned to the gallery and shook my head. "God."

"I know. I hate this wall," Ren said. "After three years of marriage, guess who still isn't on it?"

I quickly scanned the rest of the images. He was right. A new photo hadn't been added in years. I shook my head. "What's the deal? Why—?"

Ren looked around uneasily, then motioned back down the corridor. "Let's talk outside."

We slipped into the backyard, heading over to the flower garden where nobody could overhear. Much to my surprise, Ren lit a cigarette and inhaled deeply. I'd never seen him ruffled; the situation must have been harder for him than he let on.

"Gianna is an only child," Ren finally said, "and she's always been their golden girl. Their prize. A model student. A model—model. A wife and mother." He paused. "They adored Will. When he and Gianna split up, they just couldn't understand. They, you see, don't 'believe' in divorce. They 'hadn't raised her this way.' They called her every name under the sun, told her she had disgraced them, that she was a terrible mother. She thought they would get over it." He laughed. "They didn't. They moved away."

"*No,*" I gasped.

"Yes," Ren said. "Oh yes. I think they were trying to bully her into not marrying me, hoping she would break it off and get back together with Will. But of course she didn't. And she's spent the past few years trying to rebuild a relationship with them. She's made some progress. Me, though? They barely acknowledge me. I'm just the schmuck who isn't the father of their grandchildren."

"God, that's awful," I said, realizing that Gianna's mother hadn't been ignoring me out of distracted grief. "What about Clint? Are they nice to him?"

"They have no interest in Clint," Ren said flatly. "He's not their flesh and blood. Gianna dutifully sends pictures of the five of us. She says they'll come around." He shook his head. "But I really don't know."

"And Rosa is supposed to come live with you!" I suddenly remembered. "Oh my God—what are you going to do?"

"Demand some respect in my own house, I hope," Ren grinned. "But I don't know. Rosa's alone now. Maybe this is the right time for her to realize that you shouldn't turn your back on family, no matter what form it takes."

"Well, I hope it works out," I said. "If it makes you feel any better, my mom didn't really approve of me marrying Will, either. She calls him 'secondhand.' Doesn't even count the girls as her grandkids."

"People can be so stupid," Ren said, exhaling. "As if it isn't hard enough already without their little judgments and statements."

"Tell me about it," I agreed, smiling warmly. Out here in this other universe, so far away from my stepmom friends, it was so nice to have someone understand.

"So how is it with Will's parents?" Ren asked me.

"To be honest, I've only met them a handful of times," I said. "His mom's dead, and his dad and stepmom actually live in Europe. They've been perfectly nice, if not very interested." The one step-

mother I'd known before meeting Leah—my own mother-in-law!—
and the woman hadn't exactly taken me under her wing. "I guess
I'm realizing now that Gianna's parents sort of replaced his own." I
paused. "He never told me."

"It's all so complicated," Ren smiled at me, his eyes crinkling. I
could understand what Gianna saw in him—though he was at least
ten years her senior, he still had a boyish easygoing charm. "We both
deserve medals for even getting involved, don't you think?"

"*Gold* medals," I agreed.

Ren smiled and stubbed out the remains of his cigarette. "Well?
Should we rejoin the party?"

We walked back inside together. "Oh, brother," Ren breathed.

"What?" I asked. But then I saw. Will and Gianna, London and
Josie all stood circled up on the other side of the room with Gianna's
mother.

"Let's shatter the fantasy, shall we?" Ren grinned, and we separated, each of us coming up behind the respective spouse and wrig-
gling into the fold. I had to fight not to laugh when I saw the widow's
brow furrow. I caught Ren's eye just as he flashed me a devilish wink.

44

"THANKS FOR MEETING with me, Rhiannon," Brenda said, motioning to the chair in front of her desk. Brenda was one of the few people at the office who called me by my full name. "And I apologize for the delay."

I offered a pasty smile. I'd returned home the previous evening, wiped out and ponderous, and had proceeded to worry about this very meeting the entire night, even through the half sleeping pill I'd swallowed in 3-a.m. desperation. I hadn't felt this bad since the hungover dawn of my college graduation.

"I'm sure you're wondering what this is about," Brenda went on, and I smiled weakly. Was there a polite way of saying *get the fuck on with it?*

"Well, it concerns your future here at Highlink," Brenda said, her face and voice totally neutral.

I'm fired, I thought hopelessly, my heart beginning a simultaneous sink-and-race. *After all I've done here, she's going to fire me.*

Still, there was an immediate silver lining: at least if I got fired I could go home and get some sleep.

Brenda went on. "As you know, we did have that incident with Carolyn Vance a couple of weeks ago—"

I only nodded faintly. Oh, you mean the one that's been making me sick for weeks? The one that's made me choose between stepmotherhood and professional success? Yeah, I think I remember.

"—but that didn't stop me from recommending you to Lucy Shaples. As you may know, they're looking to hire within the company."

I stared back blankly, trying to understand this surprising new course of gobbledygook. Lucy Shaples was Ted's boss. In marketing. Nothing was adding up.

"They asked about you. It would be a lateral move, and honestly, you'll have more opportunities for advancement if you stay here. But the decision, of course, is up to you."

"But I'm in customer relationships," was all I could manage. I could scarcely understand what Brenda was saying. I'd never done a scrap of marketing in my life.

"That's what I told her," Brenda said. "But Lucy insisted that a bright person with good communication skills is the best kind of candidate. And they want you."

I sat back in my chair, reeling. *I'm not getting fired,* I finally realized. *I'm not getting fired!* I had to fight not to grin stupidly. Far from being a disappointment, I was a desirable candidate! Was Ted behind this? I couldn't wait to get out of the meeting and corner him.

"Well, that's a very interesting proposition," I said, nodding soberly—as though I had any doubt which move I would make. "I'll have to consider it carefully." I stopped my hand in mid-ascent, preventing an unnecessary course of chin-stroking. No need to overdo it.

"All right. If you could let me know by the end of the week, I'd appreciate it." And with a glance at her telephone, Brenda made it clear the meeting was over. I giddily half-genuflected my way out.

A week later, Will and the girls met Ted and me at a favorite restaurant close to the office. It had been my first day in my new job.

"Uncle Ted!" London cried when she saw him, weaving her way over to the table where my colleague and I were each halfway through a well-deserved stein.

"Oh—my—God!" Ted said, his mouth falling open theatrically. "This *cannot* be London Tyler. I remember her, and she was some kind of runty thing—" London scrunched up her nose and socked him in the shoulder. "Hmmm...yes...now it's all coming back to me...the cruelty, the violence...you haven't changed a bit!" The ten-year-old laughed and raised her fist again. "Have mercy on an old man!" Ted cowered. "Seriously, London, you are gorgeous. I can't believe how grown up you are!"

London flushed, grinning bashfully. Even though she often seemed older than her ten years, she was still so young. I saw the unconscious mingling of childhood and adolescence and was surprised how endearing I found it.

"And *you*—well, the last time I saw you, I think you were about *this* tall," Ted said to Josie, bringing his hand a foot off the ground and then reconsidering to about four inches. Josie giggled. "Do you even remember your Uncle Ted?" he asked.

Josie nodded shyly, but I doubted it. Though they'd all been at my wedding, most of the girls' socializing with Ted had apparently been in Gianna's party-throwing days. Josie would have been a toddler.

"Will-I-am," Ted said next, standing to give his old friend a bro-hug. "How goes it?"

I smiled, ignoring an odd twinge as we all settled down and began to peruse the menus. I was still all nervy from my first day.

"So?" Will asked, as though he couldn't wait any longer. "How was it?"

I turned to Ted for help. "Honestly, I have no idea. How'd I do?"

"She was great," Ted reported to all. "She didn't know what she was doing, but she was *great*."

The girls giggled. "Now *I'm* going to punch you," I teased.

"I'm dead serious," Ted said. "I know it's going to take you a while to get comfortable, but you're going to be great. We definitely made the right choice in whisking you away from the evil Brenda."

I felt my face stretching into a possibly lunatic grin. I'd been overwhelmed by the welcome from Ted's whole group, soothed by our boss's agreeable manner. Walking by my old, empty cube that morning, I had felt all the accumulated stress and worry falling away from me in clumps. I already felt sorry for my yet-to-be-found replacement.

"Well, it's certainly a lot more fun working with you," I said.

"To Annie!" Will said, lifting his water glass. "I'm so proud of you, sweetie."

"To Annie!" they all said. My chest burned with happiness to see London and Josie smiling at me in support.

"So tell me about yourself, kiddo," Ted said to London once we'd all put down our mugs. "How's school going this year?"

"Oh, I *hate* it," London declared with party-line ennui, but her subsequent narrative and shining eyes revealed just how much she was bluffing. She chattered on about her teacher, classmates, sports victories and A+ book reports, giving more details in five minutes than I had heard in three months. *We're going to have to keep an eye on her,* I thought, noticing how my stepdaughter bubbled and purred in the glow of male attention. Then again—this was also how she'd acted around her friend Evie. What was it that made London so sullen at home, so alive around others?

The conversation shifted. *Remember when we went to the zoo, Uncle Ted? Remember my birthday party, Uncle Ted?* The lid lifted from Pandora's jar, years of imprisoned memories streaming free. Will and Ted were talking about the old days at Highlink; coworkers that had long since moved on; parties, weekends, and poker nights. And inevitably in every story was a pajama-clad pixie or two, always good for a darnedest-thing moment. London and Josie were rapt; they would sit patiently for centuries to hear stories about themselves. *Remember, Uncle Ted? Remember? Remember?*

I sat mute. Ted was my work-friend, someone I adored but seldom saw outside of business hours. Here, though, was evidence of a history that had gone much deeper: a personal life with Will and Gianna and their children, feelings primed for rekindling. Even Josie had known Ted before I had! What had I been doing when Ted was masquerading as the Tylers' pseudo-relative? Working, clubbing with Summer? I honestly couldn't remember. I felt a strange panic that I hadn't existed at all.

"And remember when you did that amazing bellyflop off the diving board?" Ted was wheezing.

"Oh, shut *up!*" London screeched, the squirmy joy of being the center of attention overriding her embarrassment. I looked across the table at Josie, who wouldn't have remembered this particular story—but she too was laughing, tickled by the idea of her sister humiliating herself in front of her dad's entire office.

And of course they were all laughing, sopping up these good times like gravy too succulent to be left on the plate. I tried to laugh, tried to fake it, but I could hear the tinny hollowness of each forced *ha*. Ted hadn't made a single direct reference to Gianna, yet she was *everywhere,* an invading Presence, the looming ghost at a successful séance. I almost expected her face to appear, a conjured hologram, in the center of the table.

"You okay?" Ted asked as we finally hugged our goodbyes. "You've hardly said a word!"

"Yeah, it's just been a long day," I lied, weak with emotional exhaustion. "See you tomorrow."

"Bright and early, my marketing maven!" Ted beamed at me before turning to trot off to his car. Will and the girls were equally buoyant, chittering their way across the parking lot.

I walked slowly to my own car, feeling odd and disoriented. Oh, I had endured many tedious reminiscences from London and Josie—Mommy This and Christmas Eve That—but there was something different about this. I had talked to Ted so freely, so safely, never realizing how enmeshed he'd once been with my stepdaughters. He'd told me he hadn't liked Gianna, but could that really be true? Would a person spend that much time with Will's entire family if he hadn't cared for a pivotal member?

Pretending to search for my keys, I waved mechanically to Ted as he drove past me with a friendly honk. Was that even *Ted*? It was as though my friend had been body-snatched, replaced with a doppelganger that belonged to everyone in the family but me.

I fumbled into my car, tears stinging my eyes. The past wasn't Ted's fault, surely. Yet why, then, did I feel so betrayed?

45

THE DOOR CRACKED open to reveal a wizened little face.

"Ah, Yoda!" I exclaimed. "How nice of you to come. I was hoping you could teach me to use the Force."

The door swung back the rest of the way, revealing mother and daughter in matching pastels. Both looked pissed. "That is so not funny, Annie," Summer huffed. "My daughter does not look like Yoda. Or *any* Muppet."

I looked at the baby thoughtfully, trying to quash the instinct for assholery. I failed. "You're right," I finally said. "Mea culpa. She's barely even green at all."

Summer spun around and began marching into the house. "Well if you're going to be like that, you don't *deserve* to see Riley."

"Summer, come on!" I said, dashing to keep up. "It was a joke. You know. Ha-ha?" Summer stopped, but didn't say anything. "I was just teasing," I went on. "You *know* how beautiful I think she is."

Summer turned back, her mouth quivering into a smile. "Sorry," she finally said. "I'm just sensitive because there's this *woman* in the park who won't *shut up* about how beautifully perfect her baby is, and the thing is she really *is* beautifully perfect and the whole thing just makes me so *nuts*—" She shook her head. "Well never mind. Just crazy mom stuff I guess!" Her eyes sparkled as the holy m-word rolled off her tongue. "Let's go sit down."

We settled on the couch, Summer chattering about how Kevin's long work night afforded us the perfect opportunity to catch up. "I just miss my girlfriends so much, you know?" she said. "With the park moms everything's a competition."

So is this, I thought wryly. *It's just a competition you think you can win.* Still, my wariness about Ted lent Summer's friendship a new shimmer. The new mother may not have been spectacularly supportive of late, but at least she had no previous affiliation with any of the Tylers.

"Yes, it's so great to see you," I said diplomatically, glancing at the empty coffee table. "Got any chips or anything?" I was unaccountably famished.

"Oh! Yeah, I got a bunch of stuff. Do you want to hold Riley while I bring everything out?"

I reached out for the lavender bundle, laughing as Riley's maladroit little fists clubbed at my breast. "I think she's hungry too," I told Summer as she came back in the room with bowls of crackers and veggies. "I'll trade you."

"It's bedtime," Summer said, gathering up her daughter. "Help yourself and I'll be back in a few."

I didn't hesitate. I fell into a munch-induced trance, not even noticing several minutes later that Summer had returned and was watching me with a mixture of amusement and faint disgust. "Geez, Annie. Have you been fasting or something?"

I jumped, dropping my carrot. "No. I've just been *starving* the last couple of days," I said, salvaging the lost vegetable from the carpet and brushing off the hair. "I don't know. It happens to me sometimes." I ate the carrot, my eyes roving over the remains of the snacks.

"Oh my God," Summer gasped, sitting down next to me. "Annie! You're *pregnant!*"

I rolled my eyes—then stuffed in another cracker. "I'm not pregnant, Summer," I garbled through the food. "I'm on the pill."

"Ninety-nine-point-*nine* percent accurate," Summer argued triumphantly. "There is always room for *fate* to intervene!"

"Maybe someday," I said, eyeing the candy dish I could just make out on the distant kitchen table.

But Summer wasn't taking the hint. "Oh Annie—wouldn't it be amazing? You and me, moms together?"

I dragged my gaze from the chocolate and looked at my friend impatiently. "Summer, we *are* moms together," I said, trying to keep my voice light. "It's just that my kids are older." Whether I really believed that was a matter too touchy and nuanced for the likes of Summer.

Summer shook her head just as impatiently. "That's not the *same*," she insisted. "I want us to have babies at the same time, go on walks and play in the park. *And we're going to*—now that you're PREGNANT!" She began to do a happy dance in her seat.

I tried to smile. Summer was just attempting, in her clumsy, annoying way, to tell me that she wanted to spend more time with me. She was simply longing for the shared motherhood experience that sustained heaps of other young women whose friends had had the decency to be more timely and/or fertile.

Yet every word grated. The more Summer wanted me to be pregnant, the less I wanted to be. The more fantasies she launched, the more I wanted to shoot them down. I felt obstinate, ornery, argumentative. And hungry. As I reached for another cracker, the realization dawned: talking to Summer was like talking to my mother.

"We could start our own mommy group," Summer chattered on. "And go on vacations together!"

Motherhood obviously changed some women, and—though they'd never believe it—not necessarily for the better. All Summer's coolness and sarcasm had disappeared in a puff of baby powder. But even that I could have borne with patient indulgence: the baby mania would have to ebb. It was Summer's noticeable lack of interest in my life—the true fabric of it—that made me wonder how much of a friend she really was.

Oh, Summer warmed to the notion of Will's fatherhood, and as long as I had positive things to say about the girls, she was insipidly supportive. But she never asked for details, preferring to twist the conversation back to her own fascinating particulars about Riley's gas and nipple-latching issues.

Suddenly Summer gasped. "Stay *right here*," she instructed, hurrying off down the hall. I took the opportunity to make my own dash for the candy dish. I was safely back on the couch crunching malt balls when Summer returned a few minutes later with something behind her back. "I've got a surprise for you!" came the singsong voice. She pulled her prize out from behind her back.

It was a pregnancy test.

I closed my eyes and groaned. "Jesus, Summer! Will you give it a rest? I'm not pregnant!"

"Why not be sure?" Summer argued, pointing at my stash. "I *see* you scarfing down my chocolate. You said on the phone you've been tired lately. Do your boobs hurt?"

"No," I said irritably, but I couldn't help pressing a subtle hand to my chest. *Were* they more tender than usual? Fear began to tickle my spine.

"Come on," Summer was coaxing. "What's the harm in it?"

I snatched the box from my friend's hand and looked at it. "Summer, this test expired months ago."

"So it's just for fun then," Summer grinned. "Come on. You know you want to."

"Pee on a stick?" I snorted. "Not really." At least not under *these* circumstances. *Yes*, all right, I had fantasized about that mythical moment, watching happy lines appear before my and Will's elated eyes. But if I was pregnant *now*—

I looked at Summer seriously. "If I take the test will you *promise* not to say anything else about me being pregnant?"

"I solemnly swear," Summer answered with sparkling eyes.

"All right, I'll pee on the stupid stick," I muttered, heading off to the bathroom.

And then we sat in nervous silence for three minutes.

"Let's go," Summer finally whispered, grabbing my hand. "Oh, Annie," she said. "I'm *so* excited for you."

I didn't speak. Together we walked to the bathroom like the half-naked girls in a horror movie, unable to resist the deadly lure of the psycho-killer behind the shower curtain. "I can't look," I choked as I pushed open the door, but I did anyway.

And slowly I let out my breath.

"See?" I said, holding up the test. "Not pregnant. Are you happy now?" I felt the most peculiar, sickly crash of disappointment followed by a swell of relief.

"Oh, sweetie," Summer moaned, pulling me into an embrace. "I'm so sorry. I was so *sure*."

"It's okay, silly," I laughed. Despite everything, I still felt affection for my fanatical friend. "I told you I'm on the pill. It's not the time yet."

But as I looked over Summer's shoulder at the little plastic stick, I knew I'd be buying another one on the way home.

46

WILL WAS NOT happy about the news.

"You're kidding, right?"

I shook my head, cringing. "I'm afraid not."

"Well that's just wonderful," Will glowered. "Just *great*."

I looked at my husband timidly. "It might not be that bad," I suggested hopefully. "Maybe it'll even be good."

Will rolled his eyes. "I don't see how."

"Keep an open mind," I coaxed. "Where's your sense of adventure?"

"This is hardly the time for adventure," Will protested stubbornly. "Isn't that obvious?"

"Look, I know it's not what you wanted," I said. "But it's just the way things are."

Will sighed, looking defeated. "Can we get out of it?"

I thought about it. "We can, but it would be difficult." I shrugged. "Is it that big a deal?"

"Well, I guess not, but—" He looked at me in disbelief. "Cabbage ravioli?"

I shrugged helplessly. "I know. I know. But she loves cabbage. And she hates turkey."

"This is *Thanksgiving*, Annie." Will looked wilted. "It's only like the best meal of the year. And what about the kids?"

"I'll make sure she makes something else for them," I said hurriedly. "And you can make turkey the next day. Friday?" I suggested hopefully. "I just can't ask my mom to change her plans at this point. She's just *so* difficult; she'll blame you, and huff and puff about it the whole time—"

"Okay, fine," Will conceded, throwing up his hands. "Fake Thanksgiving Thursday, *real* Thanksgiving Friday."

"Thank you, thank you," I said, throwing grateful arms around my husband. "I'm so sorry. But next year—well, next year we'll maybe just run off to Italy to celebrate with your parents."

"Yeah, right," Will snorted. We could never afford the trip, and Will's father and stepmother wouldn't dream of traveling home with all the crowds. Cousin Cammy and her family were never available, either; they had their own traditions involving some kind of deep-woods backpacking, fur caps and all.

I swallowed, guilty that Will's new (so-called) family delighted in bemoaning his children and feeding him lackluster vegetables for major holidays. Why *wouldn't* he prefer Gianna's parents, who still loved and adored him after all these years? *They* probably fed him turkey.

"Wait, are you telling me"—Will suddenly asked, peering at me incredulously—"that you have *never* had a Thanksgiving turkey before? That it's always been"—he paused to grimace—"cabbage ravioli?"

"Well, no," I said timidly. "I mean, yes—I have had turkey, once, when I went to a boyfriend's house one year in college. And it's not always cabbage ravioli!" I explained happily. "But, well, usually cabbage *something*."

Will looked to the heavens with tragic eyes. "Oh, my poor girl." But then he looked at me and smiled. "This will be good, then. We will go to your mom's house for trial Thanksgiving and then, on Friday, I will make you the meal of your life. Good? Good." He kissed me and went whistling out of the room.

I sighed in relief. I hadn't realized how nervous I'd been to tell Will about the impending menu. In truth, I hadn't been very impressed by the turkey I'd eaten with Bobby Reynolds all those years ago—and I actually rather liked cabbage ravioli. But if the promise of a traditional meal would keep Will on his best behavior, that was all that mattered. It was going to be hard enough with the girls there.

Oh yes, I had made lots of throaty pronouncements and demands earlier in the year, insisting both to Gianna (through Will) and my mother (through voicemail) that we absolutely *must* have both girls with us for Family's First Thanksgiving. I had thought it was the right thing in theory—still did, really—but the prospect of negotiating this day-long event was now starting to feel like another big stupid blunder to be pooh-poohed in a preachy *Huffington Post* article. The facts were clear: the kids were unpredictable and my mother was a troll. This was probably going to be the worst Thanksgiving ever.

I sighed and went into the bedroom to change clothes for the stepmom meeting. If anyone could ensure my Thanksgiving survival, these women would be the ones.

47

"OH LOOK, IT'S *Rhi-an-non*," Kim emphasized as I approached the table. "Hello, *Rhi-an-non*."

A chorus of the Fleetwood Mac classic floated up around the table.

I stared at the group, mystified. Then I noticed the piece of paper in everyone's hands.

Kim shook hers in my general direction. "Your name's Rhiannon. So what's with this Annie bullcrap?"

"*Oh*," I said, sitting down and reaching for a copy of the member spreadsheet that Kerry had just passed out.

"Uh-uh-uh!" Kerry admonished, snatching the pile away. "Before you get one, you have to promise to guard this with your life, because it has a lot of sensitive information on it."

"Of course!" I swore, holding up a flat palm. "On all that is holy!"

She smiled and handed me one. "So what *is* the deal with your name?"

I shrugged. "Well, you know. Nothing's the deal with it. It's just what people call me."

"Well, I hate it," Kim declared. "Your real name is rad. We're calling you Rhiannon here."

"Uhhh…okay?" I said. It really didn't matter to me either way, but then again—it did feel cool having a special Society of Stepmothers identity. I could get used to that.

June suddenly laughed. "Hey, Annie Tyler sounds a lot like—"

"I know, I know, the author," I groaned. "*Yes*, okay, I should have Googled it before I changed my name. Add it to my list of a million-

and-one mistakes." I looked at the group and sighed. "Let me guess, you all kept your maiden names?" I was getting used to being the only idiot.

But I was surprised this time to see several of the women shaking their heads. "I was one of those sappy girls writing 'Kerry so-and-so' on my homework whenever I liked a boy," Kerry said. "It's what I always wanted. I don't think I'd even feel married if I didn't have his name."

Regan offered the counterpoint. "My name is timeless, and I'm not changing it for anyone."

"Yep," Kim agreed. "Once a Kim, always a Kim." I looked down at the spreadsheet, puzzled. Wasn't Kim her *first* name? But the listing read *K. Kim*—could the woman's name really be Kim Kim? Well…it certainly was easy to remember.

"I ended up hyphenating," Leah said. "At first I was going to take Paul's name, but somehow Adora found out and completely lost it at the idea of me having 'Mom's name.' Then I realized I wanted to have the same last name as my kids, too. So this way I have both."

"But doesn't it bug you that his ex still has his name and you don't?" Maggie asked. "That's my situation too, and I couldn't stand having a different name from the two of them. And, you know, I like the unity of it—Mr. and Mrs. Price. One team, one name on the mailbox…"

"…one wife that gets mistaken for the previous model…" Regan reminded her.

"Yes, okay," Maggie conceded. "I've gotten Twatwaffle's mail. She's gotten mine. And I've had the delightful experience of being mistaken for her, the crack whore, by everyone in town. But still. *I* am his wife. *I* wanted his name. It should be mine to have, not hers."

"Well, if Ryan and I do get married someday, I *will* take his name, mostly so Samantha will have a total freaking meltdown," June grinned.

"Yeah, name revenge is totally legitimate," Kim agreed. "Even I would change my name for *that*."

There was a pause, and then June clapped her hands together. "Okay. So. We all know what we're here to talk about today. So how's it all going ladies?" When no one immediately spoke up, June went on. "Well, thanks for asking. In my world it is bloody freaking murder. And why? Because Samantha found out that we're taking Annabel to *my* dad's house this year." She gave a theatrical gasp. "It's amazing how fast 'she's your responsibility!' can turn into 'but I can't stand not to be with my baaabeee for Thanksgiving!' So far, Ryan's not giving in, even though she texts him about a hundred times a day and has threatened every legal action under the sun."

"She's such a douchebag," Kim said.

"I just can't believe she can't get *over* it, you know?" June said. "We've dated for more than a year. But the longer it goes, the worse she gets! I fully expect to see her pug nose smooshed up against my dad's window this Thursday."

"Have someone test all the food before you eat it," Maggie suggested. "She could be in cahoots with the bakery people and poison your pumpkin pie."

"I wouldn't put it past her," June sighed. "Oh, *and* I have to try not to kill my stepmom. So that's fun times. How about the rest of you?"

Maggie clapped. "Things are good this year. I'm doing things *my* way, *my* meal, Twatwaffle is not in the picture—it'll be good. We usually do a big thing with relatives, but this year I just wanted it to be the four of us. One last Thanksgiving before the baby comes." I could see the *oh, crap* look in her eyes the second she spoke. "Shit, Kerry, I'm sorry."

"You can be sorry for the swear, but that's it," Kerry said primly. "I'm *glad* for you, really. But yeah, I feel pretty awful. It always happens this time of year. I *hate* cooking for these ingrates, and I *promised* myself I was going to be pregnant by the end of the year—"

"The year's not over yet," Leah said kindly.

"I know, but I just don't know how I'm going to make it through another Christmas if it doesn't happen. This is the absolute worst time of year for me."

"It's a tough time for everyone," Leah said, squeezing Kerry's hand.

"Everything okay at your house?" Maggie asked Leah.

Leah sighed. "This year we were all supposed to be together, but Curt somehow talked me into letting him take the kids on a trip." She shook her head. "And Paul's mad at me, and he should be, because we have my stepkids this year and I messed up the plan for all of us to be together." She sighed again. "I don't know what I was thinking. The kids wanted to go, and I—I just caved and messed everything up."

"Geez, the holidays are supposed to be *fun*," Kim said gloomily. "Bring on the ulcers."

"None for me!" Regan said brightly. "I don't *do* holidays. This year we'll be in Indonesia while the kids get their home-cooked meal from Mommy."

Jealous groans and napkin-wads greeted this pronouncement.

"What?" Regan said, flinging the napkins back at their original launchers. "Nobody says you have to do these god-awful things. Just bow out and everybody's happier."

"But how do you *do* that without feeling like you're doing things wrong—like you're missing out?" I asked. "I feel like now that we're married I'm supposed to do all this stuff, you know? We're going to have the kids this year, we're going to my parents' house, because *that's what people do*. That's what *families* do. And my mom's horrible, and Will's all upset because we have to eat cabbage ravioli—"

Blank looks greeted me around the table.

"Never mind, it's a long story," I said hastily. "The point is that I made all these plans because, you know, that's what you're supposed to do. And now I'm thinking about it and it sounds like a total nightmare."

"Not to sound like one of those lame-ass internet memes or anything, but the longer you do what you think you're supposed to do, the longer you're going to be miserable," Regan said. "I think we all need to dream a little bigger than some commercials for the Great Oppressor."

"She means Hallmark," Kim explained.

"But you know it's not that easy," Maggie said. "You grow up with this idea of what your life's going to be. You're going to be the perfect mom who's totally loved and adored by your perfect kids and your perfect husband. And as a stepmother you look around at all the intact families and how easy it is for them. You feel like you're never going to have what they have, like you missed out on everything."

"That's the thing, though," Leah said. "It's just a myth. Even as a young, married mother I felt like things were never quite what they were supposed to be. Everyone else always *seemed* happier than I was, like their families worked better than mine. I never lived up to the image. Nobody could."

"Exactly," said Regan. "It's bullshit."

"Maybe. But how do you break free, when you've spent your whole life wanting that?" Kerry asked.

"Easy," Regan declared. "You go to Indonesia!"

"If you'd like to fund a trip for all of us, I'm sure you'll have some takers," Kim said. "Meanwhile, the rest of us will stay home and drench our sorrows in butter and gravy. Except, I guess, for Annie. I mean Rhiannon."

I was just about to explain when a woman came up to the table and quietly sat down. The other stepmoms greeted the newcomer with surprise. "Fran! Where've you been? Are you okay?"

I thought I recognized the woman from the first meeting I'd attended. But this time her face looked gaunt and shadowed.

"It's over," she said bluntly, gulping back tears. "He pretty much kicked me out. I took the baby with me, but he won't let me see the other kids." She took a deep shuddering breath. "Anyway, I'm staying with my dad. I know I'll be okay eventually, but...."Tears were running down her face. "It's so weird thinking I'm not a stepmom anymore. I felt like they were my *kids* and I might never see them again."

The whole table looked on in shocked horrified silence. Hester's face had gone deathly white.

"I just wanted to say goodbye for now," Fran said. "I mean, I'll come back to meetings at some point, but things are too complicated right now. I just wanted to tell you in person that I'll be gone for a while." I hung back, stunned, as the other women took turns talking with Fran and hugging her goodbye.

A dismal fog hung over the table once Fran had left. Nobody knew what to say.

"Now you see why I do what I do?" Hester suddenly said, still looking like a specter. "I know you guys think I deserve better. And of course I do. But *I can't lose my kids.* Do you see that?" Hester looked at the group, her eyes coming to rest on me. She seemed to be considering whether to speak further. Then she looked away and went on.

"You know what my Thanksgiving is going to be like?" Hester said. "I'm going to be trying to have a nice family meal while my husband spends the afternoon with his mistress."

We gasped.

"Yeah, I saw the emails," Hester went on. "He's planning to tell me that he's going over to a buddy's house for part of the day. But that's okay, right? Good riddance. The kids and I will have fun. And honestly I couldn't care less who he fucks. What scares the shit out of me is that he's not even trying to hide it anymore. I'm scared to death he's going to ask for a divorce."

"But Hester—"

"I *can't lose my kids,*" Hester insisted. "I've spent the past three years doing everything I possibly can to endure this marriage. And now he's just taunting me. He knows there's nothing I wouldn't do for them and that he can take them away from me at a moment's notice." She closed her eyes. "He fucking loves it."

"But you could sue for visitation," Kim said. "You've raised these kids almost entirely on your own. They really are partially yours—"

"Of course they are," Hester said. "They are mine more than anyone else's! But I can't take that risk. Visitation? How many stepparents get that? Their mom would try to move them out to Wisconsin to be with her. And Frank would do his best to keep them from me out of spite. Even if I got visitation, that's what—a day or two a month? After raising them for all these years? I can't fathom it. It would kill me. I just...can't take the chance, you guys. I can't."

The heart-heavy silence around the table told me that variations on this no-win situation had been hashed out many times before. And yet it had never occurred to me to think about what happened to divorced or widowed stepmothers, who lost their husbands and perhaps their only children in one devastating swoop. I watched, profoundly shaken, as Leah and Hester embraced.

"Okay, okay, enough of me," said Hester, embarrassed. "It's a holiday weekend coming up, and some of us are bound to have a good time. Let's try to get in the spirit, okay? What's everyone thankful for?" She pointed to June.

"Only having two finals this semester!" June answered dutifully. "Oh, and, you know, friends and family and rainbows and stuff."

Kerry was next in the circle. "God's love, of course," she said. "My parents. Hope?"

"Oh, geez," said Kim. "I hate this question. Um. Tweezers. Lemon meringue pie."

"I'm thankful for my husband," said Maggie. "That he loves me is the miracle of the century. Having a job I love. Seeing less of Twat-waffle."

"Freedom," said Regan. "Vasectomies!"

"Second chances," said Leah thoughtfully. "Love, of course."

It was my turn. "I'm thankful for you guys," I said. "I really mean it." *And my ambivalence about the kids,* I thought as they all said *aww.* For what if I really loved them…only to lose them?

"Happy Thanksgiving, everyone," said Maggie, lifting her empty coffee mug to the group. "May we all have the grace and resilience to survive the toughest time of the year."

"Stepmom *power!*" June shrieked, and as hokey as it sounded, it filled me with warm, bubbly belonging. I raised my mug giddily and clinked.

In the parking lot, I followed shyly after Leah. "Hey—can I ask you something?" I ventured as she began to fumble for her keys.

"Of course," Leah said kindly. "What's up?"

"It's really dumb," I said, suddenly embarrassed. "I was just wondering…is Kim's name really Kim Kim?"

Leah laughed. "Ah, yes. The spreadsheet. No, actually—her last name is Kim, and that's what she goes by. But she won't tell anyone what her real first name is. I don't think anybody but her parents and her husband actually know. *I* certainly don't!"

"Huh," I nodded. "Thanks." I stalled, wanting to ask about a more serious topic but afraid to squander Leah's time and goodwill with my remedial questions. Though Leah would never be the sort to say *let me Google that for you* with techie contempt, I didn't want to be one of *those* people. I stepped back. "Well, see you next month?"

"Wouldn't miss it!" Leah said, hopping into her minivan. And I turned toward my car, reeling with the questions I was too self-conscious to ask.

That evening, though, I did my own search, my heart pattering as I typed *legal rights of stepparents* into the engine.

It didn't take much reading to confirm that everything Hester had said was true. It was the rare stepmother who'd be awarded any visitation in the case of a divorce.

Legal stranger, snotty online lawyers hissed at stepparents as ignorant and bumbling as I was. *They aren't yours. You have no more rights to those children than people off the street.*

How could this *be*? With all the millions of stepfamilies in the world? But with few exceptions the legal system just wasn't set up to dole out rights to more than two parents. So biology triumphed; the nontraditionals got the shaft.

"Hey, Annie?" Will popped his head out of his office.

"In here," I called, quickly flipping back to Facebook and praying that I gave off an unruffled vibe. But Will just asked me something about the water bill and went back to his business.

Guiltily I returned to my search. I could look at porn with less shame than this!

And why? *Why?* Would I have proudly displayed my browser window if the legal system dubbed me something more than a stranger? I didn't know. But there was something especially nasty about these facts and the smug lawyers who delivered them, as if the whole internet were laughing at the delusions of stepparents who thought they might actually matter.

And this, I understood, was why Hester was still married to a man who didn't love her. She had done exactly what the world instructed: she had loved her stepchildren as her own. But in exchange the world gave her nothing, not even the basic right to maintain a relationship with those children if her marriage didn't last.

My lungs felt punctured. I closed the computer and my eyes. How could we matter? Why would we try? Reality was peeling my fingers off the ledge. I felt beaten, ridiculous, in the face of this final, smirking catch-22.

48

"EWWWWW!" JOSIE CRIED upon tasting her first miniscule bite of cabbage ravioli, one long revolted syllable that was well suited for a playground episode involving worms.

My cheeks instantly flamed. Though my mom had conveniently forgotten to make plain spaghetti for the girls, I had also *just* delivered a long-winded lecture about table manners on the way over. "Josie, be polite," I reminded hurriedly. Normally I would have left the reproofs to Will, but I didn't want to appear out of control.

"But I don't *like* it," Josie said, both defiant and mystified. "I don't want to eat it!"

"That's what we're having, JoJo," said Will. "Try a few more bites, then you can have pie."

"Noooo!" Josie said, kicking her feet under the table. "I DON'T LIKE IT!"

And *this* is what came from allowing the girls free range of expression, no matter how uncivil, at the dinner table at home. Josie only devolved in this way once in a while, perhaps when the planets were aligned just so—but it was *so* nice of her to have saved the meltdown for this particular occasion.

"*Okay*," Will hissed. "Eat this then." He slapped another dinner roll on her plate. "And no more of this. You're being extremely rude."

Josie beamed the grin of the triumphant and began gnawing on her roll.

"I'm sorry," Will said uncomfortably to my parents. "She's, uh, picky."

"Ye-es," my mom said, unable to keep the disapproval out of her voice. My father, shoveling and munching, didn't seem to have noticed the disruption.

"Oh, Annie!" Mom said brightly, turning to me. "I forgot to tell you. Guess who's expecting again?"

My stomach dropped. Oh God, not this—not today. I tried to arrange my facial features in an appropriate configuration. "Oh, who?" I felt like an autistic person trying to mimic an emotional reaction.

"Chelsea Agate!" Mom gushed. "Her son is *so* precious, and now a daughter on the way! Her mother has to be the luckiest. I just can't *wait* to be a grandma!"

I cringed. As angry as I was with Josie, it was awful to watch the girl's face furrow in confusion. It had only been a few hours since Will and I had impressed upon the girls that my parents were in fact their newest set of grandparents.

"Mom," I said hastily. "You *are* a grandma, remember?"

"Oh, please, Annie," my mother pshawed, looking straight at Josie. "Their mommy didn't come out of my tummy, now did she?" she simpered.

"Mom," I said through my teeth, "times are changing, you know? Maybe you could read the memo? Family isn't just a matter of biology—"

Mom pouted. "Oh, fine, dear. But I just don't think it's healthy to *pretend*. These girls know as well as I do that you're not their mother."

"I didn't say I was," I snapped, trying hard not to go apeshit. "But I'm their stepmother, and that means we're all family."

"My stepmother raised me, Judy," Will broke in, pissed but controlled. "I consider her a mother and I consider Annie to be a mother to my girls. So, sorry to say, you've got some grandkids on your hands." He smiled thinly, but I could tell how much Will disliked my mother. And I couldn't blame him one iota.

"Well, no *offense*," my mom sniffed, as though she'd been unfairly attacked. "I guess I'm just too *old-fashioned* to understand how people do things these days."

"Mom just wants a *baby* to hold," my sister Stacia broke in. "That's all. Right, Mom?" Oh, Stacia had always been such a suck-up, taking every advantage of her favored position in the family.

"Well, how about you?" I teased my sister. "You're getting up there, you know!" I would never have breathed such words to any woman under normal circumstances. But a kiss-ass like my sister deserved a little rankling. Why was I always the one on the hot seat?

Stacia looked across the table at our parents. "So you haven't told them?" she asked, brimming with excitement as my mom shook her head.

Stacia turned to me. "I'm going to be doing research all next year in Geneva," she beamed. "It's a very prestigious appointment."

"Stacia will give me lots and lots of brilliant little babies someday," Mom cooed, actually pinching Stacia's cheeks. "But for now she has a *higher calling*."

"Congratulations," I tried to smile. "That's really exciting."

"Annie just got promoted to a great new position," Will broke in. "The two departments were actually fighting over her! We're really proud of her."

I looked at my husband, trying not to cry. It was such an exaggeration—but I loved him so much for saying it. I took a deep breath. "Yeah, it's been an interesting—"

And then London's cell phone went off—the song that, through no fault of its own, always made me sick inside. "Hey, Mom!" London shouted into the phone.

"Please ask to be—excused," I said feebly, but London had already shoved back her chair and stepped into the adjoining room. Josie had stood up in her chair, whining "I want to talk to Mommy!" at London's back.

I tried to drown out any smatterings of the phone conversation as Will wrestled Josie back to her seat and plied her with additional dinner rolls. "So—Geneva!" I said to Stacia, somewhat too loudly. "What's the project?"

"Oh, it's *really* important," Stacia said, and began to spew physics at me, the incomprehensible words seeming to fly from her mouth and hover around my head like a great cloud of flies.

"—no, it's some weird *cabbage ravioli*—" London was saying to Gianna. "We're having turkey tomorrow at Dad's house."

Was this really happening? I couldn't even look at my mother. "Dad, how are you?" I called across the table in evident desperation. "How're the model airplanes?"

It was truly an eleventh-hour maneuver, for my father rarely moved beyond grunts—as Will had uncomfortably discovered earlier in the day when he'd tried to engage the older man in conversation. "Fine," said my dad, smearing his bread with stuffing and cranberry sauce and sending the towering morsel home.

"I love you, Mom! I miss you soooooo much!" London was endlessly crooning. Hearing the goodbyes, Josie stood up in her chair and took a giant leap onto the carpet, managing to knock her glass of milk across the table as she ran to grab the phone and take her turn.

"Oh gosh, I'm so sorry," Will said, moving to mop up the mess with Stacia's help.

But I just threw my napkin on the table, my mother's told-you-so smirk boring into me from across the room. I didn't know who deserved the brunt of my wrath. All I knew was that I'd set out to prove we were a real family—and established instead that these girls were as far from mine as they could possibly be.

When we finally stepped from the stifling Delesio home, I gulped the freezing air like ice water. It was over. We were free!

Oh, I was mad at the girls. But I also hated myself for sponsoring this ridiculous sham. *I'll never put them in this position again,* I thought remorsefully. No matter how stinky rotten my stepchildren could be, they were pearly innocents compared to the sucktastic Judy Delesio. I thought of Regan, blissfully basking in the Indonesian sun, and sighed.

We got in the car without speaking, four crisp slams in the chilly night. I opened my mouth to apologize. But then Will said: "Well thank God *that's* over!" And the tension dissolved at once, the girls recounting in giggles everything they'd detested about the evening.

Okay, it hadn't been nice. My mother's comments had been appalling and inexcusable. But all they could talk about was the weird food and the boring conversation, picking on my father's bovine silence and my mother's hideous bedazzled brooch.

"Okay guys, that's enough," I warned, trying not to sound irritated. "I know they aren't the cuddliest grandparents in the world, but you don't have to be mean."

"Oh geez, Annie, come on!" Will laughed. "After *that* night we need to decompress—right, girls?" He grinned at them in the back seat. "I think we may have PTSD!"

Of course London and Josie didn't understand a word of this, but they brayed wildly anyway. I gritted my teeth and clenched the steering wheel, commanding myself not to speak.

And yet I spoke. "Okay, but that doesn't mean that all politeness gets to go out the window. You kids were acting like animals!"

Why was I *doing* this? I suddenly saw myself from afar, walking steadily toward a light socket with a glinting outstretched fork. *Just shut up! You can talk with Will privately!* But it was too late.

"Kids will be kids," Will said defensively. "Mistakes happen. Your mom doesn't seem to get that."

"Well *you* don't seem to get that rudeness isn't some big funny joke, Will," I said angrily. "When there are no expectations or consequences—"

"We can talk about this later," Will cut me off coldly. "Let's not make the night even worse."

With effort I swallowed my rage. No, I shouldn't have spoken like that in front of the kids. But hadn't Will kicked off the inappropriateness by involving his children in his bitching session, refusing to acknowledge let alone punish their rude behavior?

It didn't matter. He was always going to be right. I was always going to be the mean stepmother with the terrible parents. And somehow, through an instantaneous and bewildering turn, it looked to everyone like I was defending my mother—whose guts, at the moment, I actually loathed. What the hell had happened?

We drove the rest of the way in silence. "Let's get to bed early so we're all ready for *real* Thanksgiving tomorrow," Will said cheerily as we walked toward the house, wrapping an arm around each daughter. "Turkey turkey turkey!"

It was clear there would be no punishments. There would be no changes. And if I made even a minimal stink, I would be ruining this effort to salvage a holiday that my own unrealistic hopes had already blighted.

What a mess. But as far as thanks were concerned, I felt them in spades. The horrible day, after all, was over.

December

49

I KICKED OFF my shoes and flung myself gratefully on the living room sofa. Will and the girls wouldn't be home for at least an hour, part of the reason I'd felt justified in slipping away sick from the office. I wasn't faking: the tremulous feeling never seemed to leave my limbs these days. But today was no worse than any other day. I just always felt a little bit bad.

Maybe—

No. I wasn't pregnant. I'd bought a test a few days after my dinner with Summer, but had gotten my period before I could take it. So that had been that: no surprises; no upheavals; no buns in *this* oven.

And yet I had never felt so strange.

It's flu season, said Xena. *You work in an office. Hello? If you want to whiz on a stick so desperately, try one of the millions of free toothpicks we have in the kitchen.*

The voice was right. I was being ridiculous. How *could* I be pregnant? It was only the remotest possibility.

Yet no one else was home. And there was still a fresh pregnancy test just waiting to be used.

I dashed to the bathroom, my pants around my ankles before I crossed the threshold. *Just a precaution,* I told myself. *Just to be sure.* I ripped the test from its plastic enclosure and did my business, washing my hands as my gaze darted anxiously at the blinking hourglass that would calculate my hormones and decide my fate.

Calm down, I told myself. *This is just a formality.*

But I couldn't stop pacing. Two more minutes! I padded around the house, white-knuckled fist clutching the ponderous test. And then, in the driveway, I heard a car door slam.

I was so startled I shrieked and flung the test into the air. Could they all be home already? I could have sworn Will had said five o'clock!

I hunched over and darted to the window to spy. Oh God, they were all there, getting out of the car with backpacks and briefcase. I ducked out of sight, hurled myself on the test, and threw it into the closest safe spot—the kitchen junk drawer—just as the front door banged open and my family barged in.

My heart was pounding as I turned around to face them. But I could tell from the simmering look on Will's face that something was very wrong.

"Start your homework," he said, no-nonsense, and without even greeting me walked straight toward his office.

"But I don't have any," said Josie.

"But I need help," said London.

Will didn't turn. I exchanged a mystified glance with the kids and followed him.

"—how many times have we talked about this?" he was already hissing into the phone as I tiptoed into the room and closed the door behind me. "*I* didn't give any sign-off on this trip. You cannot tell them things are going to happen without talking to me first!" He listened, clenching his jaw. "It's simple courtesy, Gianna! Yeah, well tell that to your *husband*. Tell him to keep his big mouth shut from now on." And he slammed down the phone. "Gahhh!" he steamed, picking up his desk chair and dropping it down again on the plastic mat.

I held out my hands. "What's going on?"

"The same old *bullshit*," Will spat. "I get in the car to pick them up and they're going on about how Mom and Ren are taking them to Australia this summer! And now they're all excited and I can't possibly say no. It's total bullshit. I'm so sick of that asshole blackmailing me and buying off my kids."

My heart skipped a beat. The kids in Australia for one, two, maybe even three *weeks* next summer? All that time without Gianna and nightly phone calls? I wanted to throw my arms around Ren.

But I arranged my expression into a mask of stern commiseration. "I'm sorry, sweetie. That's not right." I motioned to the phone. "Doesn't Gianna agree with you?"

"Who knows," Will growled. "She said it wasn't a big deal and they were just talking about ideas for a vacation. She'll *always* defend him," he finished in disgust.

"Well, that's kind of her job as a wife," I suggested. "I do the same for you."

"Yeah, well *their* relationship is not like ours," Will said huffily. I was just about to ask what he meant when a knock came at the door.

"Daddy, can you help me with something?" It was London.

Will took a deep breath and opened the door. "Sure, hon."

I was just sidling past in the hopes of rescuing my lost pregnancy test when Will called me back. "Annie, I don't remember this stuff. Can you help?"

I sighed. My recollection of fifth-grade history was unlikely to be much meatier than his. But I smiled and agreed and the three of us relocated to the living room couch.

"Here's my assignment," London was saying anxiously. "But I don't understand this question and I can't find it *anywhere* in the book—"

"JoJo, can you keep it down?" Will called out as he scanned London's assignment. The younger girl was lost in her fantasy world, twirling and singing in nonsense syllables. I was so used to it that I'd hardly noticed. The kid could literally keep this up for hours.

"Well I *think* it's saying that you're supposed to go back to earlier chapters," I said to London. Dimly I noticed that Josie had totally ignored her father and was still getting her groove on.

"But we've never had to *do* that before," London said, panicked. "Why would we have to now?"

"Calm down, London," Will soothed. "We'll figure it out."

Josie was now whirling around right in front of us, crouching and leaping and waving a magic wand. "You and you and *you!*" she cried, pointing her instrument at each of us in turn.

"Josie, PLEASE!" Will barked. "You need to *be quiet*. And you need to *listen to me* when I talk to you!"

I looked up from London's book just as Will grabbed Josie's arm. *Oh. Good. GOD*—

"And what on *earth* are you playing with?" he was asking. I let out a helpless preventative moan. But my husband already had the pregnancy test in his hand.

Josie's eyes instantly widened, more at the mystery than her father's rebuke. "What? What is it, Daddy? What? I just found it in the drawer."

Will stared at it for three long seconds, three seconds so quiet and tortured that I wanted to jump up and down and scream just to break the tension. *It's MY test!* I wanted to yell, grabbing it away. *What the hell does it SAY?*

Finally Will looked up at me. "You're *pregnant?*"

I thought I would be sick. "Is that what it says?" I managed to whisper.

Will looked down and let out one tight, bitter chuckle. "Yeah. That's what it says." He looked at me with the coldest eyes I had ever seen.

I could barely speak. "Then I guess I am," I croaked. "Pregnant."

It was as though I'd said *dying*.

And London, sitting between us, started to cry.

50

I HAD FANTASIZED about so many beautiful things once. A man who loved me more than anything. A home that was mine to ornament and change. A young marriage, rich with adventure, that would deepen with wrinkles, children and time.

In the montage of my dream-life I had seen a cupped belly, a proud grinning father. I had seen my soul mate lift me into the air with awestruck joy, our laughter and tears mingling as we welcomed and marveled at the life within me.

I had seen so many beautiful things. But the screen was white now, the film strip flapping as the reel spun uselessly around and around. In all my varied dark days I had never imagined this kind of desertion.

Somewhere, the children had stopped crying. Somewhere, Will was sleeping, or stewing. But I sat alone in my marital bed, both desperately excited and sick with grief, hoping Google could tell me how this terrible, wonderful thing had happened.

Most pregnancies on the pill result from user error, the medical sites all judged me. But I had taken every pill, every time. Could it have been alcohol interference? But I hardly ever drank.

"It could be a false positive," I whispered aloud, my lips and throat cracked from crying. But I knew—had known, really, ever since Summer had conjured the idea out of the air—that I was fixedly, hopelessly pregnant.

And Will didn't want anything to do with me.

Frantically I kept typing. For the test to read positive, I was at least a few weeks along, maybe more. *A pregnant woman may experience spotting and think she is having a period,* the sites all explained.

I tried not to think about the evening's ugly clamor. Will had run after London, flinging back the slammed door to whirl her up into apologetic arms. "I'm so sorry, sweetheart," was all he could say, over and over, each repetition stomping my uterus like a sneering black boot. I had burst into tears; and Josie, bless her heart, had followed suit.

"It's okay, Annie," Josie had said, clutching at me and weeping, trying to play both comforter and child. "It's okay, isn't it?"

But I had been in no place to reassure my stepdaughter of anything. I was pregnant for the first time and all my husband could do was grovel and mourn.

I'd run to the bedroom, sobbing as I grabbed a bag and began to fling clothes inside. *How* could I have chosen this soul-destroying, second-rate life? Maybe my fantasy would never have unfolded the way I wanted—maybe even a different husband would have been ruffled by a baby we hadn't planned. But one thing was certain: a man without children wouldn't have gone running to pet a spoiled princess. A man without children might have put our relationship first.

Josie had hovered gnatlike behind me. "Annie, what are you doing? Are you going somewhere? Annie, why are you packing?" Distantly I heard the wringing in the child's voice. "Annie, are you having a baby? Are you going to have a baby right now?"

"Go see your dad, okay Jo?" I had said. "The baby's fine. Just—I need you to leave me alone right now. Can you do that?"

And Josie had reluctantly gone away and I had locked the door behind me, sliding down against the wall and letting the contents of my bag spill everywhere as I realized there was nowhere at all I could go.

I couldn't stand to see my mother. I couldn't bear the thought of Summer. And was there anyone else, really, to whom I could run in an emergency, someone I knew well enough to disturb out of the blue with a baby in my belly and a sad, sad story to tell?

No. There was no one. How could I face the humiliation of going to my friends, abandoned and pregnant, after a few scant months of marriage? How could I bear to hear "You knew you had kids when you married him"?

I knew the stepmoms would understand. But at the moment they were just names on a spreadsheet and I was far too embarrassed to impose.

And then Will had scared the shit out of me, pounding on the door.

"What the hell gives you the right to make this decision for us?" he'd yelled as soon as I'd let him in. "I *told* you I wasn't ready—"

I'd been so shocked I couldn't speak at first. It took a moment to absorb what he was saying. And then my rage boiled over.

"Fuck *you!*" I'd screamed. "I'm on the pill—you know that! I have no idea how this happened!"

"You're a fucking liar," Will had said. "You wanted a baby so you went out and trapped me—"

"*Trapped* you?" I sputtered. "We're *married!*"

"Yeah, that's what I thought, but marriage is a two-way street and apparently I'm just your sperm donor. So congratulations. You got what you wanted, but don't expect a thing from me. *Nothing*, you got that?"

"Oh, and how's that different from every other day of my life?" I'd spat back.

But he was gone. And all I could think as I'd cried myself sick was that London had also been a surprise—one greeted, even so, with two helpings of wonder and elation and giddy love that my own child would never know. Should I even *have* this baby? Would I be giving birth to a burden, a perpetual least-favorite?

But my entire being had snarled at the thought of casting this baby aside. *Over my dead body,* I'd thought, my very cells seeming to hunker down and cling to the life within. *Not for Will. Not for anyone.* And I'd felt better knowing I could not be pushed past this gouge in the sand.

Angelina had tried to soothe me. *A baby is a blessing! Will's upset, but he'll come around. Just figure out how this happened—and he'll have to believe you.*

So I'd run to my computer with frantic resolve. Of course there was a reason—there *had* to be a reason! I would find it and prove to my husband that I'd done everything he'd asked, everything right.

Yet site after site left me with question marks and maybes, an uneasy feeling that, at bottom, this really shouldn't have happened. Had I taken antibiotics? Not recently. Was it timing? My birth control pills were low-dose, and taking them at different times of day could have done it. But who didn't occasionally forget for a few hours? That couldn't be it.

Two hours and countless keystrokes later, I still didn't know how I'd become pregnant or what I'd done wrong. I slammed down the lid of my laptop, sputtering fresh tears. I remembered with dread the words I'd spoken to Will not that long ago: *Well I'm not waiting that long.* God! I never would have deceived him, but how could I expect him to believe me when I'd made dire pronouncements like that?

Because you're his wife, said Xena. *And he's supposed to trust you.*

But he didn't. And that was abundantly clear.

51

"HUH?" I SUDDENLY came to in the middle of the workday, startled to find Ted snapping his fingers in front my eyes.

"Hey, loony tunes. You okay?"

"What? Yeah!" I smiled with what I hoped was reassuring force. "Just one of those spacey days." *Like every day this week,* I thought. Luckily Ted was in the thick of a major project and hadn't had time to notice.

"Charlotte is wondering about the status of the storyboard," Ted went on hurriedly, and I relaxed into the safeness of the conversation. As long as the subject was work, I could remain an emotional zombie, perky on the outside and dead in the middle.

"Thanks, Annie," Ted said, rising to go. "We should get coffee or something, you know? It's been forever."

"Yeah," I agreed as sincerely as possible. "Definitely."

But in truth I'd deliberately shrunk back from Ted ever since the strange family dinner a month before. It was just too troubling to think that my friend had been a regular guest star on the barfy Tyler sitcom of yore. The things he'd witnessed—taken part in—made me shudder. I just couldn't imagine our relationship ever being the same.

Oh *why* had I taken this job? It was supposed to be fun—working with Ted every day, free from the wretched Brenda. But now I wanted yardsticks between Ted and me. And with a baby on the way, mightn't I need those famous "opportunities for advancement" that Brenda had always dangled?

I closed my eyes, fighting the tears. I was not supposed to think about this at work! *No thinking. No feeling. Only working. Be a zombie. Be a zombie!*

I gulped it all down, forcing myself to respond to neglected emails. I tapped and typed. Yet my mind kept creeping, creeping back to the purgatory at home, the cells busily thickening in my womb.

Much later, I stood zoning out in the kitchen, my sponge circling and circling the same scrubbed plate. The thought of bending over to put it in the dishwasher was unspeakably daunting. I felt like I'd swallowed some kind of exhaustion capsule.

The girls, for some undoubtedly stupid reason, had been released from cleanup duty. But I was far too tired to do the usual pick-and-nag. Better to stand there and swish the plates, trying to absorb that afternoon's shocking news.

I was eight weeks pregnant. *Eight weeks!* I had gawped in disbelief when my doctor had said it. "But I've had two periods," I sputtered.

"No," she'd cut me off. "Vaginal bleeding, maybe, but not periods. Are you concerned about the paternity?"

It had taken me a moment to understand what she was getting at. "No," I'd finally insisted, shocked by the implication. "I'm *married*."

The doctor had shrugged, as if to say, *How should I know? You're here alone, aren't you?*

Touché.

Yet as totally, humiliatingly alone as I'd been, the sound of my baby's heartbeat had sponge-bathed me in thrills.

Even now the goose bumps rose on my flesh as I thought of it. But the tears came too. First baby—maybe only baby—and Will hadn't been there. He wasn't even speaking to me.

Oh, I'd experienced the silent treatment before. But never had Will been as miffed, as sulky, as pointedly avoidant as he'd been this week. He wasn't just rubbing it in my face; he was grinding it into my pores. I'd taken the hint and made the doctor's appointment without even telling him.

"Are you hungry, kitty?" Will startled me then as he walked into the kitchen and opened the cabinet, pulling out food for Mr. Pickles.

"Hey," I said quietly. "Thanks for feeding him." But Will said nothing to me as he pierced the lid, even crooning to Mr. Pickles about his smelly canned-food dinner to make it that much more obvious that he *was not talking* to me.

"Does that taste good, boy?" he said, scratching the cat's ears. I could remember maybe one time he'd even touched my beloved pet in the past four months. I said nothing, hurrying from the room as the nauseating wet smell started to carry me over the edge.

The girls looked up uncomfortably as I rushed by. It was as though the whole family had signed an agreement to spurn reality. No one mentioned the fighting. No one mentioned the baby. And no one, certainly, said a word when I darted to the loo—as I'd done the past three nights—so I could barf up my dinner. Knowing they could hear me, knowing they knew why and yet would say nothing, made an always-disgusting experience into one of the loneliest I had ever known.

At last I flushed the toilet and crawled into bed. I supposed evening sickness was better than the usual time slot, but the conscious shunning left me wracked and humiliated, feeling punished for my very nature like a woman dubbed unclean by the Old Testament.

And then I heard the doorknob turn. *Oh Will,* I begged, the tears already pooling behind my lids as my heart began to race. *Please be with me, Will.* I was afraid to open my eyes.

"I'm sorry you're sick," came a little voice right over me. "Is it because of the baby?"

Josie. It was Josie. I discarded my initial wave of disappointment—*someone* was here. And I needed someone so much.

I opened my eyes. "Yes, JoJo, it's because of the baby," I said, my voice breaking.

"Oh, don't cry, Sugarplum Mommy," Josie said, and at the words I sobbed harder, grabbing my little stepdaughter in my arms and crushing her to my chest. Josie simply lay there, warm and wept upon, until I released her, sniffling with embarrassment.

But Josie only seemed delighted by the affection. "It's all right to cry! Crying gets the sad out of you!" she sang loudly, then kissed my cheek. "I love you, Sugarplum Mommy."

Josie was profligate with her love, but this time it was different. There was magic in these words, and I'd never needed it more. "Oh Jo, I love you too," I said, trying hard not to lose it again.

Maybe everything will be okay, I gulped, giving Josie one last hug. If only my husband could be as loving and mature as his six-year-old daughter, we might have a fighting chance.

52

NORMALLY ON SUNDAY evenings after a week with the kids, I was more than ready for an intermission. Even when the weeks were fun, or uncomplicated—and sometimes they were—everything was just *easier,* so much less tiring, without children. I'd say goodbye to the girls, politely squelching my giddiness; and Will would climb in the car with his daughters, carrying off all the noise and the clutter and the mixed and tortured feelings. I'd stretch out deliriously on the sofa, anticipating each childfree day ahead, and savor the silence until he came back to me.

But this week was different.

Please don't leave me! I wanted to scream at London and Josie. *Stay! For the rest of your lives! You don't REALLY need to see your mom, do you?*

It wasn't, of course, that the kids were spectacular companions. Josie, though always loving, hadn't skimped on her usual rascally behavior—and London had been more aloof than ever all week.

But I didn't mind. Will hadn't spoken to or slept with me in six days—and the kids had been a wonderful buffer, the *best* buffer, their mere presence hiding the dysfunction that could only be exposed now for a full catalog of painful, probing scrutiny.

I wasn't sure I could take it.

"I wish you could stay," I said to the girls, hovering around the doorway pitifully as they swept past with breezy goodbyes. "I'll miss you!" I called after them.

But they were most certainly relieved to be out of there and I knew there was no one to shield me now from my husband's contempt.

I could leave, I thought in a panic. *Go out somewhere and come back later when I'm ready to face him.* I almost ran to the bedroom to get changed.

But then I imagined us in a years-long stalemate, refusing to talk or reconcile as my body stretched, as the baby appeared. *Oh, his father doesn't want to admit he exists,* I imagined myself saying matter-of-factly to my child's kindergarten teacher.

No. Will was being ridiculous. I couldn't let this go on.

So when he arrived back at Anatevka I was sitting there on the living room couch, faintly trembling with nausea and fear. *Do not throw up,* I commanded myself.

He saw me there and his jaw tightened. He tried to walk past me.

"Will," I said, almost a screech. "Please. We need to talk."

He stopped in his tracks, not looking at me. "I'm not ready to talk to you," he said tightly. "I'm too angry." And I saw that his clenched fists were trembling too.

I couldn't stop the tears. "I don't understand," I sobbed. "Why are you being like this? You always told me you wanted more children!"

"Yes, when we were *both ready*!" he screamed at me, finally turning around. He looked at me hatefully. "I don't see how we can continue a marriage after this. I've been trying, but I just can't imagine it."

The tears poured down my face. "I don't understand," was all I could blubber. "It's just one more child. It might be inconvenient, but we can make it work. How can you be mad at an innocent baby?"

"It's not the *baby*, Annie!" he snarled. "Don't you get that? It's that you *lied* to me!"

"But I *didn't*, Will," I hiccupped, grabbing his hands. "I swear to you on everything there is that I didn't get pregnant on purpose."

He just looked at me.

"I *swear,* Will!"

And as I stood there sniffling and gasping and looking my very worst, Will's face finally softened just a fraction with attentive dismay.

"Do you really mean it?" he whispered.

I nodded, face drenched and streaked.

"It really was an accident?" He grabbed my shoulders. "Truly? On your life?"

My head had never bobbed so vigorously. "I swear to God, Will."

"Oh God," he croaked. "Oh, Annie. Jesus Christ." And he took me in his arms.

I nearly swooned with this longed-for closeness.

"The way you had talked before," he mumbled. "I just didn't see how—"

I burrowed into his chest, murmuring nonsense.

"I just was so overwhelmed and blindsided, I didn't know what to do. And I thought—"

"Shhh, it's okay," I murmured, stroking his hair. "It's fine."

You are truly pathetic, Xena said in disgust, and I could hardly deny it. *Do you have no self-respect at all?* But at that moment it didn't matter that he'd put me through emotional solitary for a week, that he'd disbelieved me and loathed me and called me a liar. It didn't matter that he'd sulked like a toddler and put everyone in the family—even the cat—before his wife.

No. What mattered was scrambling to reassemble the scattered pieces of What My Baby Deserved. I would forgive him anything if he would just look at me and love me and love our child.

We parted, and he kissed me, and wiped the tears away. "I'm so sorry, honey," he said softly. "I've been such an ass. Can we start over?"

I weakly nodded, limp with exhaustion. Will took a deep breath and took my hands. "So we're having a baby?" he asked, and his eyes were deep and teasing and full of the glimmer I remembered from a courtship that now seemed ages and ages ago.

The tears burbled over again. I nodded helplessly and collapsed into his arms.

53

"THE KIDS ARE here!" I called to Will as I opened the door. London and Josie spilled into the house with bags and backpacks while Gianna offered greetings, looking at me with a certain piqued interest that she, thankfully, declined to put into words.

I knew that she knew. And she knew that I knew that she knew.

And I hated it. She probably suspected that, too. No one—not even the kids—should know about the baby this early except my husband and me. It was tempting serious fate.

But that's...not how things had happened. And this was life with a little blabbermouth who lived in two houses.

I smiled awkwardly at Gianna and looked away. But it wasn't from insecurity, now, and that made my irritation with her premature knowledge that much easier to bear. I was no longer the junior wife, the fake, the clueless fledgling. I was pregnant; I was going to be petted and honored. I was going to be her equal in *everything*. So what if she knew it?

I couldn't help smiling a smug Angelina smile.

It had been a marvel of a week. Will and I had whispered about everything baby, from names to preschools to grand future dreams. He'd apologized for missing the doctor's appointment, promised to be there for everything else. And though I could bet we both hoped for a boy, neither of us dared to state a preference. We'd decided to call the little one "Oogabooga" until we learned the sex and picked a name.

"I loooove you, Mommy," Josie was crooning, covering every inch of Gianna's face with smacks. Where once I would have fought not to roll my eyes or huff out of the room, now I barely noticed.

As Gianna left and the evening wore on, I couldn't help but gape at how quickly—and how much—my perspective had changed. I accepted the girls in a way I never had before: they weren't just my husband's kids anymore, but the sisters of my child. My relationship with them was no longer contingent upon a marriage license; we were truly family now, no matter what. So I could dare to get close to them: my baby would link us in a way that my own efforts or love never could.

And yet…at the same time, the kids were so much less significant now. I didn't feel like I even *had* to get close to them—they were Gianna's children, after all. They were around, but there seemed to be a haze between us; their hourly annoyances seemed to strike my armor and clatter harmlessly away.

It was lovely. When London ignored my questions, I didn't even care enough to say anything to Will, let alone work myself into a froth. And when Josie tried to squash Mr. Pickles into a doll stroller, I could reprimand her without boiling over. My kitty was still my baby—but—

But it was different now. My baby was on the way.

Isn't it a little soon to become a Momzilla? Xena chided, but she was now a pipsqueak who'd lost all of her Amazonian mastery over me. I *wanted* to be a Momzilla, to recline in the ease and simplicity of obsessing about my own child. I had sure as hell earned the right.

At work I'd even been a tad warmer toward Ted, feeling so much less threatened by the past than I had just a few weeks before. *Good*

God, I thought, *Summer was actually right!* The baby wasn't even born yet and it was solving everything. I sighed happily, counting down the days till I could tell the world—and my public basking and gloating could finally begin.

Still—I was not too twitterpated to realize that we *had* to do something about London.

The girl had become a ghost. Where once there had been the hot-and-cold champion, now there was a shadow stripped of all happiness, rage and gumption. She disappeared into her room, into herself, barely speaking at meals, never joining the family unless compelled. Even her birthday the previous week had passed with little fanfare, just a small slumber party at Gianna's house and a pending dinner out with us.

I was reluctant to offer my usual recommendation to Will. I had suggested therapy so many times, always to be met with an offended *there's nothing wrong with my daughter!* But this was serious. And so I said it one more time.

"Being upset about a new baby is normal," Will brushed me off.

"Yes, but so is seeing a counselor during difficult times," I countered. "It would help her work through her feelings." God knows *I* had contributed a small fortune to the mental health community after I'd finally left home and tried to make sense of my ridiculous parents.

But Will said nothing, and I added, exasperated, "Well, will you at least *talk* to her about it? Try to reassure her?"

"I was going to, okay?" he said a little snappishly. "Tonight."

So I sat in the living room as he shut London's door behind him that evening. Josie was in bed; the house was silent. For a few moments there was muffled conversation. And then London's broken sobs rent the night.

My two hands flew instinctively to my heart and my belly. There was a tearing, rock-bottom quality in London's grief; it blanketed my body in chills.

Could she hate my baby this much?

There is something really wrong here, said Xena and Angelina in unison. And for once, all three of us agreed.

54

"CAN I DRIVE?" I asked Will as we walked out to the car Friday morning. Though evenings remained the worst time for my nausea, the slightest motion sickness could set the ball rolling earlier in the day, and concentrating on the road lessened the effects.

"Of course, my princess," Will said with a gallant bow, opening the car door for me. I grinned at him as I slid into the driver's seat.

I'd thought we'd more or less finished our Christmas shopping the week before, but Will had surprised me by suggesting that we both take an extra day off before the work holiday to take care of any straggling purchases. Now that Brenda was out of my life it was an easy transaction; our department did little of significance after mid-December, and my absence only meant missing a few hours of "work" followed by the annual office party. Since I couldn't drink anyway, I figured it was safer to bow out—Ted certainly would have suspected something if I hadn't indulged in a little champagne.

"So did you think of a lot more things you wanted to buy me?" I teased as I steered us toward the mall.

"Not a lot, just a few really huge diamonds and a Lexus with a big red bow," Will replied, reaching for my hand.

I pressed up against my husband as we walked through the mall, humming along with "Holly Jolly Christmas." It was early, and relatively quiet, though I could tell that serious bustling was about to begin. I didn't mind. There was something cozy and joyful about being a part of the Christmas scene, even if it was just commercialism gussied up with a daub of lovingkindness.

"Oh, let's go down this way," Will said after we'd grabbed some small thank-you items for our neighbor and the kids' teachers. He was leading us back toward the kiddie wing. "I just wanted to pick up a few more things for the girls."

"Are you kidding?" I laughed, really hoping he was. We'd already abused the credit cards more than we'd planned.

"Just a couple more things," Will said. "They both gave me another list."

See, Annie? I heard Xena snort. *He couldn't POSSIBLY call it quits. I mean, they GAVE HIM A LIST. You can't say no to a LIST.*

I let out a little whine. "*Will...*"

"Just a few more things," he said. "Not much, I promise." He looked back at the mayhem already brewing inside the toy store. "Here—why don't you wait for me? Go get a latte or something? It'll just be a minute."

"All right, fine," I conceded. Both the drink and the sitting sounded good.

But I had purchased and finished my latte and he still hadn't emerged from Toy Tower. I endured a few more anxious minutes and then stood up, determined. *Okay, Yes-I-Will, I'm coming in.* I threw away my cup, took a deep breath, and marched into the bedlam.

It was like swimming. I sucked down a breath and dived into the waves, fighting my way through the current. Where *was* that man?

"Will!" I cried, coming up for air. But he was nowhere to be seen, and all around me were whirlpools of wild-eyed women, shopping carts impassable as jutting crags.

I kept fighting, ducking down again into the stream. And finally I spotted him next to someone else's stuffed cart, reaching high on the shelf to pluck down something pink and plastic.

Okay, an extra thing for Josie—

And then he placed the prize in that same stuffed cart...the cart that was *his* and not someone else's after all.

NO. In two seconds I had beaten all world records, leaping the length of the store to appear at his side.

"Will, what's going on?" I asked him nervously, but he didn't even greet me.

"I told you, just picking up a few more things," he said distractedly, scanning the shelves. "Be done in a minute."

"Will!" I sputtered, motioning to the heap of presents in the shopping basket. "This is not just a few more things!"

He didn't say anything. He didn't stop.

"*Will*," I insisted. "You can't buy this stuff. We're already way over budget!"

He looked into his brimming cart and began pawing through the pile. I could feel his agitation. "I know, but I just—"

"Will, come *on!*" I said, touching his shoulder. "We can't afford this. Leave it all! We have to leave it!"

"Annie—" He looked desperately into the cart.

"Come on," I insisted. "We don't need any of this. Let's *go*." I reached out my hand to him as though he were a balky four-year-old.

He hesitated one last moment, then slumped and took my hand. Together, we walked out of the mall.

55

I WAITED UNTIL we were back in the car before I said a word. Happy shoppers laughed and slammed doors all around us while we sat in our seats, angry guppies in a parking lot fishbowl.

"Will, we can't keep going on like this," I said, gripping the steering wheel.

He didn't answer.

"The whole point of having a budget is to stick to it."

Will said nothing. I could feel it as the depleted, guilty husband who had walked out of the mall transformed into the stubborn, self-righteous model that was about to pick a fight.

Still, I was exasperated. I went on.

"We have a baby coming! You *know* how expensive that is! You have *got* to learn to control your spending—"

"Oh, I see," Will finally said, all sarcasm. "We're supposed to spend all our money on *your* baby while *my* kids go without."

I struggled to suck air through my punctured lungs. *It's OUR baby, you dumb-ass,* I inwardly screamed, even as I tried to reassure myself he didn't mean it.

"It's especially important that the girls have a good Christmas this year," Will went on reprovingly. "We have to show them that they're not less important because there's a baby coming."

"And we do that by going bankrupt?" I sputtered, dashing away my tears. "I agree they need some more reassurance, but not more gifts—"

"Oh, please, Annie," Will scoffed. "That's how kids think. In gifts! How do you think they're going to feel Christmas morning when they open all our stuff in a few minutes and then go over to Gianna's house where they'll get a scooter or a pony or a fucking zebra? Don't you get it? Where do you think they're going to want to live when they realize that we've got this small house, no money, and they're going to have to share a room with a screaming baby?"

So that was it. Forever after, every decision we made was going to be held up against the potential reactions of London and Josie, the two great emperors on the platform deciding the fate of every life choice. And Will would never allow himself to be happy about anything they didn't like.

We'll be prisoners forever, I thought miserably.

"Some kids are actually excited to have a new brother or sister," I snapped. "And I don't believe the girls think about nothing but money. They will want to be with you because you're their father and they love you. They couldn't care less about gifts or the size of our house."

"That may have been true once," Will whined, "but not anymore. Not since Ren worked his magic—"

I blew up. "Is this all about Ren? Is *everything* about Ren? I swear to God, Will, I used to think Gianna was this intrusive force in our marriage, but it's not her—it's Ren. But it's not even him! It's *you!* Ren has never been anything but perfectly nice to me and you and the kids!"

I looked over at his fuming face and felt the ugliness take me over. "You need to get over your jealousy, Will," I said in disgust. "Because it's *just fucking pathetic.*"

And with that I started the engine and drove home.

Later he came crawling, predictable and contrite.

"Annie, can we talk?"

I was about to say no. I really wanted to say no. I was furious with myself for becoming entangled in this telenovela, this joke of a life that ensured that my desires and needs would never be priorities unless they happened to coincide with a small child's. *Told you so,* taunted Xena. *Told you so!*

But when I saw my husband's red-rimmed eyes I felt my guts lurch. "What's wrong?"

Will swallowed thickly. "This is hard for me to talk about, so bear with me." He sat down on the couch, trying to gather himself. He was rigid as a golem.

I swept down beside him instantly, my heart pounding. He was about to open a secret door, wasn't he? I could hear the squeaking hinge.

Finally he spoke. "I know you think Ren's really nice. But there's a reason I don't like him."

"Okay," I said, trying to appear supportively encouraging rather than ravenous with curiosity.

"I should have told you before, but I've never told anyone," he went on. "Oh, God. Annie, this is the worst thing in the world. I don't even know how to say this." He angrily brushed away his tears.

And then he started to weep.

I sat for a moment in total bafflement. I had never seen this, never seen anything remotely like this, from this man I thought I knew.

"Honey, honey," I murmured, pulling him into my arms. "What is it? Nothing's too bad to tell me."

But he didn't speak.

"Please, Will. Please tell me whatever it is."

Finally he pulled back from me and took a shuddering breath. In a whisper he said: "I don't think Josie is my child."

There.

It was said. This thing that had always been there, this jagged quill sticking through the fabric of our marriage that had snagged us both so many times.

But I was dumbfounded. He had never even suggested that Gianna had cheated on him. "I don't understand," I stammered, trying to make the slightest sense of it. "How could that..."

"I don't know for sure," he said. "She's never said for sure. I never caught them. But I think, yes, I think they were—together. And I think that, yes, I think that Josie is Ren's"—he could barely say the word—"daughter." He started to cry again. "My little girl is that man's daughter."

"Oh, Will," I murmured. My throat was wordless.

"You can see it in her face," Will went on. "Her freckles. She doesn't look like me. And now this dyslexia? Like Ren has?" His tears had stopped, but his voice grew ever more hysterical. "Annie, what if he tries to take her away from me?"

"Shh, we'll never let that happen," I soothed. "She's your daughter no matter what the DNA says."

"I just can't stand it," he choked out. "I can't stand him."

"I know, honey," I said, stroking his hair. "I understand now. I'm so sorry, Will. I'm so sorry."

And I sat there stunned and chastened by Will's terrible secret.

56

IN THE NEXT days I realigned myself entirely with Will, hardening my heart against any outside influence. *Why* had I had so little faith in his judgment? I'd been so taken in by Ren's affable manner and superlative stepfathering that I'd secretly sided with him against my own husband! True, I hadn't known anything about Gianna's extramarital antics. But I should have never let my loyalties splatter in so many different directions. *Will* was my partner for life; he alone deserved my undying trust.

I was going to make it up to him. Through home-cooked meals and impromptu blowjobs, my husband was going to know I was forever on his side.

That weekend I hummed around the house, coddling and tousling my tender spouse. Terrible as the revelation had been, I couldn't help but see it as a positive for me: Will's confession would only bring us closer, further cementing the bond that would support and shelter our new baby. *This* child was definitely his—and some nasty little part of me even dared to hope that its unquestioned paternity would rocket it into the rank of Favorite.

Please let it look like Will! I prayed. A boy with our dark hair, Will's beautiful blue eyes. Wouldn't that be the next step in Will's healing?

I couldn't help fixating on Josie. *Did* she look like Ren? I scrutinized her every feature. "Annie, you know, it's not polite to stare," she finally informed me, and I ripped my eyes from her face, blushing crimson.

"Sorry, JoJo," I said. "You're right."

I was embarrassed to be caught. But more than that I was filled with hope and joy and such palpable relief. Will, I knew now, hated Ren because he feared losing Josie—*not* because he still loved Gianna! His feelings and fears were totally reasonable, and they cast no doubts on his love for me.

He loves me! He really loves me! I wanted to shriek. I hadn't realized how profoundly I'd doubted it.

I sighed happily, watching Will adjust the twinkling lights on our freshly severed Douglas fir. I went to put my favorite Christmas music on the stereo, loving the symbolism of decorating our literal family tree just as I prepared to add to our proverbial one.

"Okay, here's everything!" Will called out, wiggling a cardboard box through the front door. The girls squealed and descended on their father, wrestling the box to the ground and pulling back the flaps to paw in delight through their ornaments.

I peeked over their shoulders at the unfamiliar collection. I'd had a box of my own ornaments somewhere, but clearly it hadn't made it into the Christmas storage. Well, that wasn't so hard to fix. As the girls started removing the rainbow of decorations from the box, I marched into Will's office, sure I could easily track down my own stuff—

Oh, God. Were these boxes multiplying? I couldn't believe how many of my possessions were still in storage! *Screw it,* I decided grumpily, not relishing an avalanche. By next year, though, I *wanted my stuff in my house.* Was it really that much to ask?

Don't let it ruin the moment, Angelina cautioned. *First Christmas!*

I won't even mention it, I decided as I walked back into the family room, selecting a glittery silver star from the box and finding a suitable perch. "This one's pretty—"

I turned back only to see three shocked faces staring at me. Then Josie started to wail.

"You can't, you can't, you *can't!*" she screamed, now down on the floor and thrashing as I stood there in total stunned silence.

"*Nooooo! Noooooooo!*" Will and London were huddling around Josie, trying to get near while protecting themselves from her flailing feet and fists.

"She didn't *mean* it, Jo," London was saying, and I was even more shocked to grasp that she was defending me. "She didn't *know*."

"I didn't know," I echoed desperately. "Whatever it is, I didn't know. JoJo? I'm sorry?"

But it was several minutes before Josie could be convinced to sit upright and stop spraying.

"Josie puts the first ornament on the tree," Will finally explained. "After everything has been taken out of the box."

Oh, boy. The box had only been half-excavated. *Two* faux pas for the Sugarplum Mommy.

I knelt next to the six-year-old. "I'm really sorry, Jo," I said. "I didn't know that you had such an important job. I'll take this one off the tree and you can put a new one up, okay?"

Josie considered this solution carefully and nodded sulkily, giving her foot an idle kick toward me on the off-chance of making contact.

"Hugs and kisses," Will instructed, and Josie obligingly smeared her snotty face all over my shirt. Well, my pending Oogabooga would undoubtedly deliver far worse. I plucked the offending ornament off the tree and put it back in the box, clearing the way for the Tylers' precious family traditions.

"Anything else I should know about?" I asked Will discreetly as I stepped away, but he'd disappeared.

And then my favorite Muppets holiday album stopped mid-note and crooning Christmas Elvis floated through the stereo.

"Oh yay, finally!" said London, and Josie started to clap and sing along as Will emerged from the hallway doing the worst Elvis impression I had ever seen.

And just like that, their holiday spirit had grown three sizes and mine was just a Grinch's shriveled heart.

It didn't matter. It shouldn't matter. These were just details. Christmas was for children!

But here I was, still, suffocating on the sidelines. It was always going to be their life, wasn't it—their home, their traditions, me faking delight and tiptoeing around in the background so as not to offend? If I'd thought that being pregnant would make way for my own volition in this family, I'd been an idiot. My offspring would just be another warm body to be assimilated by the Borg.

57

AFTER THE KIDS had grown bored of decorating and Will had topped the tree with a tacky tinseled star, I played John Denver and the Muppets on my iPod and moved around the branches, finishing and perfecting. I'd tried to explain to Josie the principle of heavy-ornaments-for-heavy-branches, but no dice. She'd put everything, it seemed, in the same square foot of greenery—and most of it was now on the floor, being batted around by Mr. Pickles. I left him a few favorites and added the rest to the lopsided tree.

Will was outside hanging lights while Josie supervised; London, I supposed, was holing up ghoulishly in her room. Decorating the tree *had* seemed to revive her, for a time, but soon enough she'd withdrawn again, closing her door.

It was fine with me. Here with my headphones, busy redoing all the shoddy work, it was finally starting to feel like Christmas.

Oh, it was sad. I remembered my gnashing angst just a year ago as I sat beside my lonely little tree, telling myself it would all be better once I married Will and became part of the family.

Little had I known it would still be Mr. Pickles and me, forevermore. I could have saved myself the trouble and stayed where I was.

You wouldn't be so unhappy if you weren't such a control freak, Angelina scolded me. *What do you care about what music is on the stereo or how many ornaments you get to hang? Stop acting like a child!*

But I knew it was the principle—the principle that, even after four months of marriage, I still didn't belong.

I wanted to tell Angelina to stick it. But both she and Xena were too powerful to vanquish now. I'd just been starting to get them under control, to hear my own clear voice in there somewhere, when pregnancy had unearthed a whole new set of doubts. Both my daemons were always there now, larger than life as they trumpeted my shortcomings day and night.

But my brain's primal scream drowned out their words as I saw the photo ornament nestling in the back of the tree.

Will, Gianna, London, Josie. In a photograph. On *my* tree, in *my* home.

I wanted a machine gun. I wanted a crucifix. I wanted to fling holy water on the thing, to hear it sizzle and burn.

Trembling with rage, I ripped the disgusting thing off the tree, took it into the kitchen, and smashed it with a meat tenderizer. Shards of red plastic flew everywhere as I demolished the ornament thoroughly. Then I took out the scissors and cut the photo into tiny bits, taking extra special care with Gianna's face.

Finally I slumped over on the counter, relief bringing tears to my eyes. It was gone, I told myself. It was gone. But how had Will allowed this *thing* to stay in his house, to adorn his Christmas tree long after the divorce? What the hell was wrong with him?

"Annie?" came a voice behind me.

I jumped and saw London looking at me, taking in the mess. She must have known what it was.

I couldn't bring myself to care what she saw, what she knew. I had no doubt that she—after defending me to Josie!—had put this ornament on the tree herself. Was it cruelty, stubbornness, cluelessness? At the moment I just didn't give a shit.

"You okay?" she asked timidly.

"I am now," I said tightly, and pulled out the dustpan to start sweeping up the mess. When I looked again, she had gone away.

I sat down at the kitchen table, teeth chattering. My banished doubts about Will were returning in full force. *No,* I commanded myself. *It's not what it looks like. He probably didn't even know the ornament was still in the box.*

Xena gazed lazily at me as she polished her sword. *Oh, really? If you believe that, I have some land I'd like to sell you.*

"If he did know, it was just for the kids," I insisted out loud. "That's all." And decisively I got up from the table as if I really believed it.

58

THE FIRST THING I saw when I entered the Lazy O was June's beaming face. Seated at the head of the table, she was holding a ukulele and grinning like a sprite.

"Happy holidays, Annie!" she said, punctuating her greeting with a little strum.

"You too," I laughed, motioning to the instrument. "Is today's meeting a musical or something?"

"Ah, that would be cool!" she sparkled. "But I think Regan would probably implode on the spot. So no. I just wrote a little holiday song for everyone."

"Seriously? I can't wait to hear it," I said, picking a chair just as the rest of the stepmoms came dragging in. After ten minutes of chatter, June got our attention with another vigorous strum.

"Let's call this meeting to order!" Kerry said. "Maggie's out of town, but I think everyone else is accounted for. And Junie has a very special treat for us today." She turned the floor over to our youngest member.

"Okay, you guys *have* to be nice to me because I'm still learning this thing," she said imperiously, jiggling the instrument. Once satisfied that our promises were at least semi-sincere, she gave a devilish grin. "Okay, here goes. I call this 'Stepmom Christmas.'"

> It's holiday time and it's s'posed to be fun
> But nobody warns you your joy is all done
> You can't see your family; they live far away
> And custody says you must split up the day.

'Cause it's a stepmom Christmas
A gastrointestinal twist-mas
And if you survive
I'll give you a high-five
'Cause I know you're on Santa's good list-mas.

The children are running all over the mall
They're screaming and whining to get a good haul
Your husband just smiles as they claw at the loot
And whispers, all teary, "Oh, isn't that cute?"

'Cause it's a stepmom Christmas
A genuine slit-your-wrist-mas
And if you survive
I'll give you a high-five
'Cause I know you're on Santa's good list-mas.

They tell you you're mean and they tell you you're fat
They tell you, "My mommy cooks better than that."
You know that they think you'd be better off dead
So their mom and dad could be married instead...

'Cause it's a stepmom Christmas
One great gargantuan diss-mas
And if you survive
Even manage to thrive
And still have a sex drive
I'll give you a high-five
'Cause I know you're on Santa's good list-mas!

We all applauded wildly as June stood up to bow.

"You should totally sell that on iTunes!" Kerry exclaimed. "Chip away at those college loans." [1]

June looked both intrigued and embarrassed by the suggestion. "Well, maybe," she said. "If I can find some recording equipment. Anyway, enough about that. How was everyone's Thanksgiving?"

"Well, my *tan* is fading..." Regan began sorrowfully, then laughed evilly as we all glowered at her. "Indonesia was incredible. But you'll be happy to know that I'll be tortured along with the rest of you on Christmas, because Blane's parents are coming out." She shuddered.

"That's it?" June waved her off. "*That's* your torture? Please."

"You haven't met these people, June," Regan insisted. "They are absolutely *horrible*. Boring. Ugly. No sense of humor. And the worst of all?" Her voice fell to a whisper. "*Teetotalers.*"

Was she serious? Hard to tell, but everyone was rolling their eyes and smiling.

June went on. "Okay, I'll go. The good news is that Samantha didn't show up at my dad's house on Thanksgiving. But she did manage to ruin the day by calling and texting every ten minutes. Finally for some stupid reason Ryan let her talk to Annabel on the phone, and she totally worked the kid into hysterics by telling her how much she missed her and how *lonely* mommy was. We had to leave early because Annabel was sobbing and wouldn't calm down."

"She's so disgusting," Kim said.

Then June looked up, a pained expression on her face. "But here's the weirdest thing. In some ways it was easier to deal with Samantha

---

1 And she did! "Stepmom Christmas" is now on iTunes and other nifty music sites.

than my own stepmom. Because with Samantha it's all straightforward. She's wrong, she's psycho, everyone knows it. But with Sherry it's so much more complicated. I feel like—I feel like I'm almost *scared* to see her, you know? Because on the one hand, I think about some of the things I thought and said to her when I was younger, and I am so ashamed and sorry. But on the other hand I still feel these waves of visceral dislike. I get irritated when I see her and my dad being affectionate. I walk in there and I feel like it's *my* house more than hers, that my dad is somehow more mine too. I mean, can you believe it? It's, like, *gross* that I would even think to think that stuff. But it's *there*. It's like it's part of my DNA, to hate this woman because she isn't my mom. What the hell *is* this? It makes me feel like a crazy person."

"Well, it probably *is* part of our DNA," Kim shrugged. "But lots of stuff is. That's why we have minds and shit."

"I know, but it seems like my mind is no match for this," June said. "That's what freaks me out so much. I don't want to be unfair, I don't want to be that awful stepdaughter that some of you have to deal with. I just feel *so* guilty—that I'm wronging her, but mostly that I'm wronging you guys. That I'm wronging our whole, like, stepmom pride movement or something."

"We have a stepmom pride movement?!" Kim shrieked. "God I've been doing it all wrong. I don't even know the secret handshake."

"Yes, you do," Regan grinned. "The secret to every stepmom's success is 'shaking hands' with her favorite wine glass."

June laughed. "There's that. But you know what I mean, though? Being a stepmom is part of my identity, because of you guys, because we all get a bad rap. Yet in my own family, I don't try to change the dynamic. I'm just another self-absorbed, stereotypical brat of a stepdaughter."

"You're hardly self-absorbed *or* a brat *or* a stereotype," Leah said. "Not all stepmoms are great people. Even *we* know that."

"But I think what she's saying is that it's hard for her to piece out what is a genuine personality conflict and what is just the stepdaughter grudge," Kerry said. "I've been there too. And it's really unsettling."

Regan spoke next. "Well, I see how that would be hard, but I don't think you need to feel bad on our behalf. I mean, seriously—besides Leah, who here is *proud* to be a stepmom? Anyone?" Almost everyone looked sheepish, but nobody answered. "Exactly," Regan went on. "It's a liability. The stepmom thing brought us all together, and I'm grateful for that, but it doesn't mean we need a pride movement. What are we proud of? Being stupid enough to get involved with a man with kids? Not something that's going to get *me* marching in a parade, I'll tell you that."

"But even if you don't like being a stepmom, that doesn't mean you can't be proud of what you've done, how you've handled really difficult stuff," June said. "That's what I mean. I'm proud of us as individuals, as a whole group of people who try really, really hard. We rock! We should be proud of that."

"Yeah, it's amazing how much shame I still feel," Hester spoke up quietly. "I raise these kids who aren't mine, I protect them from their mean dad, I can genuinely say I love them as my own. I should be so proud, right? Yet it can ruin my whole day when someone 'exposes' me as a stepmom. And it's not just because people will think less of me. It's because *I* think less of me, somehow, every time I'm reminded of that label."

Others were speaking up to corroborate, but I was too emotional to say a word. It was exactly what I felt.

"How was Thanksgiving, Hester?" Kim asked gently. She knew we were all waiting to hear how things had gone with her philandering husband.

"It was actually great," Hester sighed. "Frank went to his girlfriend's house, I pretended not to know, and I had a really fun time with my kids. But I'm freaking out about Hanukkah tonight. It's supposed to be just the four of us, and honestly? It's almost too intimate. I don't even really know how to act around Frank anymore." She looked troubled.

"Well, this is going to be too little, too late, but you can always come to our Hanukkah party on Tuesday night," Regan said. "It's a work thing, mostly, but you're all invited too. It's not at all traditional—you know me and holidays—but everyone has fun. Lots of kids, too, alas." She sighed. "It's the one time of year I try not to be a total bitch."

"Thanks, Regan," Hester said. "Maybe it will help me shake off the ick after tonight."

Then Kim turned to me expectantly. "Rhiannon! You *have* to tell everyone your Thanksgiving story!" Shortly after the Day of Dread, I'd chatted online with Kim and Maggie, pouring out the whole thing. "It's a tragic tale of ill-mannered children, obnoxious parents, and the mysterious yet terrifying cabbage ravioli," Kim went on dramatically, hands flat on the table for emphasis.

With an introduction like that, I could only launch into the whole sorrowful tale.

"Wow. If *that* isn't an argument for disengaging, I don't know what is," Kerry said when I'd finished.

"Well, I'm definitely not doing that kind of holiday again," I vowed. "I was obviously trying way too hard and all it did was bite me in the ass. And I guess I've kind of given up on the chores and stuff." I sighed. "But it's not that I don't care anymore. I'm just so *tired*."

And, completely unexpectedly, I started to cry.

"I'm sorry, you guys," I blubbered. "Things have been awful." I wanted so much to tell them about my surprise pregnancy and Will's confession, but I just couldn't speak the words. Will's warning presence, somehow, held my tongue. "For a moment I thought things were really going to be different, but now I see that nothing ever will. I am the bottom of the totem pole and I always will be. No matter what."

"Do you want me to rough him up for you?" Regan asked me. "Seriously. There's a reason my parents named me after the kid in *The Exorcist*."

I just gawked at her through my tears.

"It's true!" she said. "Pronounced differently, but they really did."

"Well, thank you," I finally managed, "but I don't think I'm ready to resort to physical violence or, uh, demonic possession?"

"Is there anything we can do?" Kerry asked gently.

"I don't know," I said. "Just tell me...tell me that as bad as it seems, it's going to be okay. That I'm still going to be loved in this life. That it's going to be good enough." I gulped. "When I fell in love with Will I just didn't understand how much I was going to give up. Every time something happened, I just made excuses. I kept telling myself that it was how real life was, that I was living in a fantasy world if I expected anything different. But now I'm obsessed with everything I gave up. I can't think about anything else."

All their heads were nodding sympathetically. "No one ever dreams of being a stepmother," Kerry said. "At some point we all have to come to terms with the fact that we're never *really* going to have the life we envisioned when we were little."

"And we want to believe it's not different, and that we're not giving anything up," said Kim. "But it is, and we are. And it's hard."

"God, I feel like such a bitch for feeling this way," I said. "Such a whiner. I mean, I know that life isn't a fairy tale, but I guess I still want one. Didn't I know that he had kids? Couldn't I have thought it through?"

They were all so kind. "It always helps to go in with your eyes open, but you can't predict how you're going to feel as time goes on," Leah said. "This life is just so complicated. Don't be hard on yourself. Just try to focus on getting what you need from Will. The stronger your marriage is, and the more you get what you need, the less you will focus on what you don't have, what you didn't get—all the unfairness."

I nodded. Her words rang true. But how could I get more love from Will when he simply didn't have it to give?

59

THE MORE I spent time with the stepmoms, the harder it was to make plans with Summer. Instead of support I'd get tongue-lashings; instead of humor I'd get the droning lecture.

But it was Christmas. And she'd been my friend for so long.

"Oh, Annie, I can't tell you how glad I am that you're here," Summer said as we hurriedly pushed Riley's stroller away from her house. "Kevin's mom is driving me absolutely batshit, and they've only been here one day! She's *obsessed* with Riley and doesn't seem to realize that *I'm the mother.*"

Was it possible that anyone in the solar system didn't realize that Summer was the mother?

"I've practically had to arm-wrestle her just to hold my own baby," she huffed. "She's such a bitch." But then she brightened. "So this couldn't have been more perfect!"

"Oh, sure," I said, working hard to find the compliment in that. "Well, I wanted to see both of you before the craziness ensues." It was a lovely afternoon, crisp and clear, and I was glad to see as we walked down Summer's street that we hadn't been the only family hanging lights at the last minute.

Summer gasped. "Oh! I almost forgot! We are doing the most amazing thing on Christmas morning," she said excitedly, then paused for effect. "Kevin is building this incredible winterscape for Riley."

I blinked at her. "A winter-what?"

"A *winterscape*," Summer repeated. "We saw it on HGTV. It's like this fantasy North Pole scene with a little igloo and fake penguins and stuff."

"I'm pretty sure penguins only live in the South Pole," I told her.

"Who cares? It's sooo cute, Annie. You just *have* to come over and see it on Christmas. Riley is just going to *love* it!"

Riley was four months old. The pinnacle of Riley's world was her mom's ginormous nipple. But there was no point in explaining this to Summer.

"That sounds really cool," I said. "I'm not sure what we're going to do on Christmas yet. This year we have Christmas Eve and a few hours Christmas morning." I paused to grumble about the short-sighted stupidities of a custody order that split Christmas into halves. "But I'll just get burned if I plan anything," I said bitterly. "I'm sure they all have a bunch of *really great* traditions that I don't know about."

"You can't go messing with a kid's Christmas morning, Annie," Summer said sternly, as though that were anywhere near what I was suggesting.

"Well, I'm not going to," I bristled. "But you wouldn't be mad if Kevin got this winterscape idea from an ex-girlfriend and didn't want to do anything that you liked on Christmas?"

Summer thought for a moment. "Maybe I would be," she said, and I almost fell over. "But if there were kids involved...I mean, Annie, it's not *about* you anymore, you know?"

I didn't know why I bothered. At the slightest sign of my disgruntlement, Summer always put on her preachy-face, addressing me as some sort of selfish mutineer. Of course they weren't my kids—of course they didn't *really* count, would never *really* love me—but that certainly didn't mean I didn't owe them a mother's every sacrifice.

"But shouldn't there be some compromise?" I persisted stupidly. "Am I not a member of the family?"

"Yes, but you're not the most important one," she said without hesitation.

I stopped walking. "Really? Do you feel that way about Kevin?" I cried at her back. I was sure she was going to backpedal, to make excuses.

But she just stopped and turned to look at me. "Annie, don't ever tell any man I said this, but I'm telling you as a woman to woman," she said. "There is *nothing* like the love you have for your child. I love Kevin, but there is no contest. He's not even in the same league."

I felt like a force field had slammed me back several paces. I just stood there, eyes welling for Kevin and myself and all the other lonely souls who'd come up against a child and lost.

"The reason it works is because we both feel that way about Riley," Summer went on. "We're committed to each other because we're committed to *her*. Our love has produced this other person that we love a million times more. And that's how it should be."

And that's why your family can't work, she didn't need to say, but I knew that's what she meant. And wasn't she speaking the truest truth of so many mothers, a truth so unkind yet accepted that it never needed to be broached? You love your husband until he gives you a child, and then you love your child more.

I don't want that, I realized, even as I thought of little Oogabooga, the baby that Summer didn't know was there. I didn't want my baby to replace Will; I didn't want to stay with my husband through some shadowy past-life love just so we could raise a child together. I wasn't even sure we'd *had* a love strong enough to sustain that. I'd certainly never been his number one.

"I'm pregnant, Summer," I mumbled, even as the tears ran down my face. *And I'm afraid Will won't really love the baby. I'm afraid he doesn't really love me.*

But I couldn't say those last sentences out loud. Even if I had, Summer wouldn't have heard them, because she was squealing so loudly into my ear that Riley woke up and started to cry.

Summer rushed to gather her daughter up into her arms, staring at me with total elation. "Oh Annie, Annie, Annie! I am *so excited!*" She looked down at Riley. "You're going to have a cousin, honeybunny, that's right, a best friend for life!" Then she gasped and looked back at me. "Maybe you'll have a boy and he'll grow up and marry Riley!"

I wanted a boy, but holy crap, it was hard to imagine too many scarier scenarios. Still, I couldn't help laughing. "Oh, Summer, you are too much. But let's not get ahead of ourselves. I'm not quite three months." I gave a superstitious grimace.

"Right," she nodded, instantly sober, but her euphoria was showing through the cracks. She wrapped her arm around me, pressing Riley and me into an awkward group hug. The baby scent made me swoon. "I'm still so happy for you, Annie. This is the beginning of the rest of your life, and everything's going to be great now. Just wait— you'll see!"

And as uneasy as her sentiments made me, I clung to them like a limpet. I had no other hope.

60

I CRACKED OPEN an eyelid at 6:52 am, hearing the scuffling and giggles out in the living room. The creatures, it seemed, were out of their cages.

Will was still conked out, snoring softly, and as I hunted for my earplugs I was grateful that, for all the Tylers' totally arbitrary yet ironclad holiday traditions, they had *one* that made good sense: the kids got up in the morning, opened their stockings, and settled down to watch their favorite bland Christmas movie while we slept in.

Nice work, sweet, I thought as I snuggled into Will's arms, trying not to dwell on the reason that he and Gianna might have wanted to keep the kids out of their bed on Christmas morning.

An hour and a half later we stumbled, yawning, out into the daylight, groping for coffee while the girls sat chanting all the lines of *Prancer.* Will went whistling to fry eggs as I parked myself on the couch and let the warmth of the decaf slowly rouse me to life.

Carefully, I watched London. She seemed like a totally normal kid this morning, relaxed and happy, even wheezing with laughter as she watched her sister acting out the best scenes.

And yet last night I had found her huddled near the Christmas tree long after bedtime, barefoot and somber and odd.

"London? Are you okay?" I'd asked, completely startled, and she'd looked at me as though she didn't even recognize me, with that haunted look that seemed to be swallowing her alive.

"I'm sorry," she'd blurted out suddenly, flinging herself against me in a hug so wretched and brief that I hadn't even had a chance to respond before she was slipping back to her room.

"It's fine," I'd called after her confusedly. "Just get to bed."

And I hadn't said anything to Will. Somehow it was personal, this apology, and I desperately wanted to believe that London had been referring to more than a little after-hours tree-gazing when she'd said the words.

"Breakfast is up!" Will called from the kitchen as the credits rolled, and we managed to corral the children into a five-minute cramfest before heading over to the tree to dole out the goodies. Will and I settled on the couch while London donned the Santa hat. Josie flexed her fingers in anticipation, salivating like a bulldog.

Ten minutes later, the doorbell rang. The kids didn't even look up, allowing Will and me to exchange a peeved glance. Gianna was a full hour early, and we were all still in our pajamas.

Will hauled himself up from the couch and stalked to the door. I held my breath in anticipation of a beautiful reprimand. *Merry Christmas to me!*

But Will seemed entirely flummoxed as he opened the door. "... Oh!" was all he managed.

"Will?" I came up behind him to look. And there, on the porch, a full *two* hours early, were my parents.

"Merry Christmas!" my mom called cheerily, decked out in the type of bedazzled reindeer sweater that librarians and the elderly seem to find so irresistible. Past our paralyzed bodies she pushed her way inside, turning back to hurry my father, who was following in baby steps, arms laden with bags and containers of food.

"Mom, you're two hours early," I reminded her as I rescued the tottering trays from my dad's palsied arms. "We're still in the middle of things here." London and Josie were staring at us with the perplexed woe of the African kids in the child sponsorship commercials.

"Oh, don't mind us," she waved me away. "You know how early your father gets up."

"Okay," I said helplessly, turning my panicked eyes to Will. "What should I do?" I mouthed. If only we had a den I could park them in!

Will came to the rescue. "This looks great, Judy," he said warmly, leading my mom into the kitchen. "Why don't you go ahead and use the kitchen while we finish up presents and get dressed? Feel free to help yourself to anything you need."

This was the perfect answer. My mom, the steadfast snoop, would delight in poking through our cabinets and sniffing around our business, all in the guise of concocting the perfect Christmas meal. I squeezed Will's hand in thanks and relief as we headed back to the girls and their gifts.

"Who's next?" Will said cheerfully, as though Josie possessed even a semblance of the self-control required to sit politely while another family member opened a gift.

"Me!" she shouted, lolling in a sea of presents and wrapping paper with all the temperance of an eighteenth-century French aristocrat.

"I told you, you opened them all," London said irritably. "That's what happens when you rush through."

"Noooo!" Josie screamed, running her hands through the discarded paper in a frenzied search for misplaced spoils. "I WANT MORE PRESENTS!"

Will and I turned to each other in the same instant. But while my eyes held a disgusted *do something,* his housed a superior *I told you so.* To my horror, he went to comfort his daughter.

"What is going on out here?" my mom suddenly asked, stepping into the living room with both hands encased in oven mitts.

"Just go cook, Mom!" I snapped. She retreated, muttering, as Will gathered Josie into his arms.

"I think it's London's turn," I said loudly, focusing on the eleven-year-old. "How about that green one?"

London smiled at me gratefully, gathering up the package as Will cooed to Josie, rocking her on his lap. "Let's watch your sister, okay baby?" Barf, barf.

"Oooh, this is so nice!" London gasped with seemingly genuine appreciation at the soft blue sweater I had picked out. As she held it up to her body, I felt a swell of pride that the cornflower blue accented her hair and eyes just as I'd imagined.

"It looks great on you!" I said warmly, and she looked at me with such a happy smile that I felt a stab thinking how rarely I'd seen that glowing face in the past month.

"I waaant one," Josie was keening, seeming to have mistaken Christmas morning for a funeral.

"We'll get you one," Will was murmuring. "Next week, okay?"

Next week, my ass. He would never remember where I'd found that sweater, and I was *not* going to help.

"How about Annie's present?" Will suggested then, and Josie flew off his lap and into a near-crouch, determined to be the one to deliver the gift.

"Where is it?" she demanded, looking around wildly.

"Here you go," Will laughed, fetching a pink box that Josie snatched out of his hands and practically threw in my lap.

"Here it is Annie Merry Christmas I love you," she said breathlessly, climbing up onto the couch and squeezing against me like a slug. I shifted slightly, aiming for space, but Josie happily interpreted the movement as an invitation for further fusing.

"It's from London, too," Will added.

I could feel Josie's humid breath on my neck. I could see her little hands twitching. I knew she was dying to grab the present back and open it herself. And I knew that Will would have let her.

But I was not Yes-I-Will.

I slid my fingernails under the tape and carefully opened one flap, then the other. "What could it be?" I pondered out loud.

Well, that was a stupid thing to say.

"It's a necklace Annie it's a NECKLACE let me show you—" And she clambered against me, clawing for the gift that I held out of her reach.

"No, I want to open it," I said firmly, waiting until Josie stopped scrabbling before removing the rest of the paper and opening the box.

"See it's a NECKLACE but also, but also there's a drawing I made you a picture—"

Quickly palming the necklace, I let Josie's shaky fingers reach into the small box and pull out the folded piece of paper. "See? It's our family! You and me and Daddy and London and the little baby!"

And so it was, the unborn addition hovering on a cloud above the rest of us. "This is so beautiful, Jo," I said, and meant it, the tears already standing in my eyes. I looked up to show Will—and saw London for one gaunt and pale moment before she mumbled an excuse and left the room.

I stared after her, trying to squelch my bitterness. Why the hell couldn't we just have two happy children at once? Why were they always on opposite trajectories: one well-behaved while the other became a drama queen, a maniac, an intolerable whiner?

And why could Josie—the one who presumably had the most to lose—celebrate this new child, while her older sister could not even bear to hear about it?

Suddenly my eyes widened. Had my parents heard Josie? Were they marching over to jerk the drawing from my hand and demand answers? I nervously peeked toward the kitchen. But no inquiring eyes were there, and I suddenly remembered my mom's declaration that she deliberately tuned out the "screeching voice" and "constant prattle" of my younger stepdaughter in order to avoid "thunderclap migraines."

I took a deep breath, trying to conjure back some thimbleful of Christmas spirit, and took a closer look at the necklace in my hand. It was nothing I would have chosen for myself, but it was heart-shaped and hokey, and for that I loved it. "Thank you, JoJo," I said, hugging her. "These are very wonderful presents." I fastened the clasp around my neck.

"Well, we'd better get you in the bath," Will said, standing and holding out his hand to Josie. "Your mom will be here soon." He tapped on London's door on the way to the bathroom. "Time to get ready, sweetie. Mom'll be here at eleven."

That left me alone in the living room with the choice of hiding in my closet or hobnobbing with my evil progenitors. I was heading for the closet when my father stuck his head out of the kitchen. "Annie, your mother can't find the cardamom." Defeated, I slunk after him into the beast's lair.

"I don't think we have that, Mom," I said as I found my mother madly whirling the spice rack. "That's like ginger, right? We have ginger, I think—"

"Heavens, Annie, it is *not* the same thing!" Mom huffed. "You said I could cook here and then you don't have the right supplies." She held up a grimy unspecified spice. "And these bottles are disgusting! Aren't you aware that you're supposed to buy new spices every six months?"

"Aren't you aware that you're supposed to be nice to people on Christmas?" I spat back. "Just use the ginger, okay?" And I stalked out of the room to take a shower, slapping palms with both Angelina and Xena as I skipped down the hall.

But as the doorbell rang half an hour later I knew I had made a terrible mistake leaving my mom so close to the door. "I'll get it!" she called gaily. *No!* My stomach lurched and I bolted for the entryway, only to arrive just as my ridiculous mother began to fawn over the incomparable Gianna London.

"Oh, hel-LO," she said in her syrupy voice. "You must be the children's *mother*. It's such a pleasure to finally meet you!"

"Thank you," Gianna was saying with some confusion as I hurried up behind my mom to grab the reins.

"Come on in," I said to Gianna apologetically. "This is my mom, Judy."

"Of course. Hello," Gianna said politely, stepping into the house. "Thank you. I hope you're having a merry Christmas."

"Oh, yes," said my mother bashfully. "I'm just cooking up a little something. I hope you'll be staying!"

Yeah, Mom, because this isn't awkward enough already. You're quite the social savant.

"Actually I'm just here to pick up the girls," Gianna said.

"Oh, that's too bad," said my mom, seeming crestfallen. "Another time."

"Hurry up, girls!" I called, trying to keep my voice light. "Your mom's waiting!" I glanced out the window and spotted Ren behind the driver's seat. I didn't think he could see me, but he smiled and waved. Guiltily I turned away, pretending I hadn't seen.

"Mommy!" Josie said then, running into Gianna's arms. "Merry Christmas, Mommy!"

Will and London followed with smiles and backpacks.

"Oh, your children are just so *gorgeous*," my pathetic mother gushed. "They really take after you."

This from a woman who had never said a single nice thing about her step-granddaughters—or complimented her own daughter since approximately 1987. "Well, I'm sure Gianna wouldn't mind if you went along with them so you can all have a lot more time together," I said, not really realizing that I had spoken aloud until I saw the bulging eyes of everyone else in the room.

"Just kidding," I said lamely. God, why didn't I just wear a sign declaring *Morbidly Insecure?* I looked up miserably, only to see Gianna nodding sympathetically at me. Then I remembered: she had asshole parents too. I took a deep breath.

"You guys have a wonderful Christmas," I said, hugging London and Josie. "See you in a couple of days."

Now I just had to face a few more hours with my mother, the clueless traitor, and I would be home free.

✦✦

As holidays with my parents went, it would be hard to classify this one as anything but a success. Christmas had no cabbage connection in my mother's mind, so she was permitted to craft a more orthodox menu—cardamom notwithstanding—that actually approached general tastiness. I relaxed when I saw Will's hesitant mouthfuls turn to surprised gusto. He could handle most anything if the food was good.

To be sure, my mom gave us both a run for our money, blabbering endlessly about the "really annoying" women at her office and praising my sister Stacia up the wazoo for spending her Christmas in Geneva "selflessly doing experiments for the good of humanity."

"I'm *so* lucky to have her for a sister-in-law," Will answered mistily as he squeezed my thigh under the table. "What a *gem.*"

By two o'clock we'd exchanged gifts—a pretty carafe from us to them, a ceramic casserole from them to us—and sent them packing early. As we clicked the door shut, we turned to each other and burst out laughing. "You were brilliant tonight," I wheezed. "Such suckuppery! 'Oh, what a gem, Judy.' Genius!"

Will bowed modestly. "Thank you, thank you, I try," he said, heading over to the kitchen table to pick up the gifts they'd left for London and Josie. "What the hell *are* these things?" Will asked, holding up two flaccid hand puppets. "Did your mom raid a kindergarten?"

"I'm pretty sure these are the masterworks of that Patty Bates woman she spent forty minutes trashing," I said. "When it comes to love and hate, my mom likes to walk the line."

Later we went for a walk, nibbled at the leftovers, and snuggled up with a purring Mr. Pickles to watch *It's a Wonderful Life.*

It was what I'd always wanted. It should have been perfect.

But I couldn't avoid the hulking feeling that there was just something so wrong.

That night, as Will slept like a cherub, I gave in to the voices and went out to stare at the tree.

What was this uneasiness? Will had been *flawless* today, such a good sport at every turn. He'd even respected my request not to call the girls tonight, conceding that it might set him spiraling into a very un-Christmassy funk.

I sighed. He'd finally been that man I'd dreamed about all my life, the warrior to my goddess, the one who seemed to love me with all his heart.

Seemed to love me. *Seemed.*

It's just your hormones, Angelina tried to soothe. *You're just becoming a momma! There's nothing wrong!*

But there *was* something and I knew it and all I needed was to rest my brain for an instant on Will's Ren-and-Josie confession before Xena emerged from the darkness, all thoughtful malice, to administer the third degree.

I've been wondering about this, she purred. *Wondering and wondering about this.*

I wished I could stop her, but I could only stare paralyzed at the soft throb of the lights.

It doesn't really make sense, does it? Her sarcasm was oozing.

No, it makes perfect sense, I argued. It explains *exactly* why Will hates Ren so much, why he worries about Ren's wealth. He was betrayed and cheated on and he's terrified to lose his daughter. It explains *everything!*

Xena smiled at me with cold patience. *Yes, I see why it's a convenient, satisfying answer for YOU,* she said. *But to those of us living in the real world, it smells a lot like bullshit. Do you REALLY think that, if Josie were Ren's daughter, Ren would let Will raise her instead?*

"Well, maybe he doesn't know," I murmured defensively, speaking aloud now. "Maybe Gianna doesn't want him to know."

And why would that be, now? Xena asked with maddening mockery.

"I don't know!" I sputtered. "I don't even know her! She must have her reasons!" My voice was an echoey shock in the silent house, but I didn't care. I liked hearing it. And Will was a heavy sleeper. I needed to fight.

Maybe Gianna isn't sure, herself, Angelina jumped in helpfully. *Or*—a flicker of embarrassment—*she's avoiding the stigma of adultery.*

"Yes!" I said with desperate triumph, so eager to vanquish the Warrior Princess. But Xena loomed before me, mighty as ever, while Angelina whimpered and retreated. *Would a stigma keep Gianna from seeking full custody of her and Ren's child?* Xena shouted at me. *If she even suspected Ren's paternity, wouldn't she discreetly have it tested?*

Of course she would.

Of *course* she would.

"Oh, God," I groaned. I let my body slump back against the couch as Xena stood over me, smirking, her dagger grazing my jugular. There was no more pretending: Will's suspicions just didn't hold up.

And I was shaken to my cells by what it meant that he didn't realize it.

61

I HATED MYSELF as I sat in the busy café trying desperately not to puke. My fingernails tapped; I watched my cell phone with skittish fervor. I was sure that Will had seen right through my lie.

But how could I continue to live with his?

The bells on the front door jangled and I turned my head, smiling weakly at Ted as he caught my eye and made his way to the table. Only a few days after I had vowed to relinquish all other points of view, I was already betraying my husband.

"Hi," I said, trying to hide the jitters by wrapping my hands firmly around my glass of juice. "Merry Christmas!"

"You too," Ted said, signaling the waiter for coffee and a menu. "How'd it go?"

I gave him the rundown, relaxing temporarily into the storytelling as I forgot all about my mission. But as soon as I'd finished, there it still was: vicious reality, waiting to slice. It made me even sicker than the modest bowl of granola I'd ordered but still couldn't force down.

"You okay?" Ted finally asked.

"I need to talk to you," I said, forcing myself to look into his eyes. "I need to know…everything you remember about Gianna and the divorce." I had to do this without telling him Will's suspicions. "There are things I just don't understand."

He blinked at me, then snorted. "Geez, Annie. That's some ambush. Merry Christmas to you too."

"I know," I apologized. "I'm sorry. But you're the only person who was there."

He looked hesitant.

"Please, Ted," I begged quietly, tearing up. "I have to know the truth. Things are really bad right now. I just don't know where else to turn."

He still looked uncomfortable, but he swallowed and asked, "What do you want to know?"

"Just tell me how things were," I said. "Around the separation. Were things going badly before that? Was it a total surprise? Did you have any idea?"

Ted looked thoughtfully into his coffee. "Uhh...let me try to remember. It's pretty fuzzy." Finally he spoke. "I think I had wondered from time to time if there was something wrong. There was this one comment Gianna made at a dinner, something about freedom and the single life. I thought it was weird. But there was nothing that obvious, fighting or anything. When Will told me she was leaving, I was stunned."

"And was *he* stunned?" I managed to ask.

"Completely," Ted said. "He kind of came unglued."

I gulped, paling. *This is what you're here for,* I reminded myself. *Be strong.* "What did he do?"

Ted squirmed. "Annie..."

"*Please,* Ted. As your friend." I stared at him beseechingly. "I need to know."

Ted took a deep breath and nodded resignedly. "He bawled, Annie. It was like...I just had no idea what to do. I've never seen a man cry like that."

I closed my eyes against the pain of this, gripping my hands on the sides of the table. Gum squished under my nails and I couldn't even care.

I forced myself to speak. "Anything else?"

"Yeah, but Annie, you have to swear not to tell him I told you."

I opened my eyes. "I swear."

"He talked about suicide," Ted said quietly. "It scared the shit out of me. I took him back to my place that night so I could be sure he wouldn't try it."

What could I feel? I was hovering outside my body, afraid to slam back to reality and fry in that bubbling vat of pain. This had only been four years ago.

"But Annie, when he met you, everything changed," Ted rushed on, eager to get back to the happy ending.

"No," I interrupted. I wasn't done. "I need to know about more than that. The divorce. And Ren."

Ted sighed. "It was a terrible time for Will," he said softly. "He wasn't rational. And he was sure they were going to get back together. Even as he was signing the divorce papers he was saying things like 'this is just part of our story.' And then, I think about a year after they split up, he found out about Ren and it was like we were back to square one, only this time he was so angry, so livid. There were days he would refuse to see the kids because he knew he was going to say things he shouldn't. At least he never lost his grip on that. He knew that he could lose custody if he badmouthed Gianna—she was being generous with the joint custody, but she was the mother, and soon to be a multi-millionaire, and he knew he could lose it all. Keeping his kids from being raised by Ren became his new mission, which was an interesting bind because it meant he had to put that stuff behind him in order to get what he wanted."

"He's never put it behind him," I said matter-of-factly. "He hates Ren as just as much as ever."

"Maybe," Ted said. "But I'm telling you, Annie, it's not like it was. Having to be on his best behavior helped him get his shit together. And when he met you, it really was a turning point. He was excited about someone—something, anything—for the first time since Gianna left. That's why I..." He closed his mouth.

"What?"

Ted looked at me, embarrassed. "Well geez, Annie, we both kind of liked you at first. But when I saw that Will *really* liked you, I just had to step back. And it was the right thing to do. You turned his world around. And he loved you. And I could see that he was going to be okay."

"Aww, Teddy," I said, blushing up to my eyebrows. "I never knew that."

"Well, don't get *too* flattered," he said wryly. "I think we both know we're better off as friends." I smiled back, nodding. Thank God that Ted had found the wisdom, or kindness, to scoot out of the picture. I never would have fallen for him, and what would the experience have done to our friendship? To his friendship with Will?

"You feel better now?" he asked me.

But that I didn't know. It was validating to hear that my vision of myself—the woman who'd come along and restored Will to vitality—was actually true. On the other hand, the depth of Will's love for Gianna, the extent of his agony, was about as agreeable as soft-boiled eggs on a hungover stomach. *I've never seen a man cry like that.* Could I ever get those words out of my head?

"Yeah, much," I said instead, smiling at Ted. "Will just doesn't talk much about that time in his life, and sometimes I just don't know where I stand." I paused. "I feel so insecure being the second wife. This isn't exactly the life I pictured for myself, you know?"

"I know," Ted said. "But when we get to this age, everyone has a past, right? It's not like we're virgins here."

Well, maybe. But *my* past involved a couple of supremely forget-table losers. Will's involved two children and a towering love. It just wasn't the same.

"So what's more important," Ted pressed on, trying to cheer me. "Being first, or being last?" I could tell by his raised eyebrow that he thought he was being very clever.

But I'd heard this one before. "First in his heart, last in his life," I said automatically, forcing a smile. But how could I commit to the second knowing I'd never come first?

January

62

"YOU OKAY?" WILL asked me later that week.

"Oh, yeah, just spacing out," I smiled back, but of course I was lying. I was not "okay" with anything; Will's past was like a guerilla hoochie, waiting to jump out and bitch-slap me at any moment.

I've never seen a man cry like that. For days I had listened to a constant replay of Ted's voice. And every time I looked at Will I saw a man weeping and threatening suicide over a woman I'd never be.

You knew he had an ex when you married him, I heard the world dismiss and condemn me. Oh yes, I had. But it was one thing to have an ex and another to have a lost beloved, and I'd been too smitten and stupid to tease out the difference.

You're being ridiculous, Angelina snorted at me. *You're going to ruin your baby's chances for a happy home if you keep on like this! No matter what Will felt once, he is with* you *now.*

But I had the gut feeling that if Gianna came calling, begging for reconciliation, Will would drop me with a shrug. And even if that day never came—and I was pretty sure it wouldn't—simply suspecting my husband's ultimate preference was enough to make me cringe every time he tried to touch me.

What an idiot I'd been to think my pregnancy would level the playing field. I could have a dozen of Will's babies and I'd never be loved like Gianna.

I was crumbling. I didn't know what to do.

What choice do you have? Angelina tried to tough-love me. *This is your husband and you're having a baby. You'll make it work. And the baby will bring you together, pushing Gianna even further into the past.*

I took a deep breath. Okay, okay, I would go with it. Angelina and Summer just had to be right.

At dinner I looked at Will's and London's and Josie's faces, one by one. *This is my family,* I said to myself. *We love each other.* And maybe that love didn't yet flow robustly in all directions, but we would get there. I had to believe we would get there.

"Who wants more bread?" I asked cheerfully, getting up from the table to grab the rest of the baguette. But when I turned around, London was impersonating *The Scream.*

"Annie—your pants—" she stammered.

I looked over my shoulder. Even from there I could see the spreading red.

I dropped the bread and ran to the bathroom, wrenching down my yoga pants. Oh God, this was it—the reason you never talk about a baby too soon.

Will burst in. "Annie, you need to get in bed and lie down."

"No!" I wailed. I couldn't see anything through my tears. "We have to go to the emergency room!"

"You're really not supposed to," Will said gently, possessing too much knowledge as usual. "If it's—gone, they can't do anything to stop it. You just need to call the doctor tomorrow and go in for a checkup." He helped me into a maxi pad and clean clothes and settled me in bed, stroking my hair. I was both powerfully relieved and howlingly angry that he knew what to do.

I couldn't stop sobbing. "Oogabooga," I moaned insanely. The hatred was growing within me like a fiery ball ready to raze them all: Will, of course, for his wimpiness and golden past; the girls, for not being mine, for existing at all; Gianna, for everything she was and wasn't; my mother, for being a lifetime bitch; Angelina and Xena, for perpetual torment; this stupid baby, for coming at the wrong time then daring to leave early; and myself, of course, for being so optimistic and blind as to marry someone with kids who didn't love me enough to make it worth it.

I looked right at my husband. "If I lose this baby, I will leave you," I said harshly.

"Shhh," he soothed me. "Honey, just try to calm down."

He stayed with me. And though it seemed like I cried forever, eventually I fell asleep.

And then I woke to the wailings of someone else.

Startled, I looked at the clock. It felt like the middle of the night, but it was only 9:30.

I peeked at my underpants. No more blood! Was it possible that—?

I scrambled to find my discarded pants. The rusty spot looked smaller than I'd remembered, and I hadn't been wearing underwear, so maybe...

Don't get your hopes up, I commanded. *You still have to see the doctor.*

But maybe my baby was okay?

I sat down on the bed again, trying to clear my head. Then came the wailing again.

It sounded like London. *I hope you're sorry about the baby,* I thought cruelly. *You should be.*

But then I just sighed and thought about Will, bouncing from hysterical wife right to hysterical daughter. He was always on duty. The least I could do was try to help.

The second I opened the door I heard them burst out of London's room. I stopped, eavesdropping, in the hall. "What do you mean, it was Evie?" Will was shouting. "What was Evie? What did you do, London?"

"I can't say it," London sobbed. "Don't make me say, Dad, don't make me." There was weeping and then a yelp as, presumably, Will had grabbed her arm.

"London Wylie Tyler, *what did you do?*"

"It was Evie!" London screeched. "She did it! She punched out the pills!"

Punched out the pills? I shook my head, trying to understand.

Will was as confused as I was. "What are you talking about?" he snapped.

"Annie's pills," London managed between sobs. "She said that if we punched out seven pills and flushed them down the toilet that Annie would have a baby and then she would leave."

The bizarre logic was irrelevant: there were no words to describe the total crawling horror I felt. London was a dirty outhouse, a seeping pustule, a writhing maggot.

Out of my skin stepped a madwoman and I ran raving into the living room.

"What the fuck is wrong with you?" I screamed at her. "Do you have any idea what you've done?" London crumpled, bawling, and I grabbed the phone and thrust it at her. "Call your mother to come get you, because you no longer live here. NOW!"

"Annie, stop it," Will barked. "*You're* the one who left your pills out—"

What a revolting excuse-making pile of shit he was. "*Fuck you*," I said and ran to the bedroom to pack. If I stayed near Will or London for one more moment my flesh would erupt in hives.

Will followed me. "Parents don't throw children out, Annie," he lectured me. "You left your birth control out where the kids could find it! And how could you not notice that all those pills were missing? There's blame on both sides here—"

I whirled around. "You *disgust* me. And your daughter needs to be in a mental hospital." Dimly I heard her sobbing disconsolately. God knew where Josie was in this nightmare.

"You're hysterical—"

Damn right I was. I turned to roar into his face. "*YOUR DAUGHTER DID THIS TO ME!*" I shouted, clawing at my breached and hemorrhaging belly. "*I WILL NOT STAY IN THIS HOUSE WITH HER ONE MORE MINUTE!*"

Will recoiled. He only stood watching me, seemingly paralyzed, as I finished packing and headed for the front door.

But London was in my way.

"DON'T GO!" she was screaming at me, rivers pouring from her every facial orifice. "Please don't go! I'm *sorry!*"

I shook off her grasping hands. "You got what you wanted," I said unfeelingly, and slammed the door behind me.

63

WILL HAD BEEN calling and texting all day, but I hadn't answered. Then Summer had called. And my mother. I'd ignored them all.

As I walked out of the clinic I texted Will four words: *The baby is okay.*

Seconds later he was there: *Thank God. How are you?*

I didn't answer. After five minutes he called, but I let it go to voicemail.

How was I?

I was so happy to be pregnant. I was so angry at London.

I was so happy to be pregnant. I was so angry at Will.

I was so happy to be pregnant—but I felt so smothered and caged. Now I couldn't leave Will even if I wanted to. Now I was one of those desperate women who stayed because of a baby.

Yet—what if the baby's very *existence* was a message from the universe? No matter what Evie thought, Oogabooga's conception had still been a statistical unlikelihood. And for the little waif to hunker down and survive a miscarriage scare…was it somehow meant to be?

Or maybe I was just meant to be in the nuthouse.

The thought of going home sickened me. The thought of talking to any of the Tylers made the steam billow from my ears.

But what could I do?

Don't make any decisions yet, I heard the voice say. And it was not Angelina or Xena. It was just me.

After calling in sick, I crept home, parking halfway down the block so I could sneak up on the place and make sure Will wasn't there. After securing the premises, I came in quickly, adding to my stash of work clothes and taking two photos that would keep my mind on what mattered.

And then I called the only person I could trust.

64

"COME ON IN," Leah said with a warm and sympathetic smile.

I hesitated. "Are you sure about this? I mean, I would totally understand if—"

"You're welcome here as long as you like," Leah assured me, and I could tell she meant it. I had to fight back the tears.

"Thank you," I sniffled, following her inside. "I can't tell you how much I appreciate it."

"We've all been there," Leah said as she led me down the hall. "Now don't get too excited, because it's not much of a guest room, but it's yours."

I saw crooked family photos on the walls, dust bunnies in the corners, sneakers discarded in walkways. And printouts of *StepMom* magazine, right on the coffee table. How brave she was, I marveled, how unashamed to be a stepmother, how proud of her family just the way it was. *Someday,* I thought to myself.

And then I remembered that I might be subscribing to *Single Mom* instead. I took a deep breath.

"Here it is," Leah said, stepping inside a small, cluttered room with an ancient plaid sofa against one wall. "It's a foldout, and it will probably realign your spine permanently, but it's yours for as long as you need it."

"Oh Leah, thank you," I said, putting down my bag and reaching out to hug her. "It's great. It's perfect."

She smiled at me when we parted. "You want to talk about it?"

"Yes," I groaned, "but I don't even know where to begin."

Just then we heard the door slam. "Whoops—school's out," Leah said. "Let me do the greetings and then we can get back to it."

"Oh, it can wait," I smiled. I was dying to meet her kids.

"In the guest room, angel," Leah called out as we left my bag behind and headed back into the hall. A tweenish girl with light brown hair nearly trampled us, giggling as she threw her arms around Leah.

I looked away politely at the affection, but I couldn't help peeking out of the corner of my eye. *This could be me and my own daughter,* I thought mistily. *Would it be so bad, just the two of us?*

"Casey, this is my friend Annie," Leah explained. "She's going to be staying with us for a while. Her stepdaughters go to Brighton, too!"

"Hi!" Casey said with a brilliant smile, reaching out to shake my hand.

I was so stunned I almost didn't take it. This was Leah's *step*daughter, just a year older than London. With a new haircut, she looked totally different from the girl I'd seen at the school. "Nice to meet you," I finally managed. "I hope you don't mind me camping out."

"No way, we love guests. Right, Leelee?" She tucked her arm into her stepmother's and grinned. "Come on, we gotta do snack time."

Leah looked at me over her shoulder as we marched back down the hall and through the living room. "Casey gets out earlier than the other kids, so we do a thing where we make them snacks after school."

"Well, count me in," I said.

"I was thinking maybe some crostinis today," Casey said seriously as we entered the kitchen. She started pulling out cheese and mushrooms. "Those are like little cheese melts on bread," she explained for my benefit.

"That sounds great," I nodded. "But let me get this straight...you *cook* for your *siblings?*"

Casey giggled.

"Casey wants to be a chef," Leah told me, pulling out a knife and a partial loaf of French bread. "I'm not much of one, but I show her what I can. Mostly she learns from the Food Network."

They put me to work chopping fresh herbs. In fifteen minutes we had a tray of luscious crostini suitable for a wedding reception. I stuffed my face.

"This is amazing!" I managed through my full mouth. "Seriously, Casey, you should open a catering business, like *right now.*"

Her smile was radiant. Gosh, what did Leah do to get a kid like this, a relationship like this? Did cooking with kids really create magic, just like those revolting commercials for chocolate chips and Ranch dressing had always promised?

Suddenly the door slammed. "Bite me!" a girl's voice shouted, followed by a male jeer. "MOM!"

"And the diners have arrived," Leah said with a mock-sigh. "Service!"

Casey brought the tray out to the dining room table. "Come on, guys, it's a really good snack today!"

Toilets flushed, backpacks thumped, and two unkempt boys stormed the table. The bigger of the two was the spitting image of Leah—sandy-haired and freckled—though about twice her size in total bulk. The smaller boy was also blond, but much slighter. I detected a slight resemblance to Casey.

"Guys, this is my friend Annie," Leah introduced me. "She's going to be staying here for a while."

They nodded in my general direction, shoving in crostini with both hands. "Hey," the older one said.

"These are my boys, Andy and Kyle," Leah said, pointing first to the oldest, her biological son. "And...I don't know where Paige is."

"Having her period," Andy snickered.

Leah shot him a look. "Don't be gross. What happened?"

"Who knows. She's just being a B as usual."

Casey, noticing the hasty disappearance of her creation, gathered up two crostini on a napkin and went down the hall. I could hear her tapping on a door.

"Paige? You want some snacks? I saved some for you!"

"Go away. I don't want anything," Paige yelled.

I could hear Casey sigh. She appeared a moment later, taking a bite out of one of the rescues. "Mmm, these *are* good!"

"Yeah, if you like dog food," Kyle guffawed. Given the number of crumbs flecking his jacket, he apparently liked it very much.

"Don't be rude, Kyle," Leah warned. "Nobody has to make you snacks, you know."

"I was just joking. *Geez!*"

Leah looked at me. "Ah, teenagers. Aren't they fun?" But there was a twinkle in her eye that I knew for a fact had never appeared in mine.

That night I received an email.

Annie,

I love you. I was totally out of line in blaming you. I just lost it. I hope you can find it in your heart to talk to me and work on this. I don't know what I can possibly do to make this better but I'm trying. I hope that wherever you are, someone is taking care of you. I'm sorry I called Summer and your parents, but I was trying to find you.

I talked to London for a long time and I think I understand what happened. But she wanted to write to you so I'll let her say it in her own words.

Dear Annie, please come home. I am so sorry for what I did. I was afraid to say no to Evie. She said that if you had a baby you would move away because all you wanted was a baby of your own. I guess she saw it on TV. I didn't want you to move away but I was scared to say no to her. I didn't know what the pills were. I was just hoping that nothing would happen. Then when you were pregnant I was too scared to say anything. I'm so sorry, please come home.
Love, London Tyler

Annie, I am trying to come to terms with what London has done. I feel like I've been shattered to the core. I always thought of London as so mature. Give in to peer pressure? Not my kid. I don't even know what to think.

I have talked to Gianna about this. Of course she is horrified. We agreed that London is not allowed to see Evie anymore. She will be seeing the school counselor tomorrow. You were right about that all along and I'm sorry I didn't listen. Gianna has offered to keep London at her house as long as we want.

I don't know what you want and I can't imagine how you are feeling. All I know is that I want us to be a family again. If you want to talk, meet, whatever, please let me know.
I want you. I want our baby. Please come home.
Love, Will

Could I let this melt me? No.

I read it four times, shut down the computer, and curled up in bed to stare at my two salvaged pictures.

65

THE NEXT MORNING I woke slightly refreshed and marginally in control of my life. It was a vast improvement.

Strolling into work felt surreal. I looked the same, I talked the same, and no one would ever guess that I was living apart from my husband. Yet I felt the difference like a scarlet letter. How long could I pull this off? And how many of my coworkers had their own classified arrangements? I spied at them surreptitiously, scanning for secrets.

At my desk I called my parents' house, knowing my mom would be at work and my dad busy with his jam-packed retirement regimen. On the answering machine I assured them both that we'd had a (hilarious) misunderstanding and everything was just peachy.

Just *peachy*!

And then I pulled out the old *Rhiannon Delesio* placard that I'd stowed in my desk, my eyes slowly filling with tears as I stared at my maiden name…my potential future. God, I'd only been married a little over four months. What a fucking failure.

"Hey, feeling better?" Ted suddenly said from somewhere in the background, startling the hell out of me.

"God, Ted!" I shrieked, pushing the placard back into the drawer hurriedly. "Yes, thank you," I answered, clearing my throat to suggest the remnants of my dreamed-up illness. "At least I *was*. How are you?"

"Oh, fine," he said, but he was looking at me with concern. I knew he had seen me staring at my old name. "How are…you know. Things?" he asked tentatively.

"Oh...we can talk later," I said with a sad smile. I didn't really want to tell him anything, but after I'd forced him into disclosure the previous week, I figured I probably owed him some version of the truth.

Ted nodded, the concern deepening. "Well, let me know if there's anything I can do," he said before awkwardly slipping away.

How about throwing me in a time machine? I thought instantly. But would I really go back to being Rhiannon Delesio—kissing Will and my just-thickening waistline goodbye?

Maybe. Maybe I would give anything—the child in my belly, the clothes off my back—not to be faced with this horrible choice.

At lunch I slipped out early and walked the fifteen minutes to a park I was reasonably sure would remain coworker-free. I didn't want to deal with Ted or the whole chummy marketing department, whose fondness for me—while initially touching—now only made me feel cloistered and false.

I scanned the grounds nervously, recognizing no faces. In relief I settled on an open bench and pulled out my cell phone and Leah's incredibly thoughtful home-packed lunch.

I was shocked when Summer picked up on the first ring. Since Riley had arrived, Summer hadn't once answered her phone. "Uh, hi," I stammered, unprepared. "I just wanted to apologize..."

"You'd *better* apologize," Summer cut me off. "Where the hell have you been?"

I blinked. Was she serious? "It's a long story," I started to explain.

"Well it's not cool, Annie. Not cool. Your husband calls me looking for you? You don't answer your phone? I mean, what was I supposed to think?"

"I'm sorry, Summer," I said. "I really am. Things are just so fucked up right now."

She snorted. "Don't make excuses."

"I'm not making excuses," I said. "I'm just trying to explain—"

"Ex-*cuuuuse!*" she trilled. "You're going to be a MOM, don't you get it? You can't just disappear on people—you have to *be there!*"

Oh, good Lord. "Yeah, I get that, Summer," I said irritably. "Although, you know, a lot of people count on me already. I'm pretty reliable, it turns out."

"Well that's not what I'm seeing," Summer huffed. "I'm seeing a person who just *disappears*—"

And that's when I snapped.

"Look in the fucking mirror, Summer!" I hissed. "*You're* the one who has disappeared from our friendship, not me! You just check your phone and email to see how many times I've tried to reach out to you since Riley was born. But everything has to be on *your* schedule, *your* timetable."

"Riley needs—" she began indignantly.

"And *don't* tell me it's because you're some great mother," I cut her off, "because the truth is that you just use Riley as an excuse to get whatever you want, all the time. You're not fooling anyone, Summer. You pretend to be so selfless, but it's a complete joke. You're the most selfish person I know."

There. I'd said it.

"You're just jealous," Summer snarled at me. "You're just jealous because I'm a real mother and you're some mean stepmother who nobody wants or needs anyway."

"Maybe I am," I said, "but I would rather be a mean stepmother than the ridiculous human being and god-awful friend that you've turned out to be."

And then I slapped the phone shut and ate my lunch in peace.

66

AS LEAH AND I walked into the restaurant, I wanted to duck back out and hit Jack in the Box instead. I was unstable! I'd already told off one friend today—was it really a good idea to unleash me on a whole new batch? *Please,* I begged myself, *don't burn any more bridges.*

But Maggie and Kim were smiling at us from an inviting candlelit table and I took a deep breath and smiled back. Surely, for an hour or so, I could cage the harpy within.

"Hi, guys," I said as we sat down across from them. "Thanks for being here at such late notice."

"Hell yeah!" Kim said. "Stepmom rescue patrol, at your service! We don't call ourselves SOS for nothin'."

"This is actually great," Maggie said, ogling the menu. "I was dying to get out of the house today. And I've been trying to take advantage of this kind of thing until the baby comes and totally tanks my life." She laughed. I knew she was joking, but I also knew she was no sanctimonious Summer. I was safe here.

"So what's up?" Kim grinned at me. "The price of our company is spilling the dirt."

I looked down at my hands fidgeting on the tablecloth. "I'm just really struggling right now," I finally said. "I just…don't know if Will really loves me. And I don't know if I can stay married to him."

"That fucking model," Kim growled. "What did she do now?"

"Nothing," I sighed. Across from me Leah quietly beamed her support. "Nothing. It's me. It's Will. I think it's always been. I just… never knew how unbalanced my life with him was going to be. He's lived a whole life already. And it's easy for me to blame the kids or Gianna, but doesn't it come back to us as a couple, whether we're really right for each other?"

"Sure," said Maggie. "It always does."

"What makes you think you're not right for each other?" Kim asked.

It was hard to put into words. "I've just never known how to gauge what to expect from a man with kids," I finally said. "I haven't been happy with our relationship, but I always told myself I needed to try harder to understand him and the situation, that it was just 'real life' rather than a fantasy. Like when he was obviously jealous of Gianna's new husband, I told myself I didn't know what it was like to have kids with someone. Or when he would cuddle with London on the couch instead of me, I told myself that he knew best because he was the parent and I wasn't. I always made excuses for how he was hurting me."

"...and so did the rest of the world, I'm sure," Maggie smirked.

"Yeah. Everyone. I know it's not reasonable to expect that a stepfamily would be like a nuclear family, or that a second marriage would be like a first. But I didn't know that before. And I guess what I'm saying is that if Will acted this way and he *didn't* have kids, I would have dumped him a long time ago. So how do I know what is reasonable to expect? How do I know if he's treating me well? How do I know if he really loves me?"

They absorbed my weighty questions.

"I'd like to say that you should use the same criteria that you would with any relationship," Maggie answered. "But the reality is that you can't. A man with kids is *not* the same as a man without. You will get less time and attention than you would from a childless guy. A lot of times you'll get less love, too. It's just the reality of it."

Less love. I winced. London, Josie, Gianna. How far down the list was I? Yet I had given Will my whole heart.

"But he still has to treat you as his partner," Kim said. "Yeah, you need to be flexible and understanding. But the adult relationship is still the foundation of the family. You still deserve to be respected as his wife."

"It's all so vague," I whined. "And what about with Gianna? I just want to tell him he can't see her anymore, but of course that's impossible. How am I supposed to stand him being around her?"

"I know how hard it is," said Leah gently. "It's really easy to get bogged down in comparisons and jealousy. But I've seen women ruin good relationships by losing themselves in competition and hatred for the ex and the kids and the past. You just have to try to block her out, focus on you and Will."

"Yeah, but it's easy for you to say, Leah," Maggie said. "You and Paul married on even ground. You'd both been married before; you both had kids. It's not the same for me or Annie or Kim. I mean, I'd been married before, but I didn't have kids. It changes *everything*. It's *so* hard."

"I know that," Leah said. "Believe me. But I also know from experience that love isn't just a one-time thing, and that if you focus on your partner's past then you'll never be happy in the present."

I nodded. "Yeah, that makes sense. But I also just *know*"—I took a deep breath—"that I love Will in a different way than he loves me. And the way I love him is the way he loved Gianna." I gulped back the tears, fiddling in my purse for the pictures I'd taken from the house.

"I mean, *see*?" I said, slapping the two photos on the table. "See how he looks at her? How he looks at me?"

They were wedding pictures. I'd crept into London's room, where the horrid *Our Wedding Memories!* album had been secreted, and found that spine-tingling photo I'd seen hanging so proudly on Gianna's parents' wall.

"Oh, Annie, this is not going to help you, honey," Leah murmured in dismay. "They're just snapshots; they don't mean anything. They're just going to drive you crazy—"

"Look, I know it's sick, okay?" I conceded, dashing away tears. "But *this* is my reality. *This* is what I'm up against. It's my life on the line. And *no one*"—I pointed at the picture of Will and Gianna—"has ever looked at me like that. Do you get that? If I stay with Will, *no one ever will.*"

There was a collective sigh as they gazed at the two photos, two brides, one groom.

"Annie, I so understand where you're coming from," Maggie said finally. "Believe me. But I really don't think the pictures are a good idea."

"Yeah," Kim murmured. "They'll drive you to madness, seriously."

"Fine," I gave in gruffly, snatching the photos out of sight. "No pictures. But let's just say the pictures are right. Let's just say that everything I see in them is totally true. Then what? How do I know if Will loves me—enough?"

No one said anything for a moment.

"I think you're comparing something that can't be compared," Leah said. "Love isn't about quantity. I can't compare my love for my kids to my love for Paul to my love for my parents to my past love for Curt. Each one is different." She looked at me kindly. "I'm sure Will didn't love Gianna *more* than he loves you now."

"Yeah, but the nature of the love does matter, doesn't it?" Kim asked. "I think what Annie's saying is that Will had a certain kind of *passion* for Gianna that she doesn't think he has for her. And I for one think that matters. I think Annie deserves passion. I think everybody does."

Leah considered this. "I suppose I had more passion for Curt than I do for Paul. But I'm older now. It really doesn't mean that I loved him more. You guys know that Paul is my everything."

"Yes, but that's the crux of it, again," said Maggie. "Annie and Will are in different places in their lives. For Annie, Will is that first-time love, that passionate love. But she feels like he's already had that with Gianna. She stays with him, she never gets that."

I nodded. "Exactly. I'm *not* older. I don't *want* to be Will's quiet, mature love. I don't mean anything bad about you and Paul, Leah. Hands down you have the best marriage I've ever seen. But with Will, things are uneven. And I *do* want someone to be passionate about me—I want the mutual feeling, not just someone who's been there, done that. And that's how it feels sometimes. A lot of the time."

"I totally understand that," said Kim. "Honestly, the main thing that makes this life worth it for me is knowing that Nate never really loved Zoey. I know it may sound petty and mean—and that's fine, because I am—but it's the God's honest truth. I have to raise their kids and never get one of my own? I *hate* it. But I have his heart. I have something of my own that she never had and never will." She sighed. "It's the only way I can keep myself from going off the deep end."

"Yeah," Maggie nodded. "One of the biggest struggles I've had is facing that my husband, for a time, actually was *in love* with a woman who has made our lives so unbelievably miserable. She's a deadbeat, druggie, worthless drain on society. Yet my husband was *in love with her,* long enough to have two children. Even today he can't really say that they didn't have good times. And yeah, it was like fifteen years ago. But that doesn't mean it doesn't kill me. It feels like betrayal in every sense of the word. If not betrayal by him, betrayal by *life*. It's hard not to keep wondering why I deserve this, why other people have it so easy and I have this lunatic in my face."

"So what makes it worth it for you?" I asked.

Maggie thought for a moment. "I know Dennis loves me," she said. "Even if he had greater passion for Twatwaffle—and maybe he did, I really don't know—I know our relationship *works* in a way that his never did with her. And we run the house together; we parent together. I know he'd make the kids mine if he could. And he's willing to have our own, even though it probably wouldn't have been his first choice. Sorry, baby." She patted her belly and laughed. "So, you know. I handle what I have to handle because I have a man like that."

I nodded, feeling the twinges of jealousy. As stressful as it would be to have a delinquent bio-mom always mucking up the works, at least it cemented the new couple as the team, the parents. Maggie was no outsider in *her* family. She was a stepmom to be reckoned with.

And Kim? She was the love of Nate's life.

And Leah? She had a wonderful man and stepkids she adored.

All their reasons made sense. But I still was struggling to find mine.

"I guess I know the answer," I ventured in a faltering voice. "I guess I know that I want more than what Will has to give me."

Kim's and Maggie's faces were creased with concern in the dim light.

"But there's a big complication," I added, looking up at them ruefully. I'd concealed it deliberately, trying to set my friends' microscopes on the relationship alone.

But to pretend it didn't change things was ludicrous.

"I'm pregnant."

They looked back at me in shock. Leah sat quietly, radiating support.

"Oh, fuck," Kim finally said.

"Yeah," I said, laughing in spite of myself. "Exactly."

67

"SO, DID LAST night help you at all?" Leah asked me as we sat together in her den folding laundry.

"Oh, it always helps to hear from other people," I said. "I still don't know what to do, but it's reassuring to talk to people who've done this a lot longer than I have."

We folded for a few moments in companionable silence. "Have you heard anything from Summer?" Leah finally asked.

I shook my head. "I just can't deal with her right now," I said. "I feel bad, but at the same time I have nothing else to say." I paused. "Is it just me? I feel like it's so hard to have *any* friends who aren't stepmoms. Some people try more than others, but not many seem to really get or even care what it's like."

Leah nodded. "Having stepmom friends is absolutely necessary to keep your sanity," she agreed. "But I think it's still good to get other perspectives too. And you know—keep in mind that having kids is always hard on friendships. I went through all sorts of things with people and I wasn't even a stepmom back then." She shrugged. "Anyway, it's just hard. To be honest, Summer might need to focus on friends who understand what *she's* feeling right now. Maybe you both need to take a break until you reach a point when you can be good friends to each other again."

"Yeah, maybe," I sighed. As remote a possibility as it seemed, I was willing to consider that I'd somehow been quashing Summer's tender mothering spirit. "And I don't know how to feel about Ted either." I had given Leah the rundown on that whole situation. "He means a lot to me, and it's great to have a guy friend. On the other hand, he's too entangled in Will's old life. On the other *other* hand, I took advantage of that for information." I shook my head. "God, I don't know. I owe him an explanation and friendship but I'm just so *tired* of dealing with Will's past."

"Honey?" said Leah's husband, poking his head into the den. "Hi, Annie," he acknowledged me with twinkling eyes, and I practically blushed. I hadn't been lying last night—Paul was some kind of Wonder Husband, cute as a cupcake and so perfect for Leah that he'd make a skeptic believe in soul mates. "Are we doing the burgers tonight?"

"Sure, that sounds good," she smiled, and their eyes held for just a sweet, practically unnoticeable little moment that made my heart lurch with longing.

That's what I wanted with Will. It's what I'd always wanted. That constant affection, that glimmer of admiration, that daily conscious *choosing* of the other as a partner and a love. Being in Paul and Leah's home, I'd seen with my own eyes how well remarriage could work. Sure, there were tense moments and disagreements. Sure, the kids fought. But there was no doubt in my mind that this was a *family,* where everyone fit and counted and belonged.

It was possible to be happy in this life. It was possible to be a second wife and still be supported and adored.

But was it possible for me?

"You'll be here, right Annie?" Paul asked me.

I shook my head regretfully. "But I wish I could be. It sounds delicious."

"We'll save you some," he promised.

Once Paul had left, Leah looked at me expectantly. "Are you ready for tonight?"

I shook my head. "Not even a little bit. But I just have to know."

68

WHEN I FIRST saw Will, he looked like a stranger, some deeply handsome stranger who'd never speak to the likes of me. And when he came toward me I felt the usual giddy excitement, the fluttery chosen feeling that had sucked me into this mess in the first place.

But when he leaned over to kiss me, the gates came crashing down. I stiffened, leaning away, securing the proverbial broomstick where the sun don't shine. He'd reduced me to mulch too many times to take any chances.

We sat at the table in silence for a few uncomfortable moments. This time I wasn't going to rush to forgive, to frost over the gouges in this cake.

"Well, London saw the counselor today at school," Will finally said. "She said it went well. She only gets a few sessions there, but the counselor said she'll give us a referral to someone in the community…" He went on with the details, trying to reassure me of progress.

London! That's what he thought this was about! Oh, Will. So much has happened and you don't have an inkling.

"Will," I gently interrupted, "I think we need to talk about us."

"What do you mean?" he asked, looking so confused and innocent that I almost laughed.

But I kept my expression serious when I spoke. "I've been doing a lot of thinking. And I'm not sure it's the best thing for us to stay together."

"What more do you want from me?" he spouted. "London's in counseling, she's not seeing Evie, she can stay at Gianna's house—"

I shook my head. "It's not about London, Will. You're doing great with her, and I appreciate it." I paused. "It might take some time, but I know I can forgive her."

I meant it. Someday I might even *thank* London for the child she had foisted on me.

But that, bizarrely, was all because the baby was okay. I knew equally strongly that if Oogabooga had been lost, my involvement with all the Tylers would now be over.

Will looked so thrilled. "Oh, Annie—"

I shook my head gently, trying to squelch his premature elation. "But that's not the end of it. I'm just not sure that *we* have what it takes."

He looked back at me, flabbergasted. "This is crazy, Annie. I love you. You love me. Just—come home and everything will work out."

I looked at him thoughtfully for a long moment. "Josie is your daughter, Will. There is no way she isn't. The fact that you would hold on to this delusion for all these years tells me that you're not over Gianna and that maybe you should never have married me."

He only stared at me, completely taken aback.

"While we've been together I've seen you use me to try to make Ren jealous. I've seen you freak out at the slightest mention of his name. I've heard you tell me things about your 'complicated feelings' for Gianna. What conclusion can I draw from all this except that you still want to be with her?"

"It's not really about that," Will mumbled. "It's more like a matter of principle. And the kids. I'm just a jealous person—"

"If you're such a jealous person, then why doesn't it bother you that Ted and I are friends?" I argued. "He's a guy, isn't he? A guy who used to like me?"

He looked surprised that I knew that. "Yeah, but I *trust* you, An-nie," he said. "And Ted likes a new girl every week. It didn't mean anything."

I closed my eyes. "Just cut the bullshit, Will," I murmured. "Tell me the truth! Do you love me or do you still love Gianna? It's not a hard question."

He looked at me, frozen, as though it were the hardest question in the world.

Exasperated, I got up from my chair and turned to leave.

"Annie, wait," he said. "Please don't go yet. I want to talk to you. But not—here. Can we go somewhere else?"

I exhaled in frustration but relented. "All right. Wherever you want."

We left our half-empty coffees on the table and went out into the dark. And as we walked up and down the slick winter streets, Will talked.

And for the first time I was determined and distant enough to hear the truth.

He had been so happy when he met Gianna. Not looking for love, not looking for anything, just young and free and proud of his tan, proud of his wallet, his surprisingly decent post-college job. But into his life she'd walked anyway, this glorious blond breathtaking thing, a puzzle piece too perfect not to fit into place.

He'd had to pinch himself. Could she really want *him*? He was reeling with her, with the way people stopped to stare at them as they went by. *The perfect couple*, everyone said. Were they right? Even her parents adored him. It had started to feel like fate.

He'd careened into love like a man on a mudslide. He, who'd never thought once of marriage with anyone ever, was down on one knee after six months. And marriage was some staggeringly hot combination of porno and dorm room, too good to be true, all giggling and sex and cheap furniture that is perfectly suitable when you're twenty-two and married to the most beautiful woman you've ever seen.

Then there was that gear-screeching day. Not exactly the plan, of course, but they'd been sloppy; what could they expect? Gianna was so quietly elated. And though it meant the end of so much, law school and modeling chucked out the window, the knowledge that he'd *fucked this into her* made him feel more powerful and delirious than he had at any other moment in his life.

The babies came, so much harder than he'd expected, yet they tempered him in the fire of their demands, forcing him to stretch and twist and grow up alongside them. Gone were the porno dorm room and their extra cash. Gone, most days, was unexhausted happiness. But he was proud of what he'd become, what he'd provided. He was a beaming father. He was a husband eight years in and still positively in love with his wife. They were going to grow old together.

And then one day, out of nowhere, she'd mashed him like a goddess crushing a beetle.

There were tears, yes, but tears of apology, not grief; she was sorry to break up their family, so sorry to hurt him, but it was just... he was just...not her answer anymore. She wanted a break.

And there was nothing he could do.

The pain was astounding, like every joint and tendon being ripped, plinking, from its housing. He sobbed and railed and made bargains both fruitless and insane. He wanted to hurt her. He thought of his life and his children and his unrazored wrists.

He left them unrazored. But his life was murk and humiliation. He believed, because it made him get up and shave and go to work, that she would come begging back. He cried when he masturbated. He cried when he held his confused and aching children in his arms. He hated their mother as much as he loved her.

She didn't come begging back. She took up with a man tall and rich; after a year she cautiously told Will, newly and officially ex-ed by the courts, about her new relationship. Will faked tranquility, yet the thought of that man sharing a bed with his wife kept him awake for countless full thrashing nights.

He would have killed the man in cold blood if he'd thought he'd get his life back. But even through the film of his rage and disgust he could finally see that it was over between them, that Gianna had found her new answer. And then she married him to prove it. And that man began cuddling and raising Will's daughters every other week.

And life was murk and humiliation for another year more.

When the kids were gone he pursued the horny and brain-dead, rarely calling after an encounter. He had no interest in anything real.

And then he'd met Rhiannon Delesio.

Just as Gianna had fallen into his life unpursued, snagging him at his very best, so Annie appeared, unbidden, in his darkest hour. He clowned with her—for some time he had been capable of faking happiness at work—but was shocked to admit *feelings* stirring in those internal ashes. Was it real? He knew he couldn't possibly be ready for a relationship. Yet she was fun and smart and beautiful, though nothing like Gianna—dark hair, dark eyes, warm and comforting as a treasured family recipe. Spending time with Annie he realized how absent Gianna had truly been, at least in the later years of their marriage. For the first time in a serious relationship—this was only his second—he felt safe.

Maybe it had been too soon. Maybe—certainly—there were years of love, broken trust and ignominy he should have unpacked instead of lugging it all into another marriage. But if he had acted in haste and ignored his old wounds it had only been because he'd seen Annie herself as the healing salve.

He'd fallen in love again. And certainly it was different this time. He was no more the lusty adolescent, but a hopeful thirty-two-year-old man mangled by heartbreak and divorce. He couldn't say, exactly, that Gianna wasn't still roaming his soul in the manner of all unresolved devastations. But it didn't matter, because she was just an ex in every practical way, and he loved Annie with everything his crushed and reconstituted heart could manage: as his savior and his future, a wife who was a partner and not just a prize.

He knew, without a doubt, that she was the real thing.

"Thank you for telling me this," I whispered, kissing my husband's cheek.

But I still didn't know where it left me.

69

ON A SATURDAY in January I folded away the plaid couch and hugged Leah goodbye. "I can't thank you enough," I said tearfully. "I hope I never have to return the favor, but if I do…"

"It was my pleasure," she assured me, warm as ever. "You are always welcome here."

In the living room I went through the gauntlet of hugs—Casey, Leah's amazing stepdaughter, who squeezed me with an enthusiasm untraveled by the average preteen; Kyle, who hugged in haste, all clumsy avoidance of my bosoms; and finally Paul, this man who'd opened his home to his wife's friend without asking a single question, who kissed my cheek and wished me well. Leah's biological children, Andy and Paige, had left the evening before to spend the weekend with their father.

"I'll miss you guys," I waved, choked up, as I walked away from their happy home toward a tottery future.

But at least I'd finally made up my mind.

When I was halfway there I panicked and pulled over. *This is irreversible,* I told myself with a thwacking heart. But even as I thought the words I knew it wasn't—though I also knew I wanted it to be.

I started the car and drove on.

I had no idea what was going to happen, whether this would be better or worse for Oogabooga and me. But as I turned into the driveway I knew I was happy to be taking the chance.

A huge sign stretched across the garage door. Painted in reds and blues, sloppy with childish hands, it read *Welcome Home Annie*. And there they all were, my expectant little family, hovering nervously under the sign.

I took a deep breath and stepped out of the car. My eyes were already brimming. I didn't know what to say.

As usual, my sweet Josie leapt the social crevasse, running headlong into my arms. "Sugarplum Mommy," she said, crashing into me. "I missed you soooo much!"

"Me too, JoJo," I said, kissing her. "I'm back now."

But she was the easy one. As I stood and gazed across the concrete at London, I swallowed. I was the adult, the one charged with bestowing forgiveness, and I knew I would have to make the first move. "London—" I began.

But that was all I had to say. She slowly came toward me, crimson-eyed, and fell sobbing against me. "I'm so sorry," she cried, clinging to me with novel ferocity. I could feel her trembling.

"It's okay," I soothed her. "Everything is all right. See? The baby is fine." And even though there was nothing to feel, almost nothing to see yet, I put her small hand against my belly. "I accept your apology," I said, looking into her eyes. "And I forgive you." Her head bobbed, tears still streaming.

And finally there was my husband. I could see he was already crying. And then he came for me, crushing me against him, grabbing my head as he sobbed into my hair. "I love you so much, Annie," he said. "Thank you for coming back."

We had negotiated, before this day could come. He had agreed to counseling, for himself, for us; he had agreed to listen more, to commandeer less.

He had agreed—so minor, so major—to make room, immediately, for all of my stuff in this house.

Today, it was all I could ask. I didn't know if he would ever get over Gianna. I didn't know if I would regret never finding that man who could unhesitatingly call me his soul mate.

But he was still the man I loved; and for now, I had to try.

"Well?" he smiled, brushing away his tears. "Do you want to go inside?"

I nodded, dumb with emotion. *Yes-I-Will.*

He took my hand. I didn't hear a peep from Angelina or Xena.

And surrounded by my family-in-progress, I moved back into my house.

The Spreadsheet

Member	Partner	Children	Stepkids
Leah Barlow-Michaelson	Paul	Andy Paige	Adora Kyle Casey
Fran Elmore	Jason	Reina	Holden Brianna
Regan Holloway	Blane		Shaena Timmy
June Karras	Ryan		Annabel
K. Kim	Nate		Chloe Marty Scott
Hester Levine	Frank		Caleb Gabby
Kerry Lindsay	Derek		Destinee Maddox
Maggie McConnell Price	Dennis		Laurel Jude
Rhiannon (Annie) Tyler	Will		London Josie

Author's Note and Acknowledgements

THIS IS A work of fiction, all resemblance to persons living or dead is entirely coincidental, and all that good stuff. But in Annie's story, and in the stories of her friends, are the threads of countless lives that have touched mine with their honesty, humanity, vulnerability, courage, and resilience.

I lucked out big time in the stepfamily department. But even I was knocked flat by the emotions I was unprepared to have and ill-equipped to process. In a moment of exquisite sadness and desperation I reached out for help and understanding, and in that moment I stumbled upon a silver lining so bright that for seven years it has been one of the most meaningful parts of my life.

I'm talking, of course, about friendship—about love, compassion, and support generously given by other stepmoms. In this book I have tried to explore the issues with identity, competence, value, and life meaning that loomed large in my own first years as a stepmother. I have tried to crystallize an experience that, for whatever reason, seems difficult to imagine for those who haven't lived it. In steplife there are few sure-fire "fixes" and few solutions that apply to everyone; the purpose of this novel is primarily to paint an authentic picture of the struggles and emotions, not to offer clear-cut answers that simply don't exist. But if there is a message or moral here, it is that friendship matters. Friendship saves. This book is an ode and testament to the women in my life who daily lend their wisdom, humor, validation, unconditional acceptance, and occasionally even their homes and resources to other stepmoms in need.

Along with my panoply of editors, many of these friends read this book in its early and final forms. I am so grateful to all of my readers for their diligence and enthusiasm! For their detailed feedback on the first complete version, I particularly want to thank Emily Autenrieth, Ellen Fortini, Shanon Johnson, Elizabeth Lambert, Elsa Ouvrard-Prettol, Gwen Rivera, Penni Siemens, and Andrea Stewart. You improved this book in so many ways.

There are many reasons that stepfamilies succeed, but there's no question that a stepmom's partner can make or break the whole enterprise. In this and in all things, there are not enough superlatives in the world to describe my husband John. We sidestepped many common stepfamily pitfalls by virtue of good luck or personality; others we needed to spend some time resolving. But no matter what, he has never been anything but my best friend, biggest fan, and steadfast sweetie. I am beyond grateful for his love of me (and for his conviction that every stepmom's husband should read this book!). Would that every stepmother had a partner to listen to her experience without becoming defensive, to strive to understand and adjust, and to compromise as needed to ensure a happy lifetime with both her and the rest of the family.

And there are others. My stepdaughter has always looked for the best in me and in a difficult and confusing joint-custody life; her positive attitude and easygoing love made us a family. Her mom, one of the most gracious ex-wives on the planet, encouraged her daughter to love and thrive at both houses. My parents and siblings and friends embraced my "secondhand" husband and "pseudo-child" with open arms, wisely understanding that the job of a loved one is simply to love.

But not every stepmother has so many advocates. So I really must insist: if you're a struggling stepmom, please reach out. Type "stepmom support" into a search engine right now. You deserve understanding. You deserve to have your feelings heard. And you never know—some of the best friends you'll ever have might be waiting to meet you right now.

Lisa Adams
July 2014

Discussion Questions

1. One of the recurring themes of the book is Annie's inability to get her "footing," as illustrated by the Fiddler on the Roof concept and other motifs. She feels she is "always groping for a light switch, trying to read a code without a cipher." Many stepmoms never feel quite settled and secure in their families. Do you think that being a stepparent is inherently tenuous? What factors make it possible for a stepmother to feel more confident and secure in her role, life, and relationships?

2. Annie personifies her internal critics in the characters of Xena and Angelina ("independent (selfish) woman versus abnegating (tedious) mother"). What does it say about Annie and our culture that she casts Angelina in the "angel" role and Xena in the "devil" role, when both voices can actually be quite harsh and unkind? How would you characterize your own internal critics? Do you have any tricks for banishing them?

3. Stepmoms frequently blame themselves—and outsiders frequently blame them too!—for friction at home. Annie feels like "a pathetic, unbalanced, unlikable and clueless moron." But, of course, responsibility for change doesn't lie with just one person. What could all of the characters do differently? Annie herself? Will? The kids? Gianna and Ren?

4. On more than one occasion, Annie feels a tremendous shame about being "outed" as a stepmother. Where do you think this shame comes from? Have you felt it?

5. Annie observes, "Reading the news…you'd think that blended families were modern-day locusts….So where the heck were they *hiding?*" If stepfamilies are so common, why is our society so ill-equipped to support them? What would need to change, legally or socially or institutionally, to make stepparents more visible and welcome?

6. Children can bring stress to any relationship, but one of the most difficult aspects of a stepfamily is that the two adult partners often have vastly different feelings toward, and expectations of, the children. Annie realizes that instead of maternal love, she feels like "a nanny without a paycheck," and this disparity undermines her connection with Will. How has that played out in your life? Is it possible to overcome this "feelings gap"?

7. Jealousy is a struggle for both Annie and Will, and we see how it affects their lives and family. Leah notes, "I've seen women ruin good relationships by losing themselves in competition and hatred for the ex and the kids and the past." Yet jealousy is an extremely difficult emotion to overcome, especially for those whose needs are not being met. Have you felt jealous in your stepfamily? How have you dealt with it?

8. As Annie's life changes, so do her friendships. By the end of the book, she says to Leah, "Is it just me? I feel like it's so hard to have *any* friends who aren't stepmoms." We see the strain on her relationship with Summer and with her mother as she feels increasingly judged and misunderstood. At the same time, Annie wonders if *she* is the one being paranoid and causing distance in

old friendships. What do you think? Is it possible and beneficial to maintain old ties when friends are moving in very different directions? Are there dangers in having only other stepmoms as friends?

9. Annie worries that Will doesn't love her as much, or as passionately, as he loved Gianna. Is she right to be concerned? Do you think Will loves Annie "enough" to justify the difficulties of living in a stepfamily? What justifies the difficulties for you?

10. Annie comes to see that there's no one right way to be a stepmother. Is this fact more liberating or disconcerting to you? Would you rather have set expectations for your roles and duties, or the freedom to create a more customized role to fit your personality and family?

11. In the novel, Annie connects easily with one stepchild (Josie), but struggles with the other (London). Has this been true in your life? How have you dealt with it?

12. Should stepmoms assume they are welcome or not welcome at events for mothers? Do you agree with Monica (the angry woman at the mommy group) that stepmothers should not do certain things with their stepchildren out of respect for the biological mother?

13. Was Annie's reaction appropriate when she discovered that London had tampered with her birth control pills? Would you be able to forgive a stepchild for a similar violation?

14. Briefly, Annie feels that her pregnancy will solve all her stepfamily problems. Realistically, what impact do you think her pregnancy will actually have?

15. The issue of legal rights for stepparents is a complicated one: some stepparents don't see themselves as parental figures at all; others are more active parents than the biological parents; many others lie somewhere in between. Should we as a society move away from the absolute supremacy of biological parenthood? Is there a way to give some legal rights to stepparents without diminishing the rights of biological parents?

16. This novel focuses on the issues of a childless stepmother in a joint-custody arrangement. How might the story have been different if Annie had children from a previous marriage? If Will were a childless stepfather and Annie the biological mother? If Gianna were dead?

17. What do you think the future holds for the Tyler family? If you were Annie, would you have moved back into the family home?

www.ingramcontent.com/pod-product-compliance
Lightning Source LLC
Chambersburg PA
CBHW050912250626
47155CB00001B/204